Praise for **THE LUK**
The Cascade Killer, *Casc*

"Luke McCain is back in action! The iconic Washington game warden and his canine partner, Jack, are tearing around Washington's central Cascade Mountains in search of an escaped – and maybe dangerous – Bengal tiger! A fast-paced story that will challenge you to figure out how, and even if, Luke and Jack can pull the loose ends together and nail this case shut. I didn't want to put the book down."
–Bob Mottram, author and outdoor writer

"*Cascade Predator* is a well-blended stew of Northwest icons, a reflection of Rob's intimate knowledge of wildlife, outdoor realism, and page-turning curveballs that is just flat tough to put down. This latest edition to the Luke McCain series confirms Rob Phillips's standing as a skilled mystery writer. Already I want to read another."
–Terry W. Sheely, northwest author and writer

"*Cascade Vengeance* takes readers on a thrill ride through the dual worlds of drug dealing and big-game hunting deep in Washington's Cascade mountains. Rob Phillips uses his extensive knowledge of the region to tell the fast-moving tale . . . on the way to the story's harrowing and heartbreaking conclusion."
–Scott Graham, National Outdoor Book Award-winning author of *Mesa Verde Victim*

"Luke McCain and his wonderful yellow lab Jack are back for another fast, fun read in a series you won't want to miss. The big Mexican drug cartels have moved into the Cascade Mountains of Washington State where thousands of miles of forests provide endless opportunities for illegal marijuana grows, and the men doing the growing and harvesting are being stalked and killed. Luke must use all his experience and knowledge to help his girlfriend FBI Agent Sara Sinclair discover who is doing the killing. This is crime fiction at its finest – the perfect blend of a compelling mystery, a fabulous

setting, the best dog ever, and a very likeable hero you won't forget."
—Christine Carbo, award-winning author of the Glacier Mystery Series

"Rob Phillips delivers another page turner. *Cascade Vengeance* is full of murder, intrigue and suspense. And just when you think the case is solved, Phillips throws you a curveball. If you enjoyed *The Cascade Killer*, you'll love Phillips's latest in the Luke McCain series."
—Pat Hoglund, publisher of *Western Hunting Journal*, *Traveling Angler*, and *Salmon & Steelhead Journal*

"*Cascade Vengeance*, the second book in the Luke McCain series, is another hang-onto-your-hat, nonstop action episode with Luke, a Washington State Fish and Wildlife officer, his FBI girlfriend Sara, and Jack, his loyal yellow Lab. I felt like I was riding shotgun in Luke's Ford pickup, bouncing along forest service roads where very bad guys might be lurking."
—Susan Richmond, owner of Inklings Bookshop

"Another fast-paced, exciting chapter in the Luke McCain series that remains true to the Pacific Northwest. Phillips leaves readers with a splendid conclusion, helping us wonder when the next Luke McCain volume will be out. I am truly a fan of Luke and Jack!"
—Vikki J. Carter, host & producer of *Authors of the Pacific Northwest Podcast*

"If you're looking for an enjoyable read out in deer camp or for just sitting next to your fireplace, then *The Cascade Killer* is a definite winner."
—John McAdams, author of The Big Game Hunting Blog & host of The Big Game Hunting Podcast

"Real! Captivating! Once you start, you can't put it down! *The Cascade Killer* is VERY well done!"
—Scott Haugen, host and producer of *The Hunt* and author of numerous outdoor books

Also by Rob Phillips

THE CASCADE KILLER

CASCADE VENGEANCE

CASCADE PREDATOR

CASCADE PREDATOR

A LUKE MCCAIN NOVEL

ROB PHILLIPS

Cascade Predator

Book design by Kevin Breen
Cover image derived from Adobe Stock photos

ISBN: 978-1-7360127-4-1
Cataloging-in-Publication Data is available upon request

Manufactured in the United States of America

Published by
Latah Books, Spokane, Washington
www.latahbooks.com

The author may be contacted at yakimahunter@yahoo.com

Prologue

Sam Banister felt like he'd driven 50,000 miles. In reality, he'd driven just over 2,900 miles from his home in Orlando, Florida. The journey had taken him the better part of six days, stopping here and there as needed. He was definitely looking forward to getting to the Washington State Fair in Puyallup.

When he'd signed on for the gig several months ago, he hadn't thought about what the Northwest weather would be like in September. Heck, in Florida, it was the same temperature just about any month of the year, except for July and August, when it was so hot even the reptiles were ready to move north.

When he had checked, the summertime temperatures in the Puget Sound area didn't look too bad. What Banister hadn't figured into his plan was driving through several western states during some of the hottest temperatures of the year. His precious cargo had trouble dealing with hot temperatures, and it caused him to take his time, often driving at night to avoid the heat of the day. Still, the draw of the $19,000 appearance fee, plus expenses, kept him headed north and west at a plodding pace.

When he pulled into Ellensburg for fuel and yet another fast-food burger, Banister checked the map app on his phone. He was almost there. Another two hours, and he'd be done driving for a while. He checked the outside temperature gauge on his truck. It read ninety-four degrees.

He thought about his cargo again and decided it would be best to stop for the day and get an early start in the morning. Banister pulled into one of the cheaper motels just off I-90 to get some much-needed sleep. He parked his black GMC 2500 diesel pickup and forty-foot cargo trailer under the shade of a couple big cottonwood trees and went to get a room.

After he checked into his room, Banister went out to the trailer to tend to his girls. His Wild Cats of the World traveling show featured a caracal, an ocelot, a bobcat, an African lion, and the star of the show, a Bengal tiger named Timba. The cats had made the trip surprisingly well, considering the amount of time they'd spent in the trailer. They were housed in shiny, stainless steel enclosures inside the long trailer. All had plenty of room to lounge and walk around, and each of the enclosures included cedar shavings on the floors, with big, padded beds in the corners of the cages. The specially designed trailer was insulated, and when needed, it was cooled twenty-four seven by a small refrigeration unit.

Seeing that the cats seemed calm and comfortable, Banister fed each one their rations of raw meat, and as he did, he talked to them calmly. All the cats, except for the bobcat, came over and rubbed along the stainless bars. Banister reached in and scratched their ears and backs. The tiger actually licked Banister's hand.

After they ate, Banister made sure each cat had water in their small watering troughs, continuing to talk to them calmly and quietly as he filled the tanks. When each had moved to lie down, he double-checked the locks on their cage doors, told them goodnight, shut off the interior lights, and closed the door.

Banister was always a little antsy about leaving the cats in the trailer basically unattended, but this would be the last night like this for at least three weeks. He again thought about just bagging the motel and driving on to Puyallup, but he was beat. And now that the cats were settled in for the night, he decided a good night's sleep was what he needed more than anything.

When Banister woke up the next morning, he was surprised to discover that his truck and trailer were nowhere to be seen. He was admittedly tired when he parked the rig, so he just figured he was turned around and was looking at the wrong parking lot. But when he went around to the other side of the motel, and his truck and trailer were not there either, he became frantic.

Why in the hell would anyone steal a truck and trailer like that, and where would they go, he wondered.

More importantly, what was going to happen to his cats?

Chapter 1

The Department of Fish and Wildlife's Region 3 in Eastern Washington covers about a hundred thousand square miles and three counties. With only six Washington State Fish and Wildlife police officers to cover that area, each of those officers has the challenging task of keeping the region safe for the area's fish and wildlife, as well as the humans who enjoy recreating there.

Luke McCain was working in Kittitas County when a call came through on his radio.

"APB on a 2015 GMC 2500 pickup, black with Florida plates, pulling a white cargo trailer," the dispatcher's voice crackled over the radio. "If located, approach with caution. Cargo includes several exotic cats, including an African lion and a Bengal tiger."

McCain did a double take. What had he just heard? He looked at the radio as if it would explain the call. He was about to ask for the dispatcher to repeat the information when one of the other officers, probably a Kittitas County deputy sheriff, beat him to it.

"Repeat that please."

The dispatcher gave the APB again.

"Are they live lions and tigers?"

"Ten-four."

"Can you describe them?" the deputy asked.

The dispatcher sighed. "I'm guessing if you run across any lions or tigers, they will be the ones we're looking for."

"Are they full-grown animals?" the deputy pressed.

"Yes, they are," the dispatcher said impatiently.

McCain listened with amusement at the back and forth. He almost asked if one of the cats was driving the rig but figured the dispatcher was in no mood for his weak attempt at humor.

"We better keep our eyes open," McCain said to his Labrador retriever, Jack, who was riding in the back seat of his state-issued Ford F-150 four-by-four pickup. The dog rode with McCain during some of his patrols, and with the call that just came in, he was glad the big yellow dog was with him.

McCain was a sixteen-year veteran law enforcement officer for the Fish and Wildlife Department. Standing close to six-foot-five, weighing in at two hundred and twenty-seven pounds – give or take a couple – he liked to stay in shape to handle calls like this. Of course, it didn't hurt to be tall with a good build when it came to dealing with the occasional belligerent hunter or angler, too. He knew how to handle himself in almost any situation. Dealing with a tiger or a lion, well, that was a new one for him.

McCain had been called on all kinds of wildlife situations through the years. Skunks under houses, bears in trees, cougars on back decks, raccoons in dumpsters – the list went on and on. Sometimes, McCain had to put the animal down if it was causing major trouble or was a threat to humans or pets, but most of the time – usually with the help of other WDFW officers and sometimes a biologist or two – he was able to dart or trap the animals and relocate them.

Besides being called in to help find and capture a twelve-foot Burmese python that had escaped from a house in Mabton, one of the smaller towns in the Yakima Valley, McCain had never dealt with exotic animals. Not that he was surprised there were big cats like these living in the United States. He'd once read that the number of exotic cats living in the U.S. was in the tens of thousands. They are kept as features of roadside zoos, or just as family pets. The story went on to say that twenty-one people had been killed and some 250 had been mauled in the U.S. by big exotic cats since 2000. McCain even remembered hearing a radio commercial on one of his favorite sports channels that said there were more Bengal tigers living in captivity in the United States than wild in their native India.

What the cats had been doing in the trailer, he didn't know. But whoever stole them was in for a surprise when they opened the trailer door.

McCain guessed that the person who had taken it probably thought they were getting a trailer full of motorcycles or four-wheelers. Eastern Washington has some fantastic trails and hill climbs, and those areas were a beehive of activity in the summer. Besides the designated areas for motor sports, there were hundreds of miles of roads throughout the Cascades where thousands of people enjoyed buzzing around the national forests on their motorcycles, four-wheelers, and side-by-side ATVs.

More and more ATV owners now carried multiple four-wheelers in enclosed cargo trailers for transportation to the good mountain trails. With that in mind, McCain decided he'd run up the interstate toward Snoqualmie Pass to check some of the riders' favorite parking spots.

As he drove up the freeway, he glanced over into the rest area at Indian John Hill to see if any trucks or trailers matched the ones the dispatcher had described. Seeing nothing there, he then took a little bypass to drive up through the old mining town of Cle Elum. He saw nothing of interest there either but did stop at the bakery in the center of town for one of their famous bear claws. He pulled into the parking lot, told Jack he'd be right back, and went into the bakery.

When McCain returned to the truck with the pastry, Jack immediately had his head through the space between the two front seats, looking for a bite.

"I see you missed me," McCain said to the dog. "Or do you just want a bite of my breakfast?"

The big yellow dog was staring at the bear claw, which gave McCain his answer. As usual, he gave Jack the last bite of the pastry. And as usual, the dog swallowed the treat without even chewing it.

"That can't be good for your digestive system," McCain said. "And I know you didn't even taste it."

Paying no attention to his human partner, Jack was nosing into the white bakery bag in hopes of finding some pastry crumbs.

The old road through Cle Elum led up to the even smaller town of Roslyn. With a couple of microbreweries and a tavern or two, Roslyn's big claim to fame was it was the town where some episodes for the TV show *Northern Exposure* were filmed in the 1990s. The show followed a doctor and a group of eccentric residents in a fictitious Alaskan town.

Seeing nothing there that resembled the truck and trailer, McCain went on up the road to Cle Elum Lake to take a look around a couple of the campgrounds there. As he drove, he thought about the trailer full of cats and the person or persons who took the rig. Would they pull over and inspect the contents of the trailer right away, or would they keep driving to Seattle or Spokane where they could get lost in the bigger cities?

He was sure the State Patrol was all over the APB on the truck and trailer, and if the person who stole the outfit had any smarts, they'd know to stay off I-90. But if the truck-and-trailer thief made it to Seattle or one of the other cities in the Puget Sound area and then let the cats loose, either accidently or on purpose, it would create some real mayhem.

For the sake of the animals, McCain hoped the outfit would be found quickly and the cats would soon be back with the person who knew how to care for them.

*

Cassidy Sutcliff had been a member of the World Wildlife Federation, the Animal Justice Project, the Animal Liberation Front, and a couple of other animal rights organizations for a number of years. But for her, those groups – while meaning well – were way too passive. She believed hunting of all animals needed to be banned and people who kept wild animals as pets should be prosecuted and imprisoned. The animals could not speak for themselves. Someone needed to step up and act on their behalf, and she believed she was that person.

Sutcliff grew up in a house where people treated each other poorly. From an early age, she found refuge and love amongst a group of cats that lived out in the barn on their family farm near Concrete, Washington. She would spend hours out there with the cats, away from the constant screaming and bickering going on in the house.

As soon as she was old enough and had the means to do so, she loaded up and headed south. Sutcliff had read just about everything she could on the different groups out there trying to help the animals of the world, and she was hell-bent on doing her part to make a difference.

Being a tall, athletic brunette, Sutcliff had the kind of beauty that got looks from people when she entered a restaurant or some other public place. After working on a county survey crew for a couple years in Oregon, Sutcliff had saved enough money to get to Australia, where she found a job as a crew member on the anti-whaling ship, the Sea Shepherd.

For eighteen months, she worked on the ship as it voyaged around in the South Pacific, trying to stop the Japanese whaling fleet as they hunted Antarctic minke whales. The Sea Shepherd had some limited success in harassing the whaling fleet, but Sutcliff came to the realization that their efforts were mostly in vain. She believed more needed to be done. Blocking the whaling ships and screaming at them through bullhorns was a minor irritant. She believed that sending a torpedo through the hull of the ships would be way more effective.

Sutcliff discussed some of her radical thoughts with the captain and crew, but in the end, she knew her ideas were not being seriously considered. Only one other person on board, another crew member, Cory Spearman, seemed to empathize with her.

Spearman, who understood the irony of his name as it pertained to whaling ships, would sit with Sutcliff for hours and talk to her about what really should be, no, what had to be done to stop the bloodshed and senseless killing of the minke whales.

Of course, Sutcliff wasn't totally naïve, and understood the guy might have ulterior motives for agreeing with her – like trying to get into her pants – but she liked having at least one person who she could talk to about her ideas. It didn't hurt that Spearman was a good-looking guy about her age with long blond hair, a surfer's body, and several tattoos on his oversized biceps, including one that said, "Save the Whales." And talk about a six pack. Sutcliff believed Spearman could have been a model in one of those ads for men's cologne if whaling ship harassment work ever dried up.

A few weeks later, when the Sea Shepherd put into port in Perth, Australia, Sutcliff – with Spearman in tow – jumped ship and headed to the airport to catch the next flight back to the United States.

The couple ended up back in her native Northwest. They were working as waitstaff at a fashionable restaurant in Seattle when Sutcliff saw the commercials on television for the Puyallup Fair, featuring daily appearances by the Wild Cats of the World show.

"That pisses me off so much," Sutcliff said to Spearman after seeing the commercial one morning. "Why do people do that? And who would pay money to go see them?"

"It's all those people who grew up in the city," Spearman said. "Hell, most of them have never seen a live cow or pig or chicken and have no clue how cruelly the animals they eat are treated before being slaughtered."

While he knew the words Sutcliff wanted to hear, deep down he didn't really believe them. Sutcliff was a vegan and believed Spearman to be as well, but when she wasn't around, he would eat the leftovers at the restaurant where they worked, enjoying the chicken, veal, and pork the chef prepared nightly. You didn't keep up the muscles and the body he had without some good old-fashioned animal protein.

"We really need to do something about this," Sutcliff said, getting more and more worked up by the minute. "I'm going to find out about this cat show, and we're going to put an end to this."

"Before you do," Spearman said, grabbing his girlfriend by the waist. "We have about a half hour before we need to catch the bus to work. Let's go work out some of these frustrations."

Chapter 2

Carson Dobbs didn't hate people because they ate meat or held wild animals in captivity for capital gain; he just hated people in general. He especially hated people in the big cities and never understood how anyone could live all crammed together in neighborhoods that sat jammed against each other, one after another, stretched out for miles.

He hated that the people who lived in the big cities all had cars that filled the freeways just about any time of day, spewing exhaust, fouling the air he was trying to breathe.

And he really hated people telling him what to do, how to do it, when to do it, and where to do it.

Dobbs had left urban life behind a few years ago and successfully learned how to survive in the mountains, living in a small shack that, to the rare few who ever saw it, looked uninhabitable. He killed the occasional deer or elk or bear when he had to eat, and he spent much of his time reading. He read *Mein Kampf*, the political manifesto by Adolf Hitler, and *The Communist Manifesto* by Karl

Marx and Friedrich Engels and many, many other books that were, to him, the obvious solution to what he believed to be the problem with modern America.

He also wrote. Over the three years Dobbs had lived in his little shack, he had written over 1,300 pages of his own manifesto, with many of his own ideas on where the future of civilization in the United States and the world was headed.

As much as Dobbs hated the people who went about their mundane days like a bunch of sheep, living what they thought life should be based on the teachings of the churches and the educational system and Hollywood, he really despised the people who came in bunches out into the forests on their noisy machines, breaking the perfect silence he enjoyed so much. In the summer, they would ride their four-wheelers and dirt bikes, and they'd run their chainsaws and generators at the campgrounds. In the winter they'd ride all over the place on their loud, obnoxious snow machines, scaring the critters and ruining his reading and writing time.

The noise of the machines would drone on and on in his head until he felt like his brain was going to implode inside his skull. Every year, every month, every week, every day he had to listen to the incessant buzz of the machines, he got closer to a breaking point.

He was going to have to do something soon.

*

After checking a few spots around Cle Elum Lake that McCain knew were parking areas for the ATV crowd, and finding no sign of the missing truck and trailer, he decided he'd go back down and see if he could have a little chat with the guy who'd reported the vehicle missing. He grabbed the microphone to his radio and pushed the button to make a call.

"Wildlife 148 requesting the location of the owner whose exotic cats have gone missing."

"Stand by," the dispatcher said. Fifteen seconds later, she was back. "The man's name is Sam Banister, and he is at the Econo Lodge off of I-90, exit 106."

"Copy," McCain said before doubling back toward Ellensburg.

When he arrived at the motel around lunchtime, there was one Kittitas County sheriff's SUV parked in the lot. McCain parked next to it, told Jack to stay, left the truck on with the air conditioning running to keep the dog cool, jumped out of the truck, and headed inside. In the lobby, he found Deputy Alivia Hernandez talking to a slender man of about forty-five with dark hair in need of a trim.

Hernandez saw McCain and waved him over. She knew the wildlife officer from a couple different cases they'd worked together, most recently helping to find a hunter who had gone missing. McCain and Jack had located the man's body in an illegal marijuana grow in the mountains west of Ellensburg.

"Deputy Hernandez, how are you?" McCain asked.

"Good, Luke. This is Sam Banister. He's the proprietor of the Wild Cats of the World exhibition and the owner of the missing truck, trailer, and cats."

After shaking hands with the obviously distraught Banister, McCain cleared his throat.

"Sorry if Deputy Hernandez has asked you some of these questions already, but I'd like to know a few things," McCain said.

"No problem," Banister said. "Anything to help get my girls back."

"I guess the first question is how dangerous are the cats if someone happens to get into the trailer with them, or accidentally lets them out?"

"They're pretty tame, but you never know with animals that are supposed to be living in the wild. I can't say what might happen. Heck, look at what happened to Roy Horn in Las Vegas. He worked with those tigers every day for years without an incident and then bam, something triggered one of the tigers to attack. That was it."

McCain remembered something about the popular magician act of Siegfried and Roy and the attack by one of their white tigers during a performance at one of the big casinos several years ago.

"Have you ever had any issues with your cats?" McCain asked.

"No," Banister answered, "but I've been working with these animals since they were very young. I'm like one of the family. But someone new and different might have issues."

"Do the cats still have their claws?"

"The big cats do. I had the caracal, ocelot, and bobcat declawed. They all have their teeth though, which can be way more dangerous than their claws."

"What kind of set-up did you have for them in your trailer?"

"They're all in big steel cages, and each of the doors is locked with a heavy-duty padlock. It would take quite a bit of work to get them out without a key. And I've never had a cat get out on its own."

"So, if someone pulls over somewhere to look inside the trailer, sees what's in there, and decides to just abandon the rig, how long can the cats stay in their enclosures before they'd need someone to attend to them?" McCain asked.

"Well, they all ate yesterday, and I left water for all of them last night, so they'd be good for a day or two. Like most animals, they'd be fine for a few days without food, but they do need water, especially in these hot temperatures."

"And what about the heat? This time of year, that trailer might become an oven."

"Yeah, that wouldn't be good. The trailer is insulated, and I run a small refrigeration unit when we're traveling in the heat, but if they're left alone for too long without refrigeration or water, it could get serious within twelve hours or so."

McCain asked the man if he happened to have a photo of the trailer and truck. He did, and soon sent it to McCain's phone.

"I assume you sent this out to the other officers, including the WSP?" McCain asked Hernandez.

"Yes, we did. Sorry you didn't get it," the deputy said.

"That's okay. At least now I know what I'm looking for," McCain said. "Don't worry, Mr. Banister. You have about a hundred officers keeping an eye out for your cats. We should find them soon."

But after he said it, McCain could see his words didn't really soothe the man's concern.

"Thank you, officer. I really hope that is the case."

*

They were parked at an interstate rest stop when Cassidy Sutcliff spotted the truck and trailer driving west on I-90 near Moses Lake. She knew immediately that it was the one. She had done a bunch of research on the Wild Cats of the World show and had seen photos of the truck and trailer on their website.

"That's it!" she shouted when she spotted the black truck pulling the long white trailer. "Let's go."

Cory Spearman woke with a start in the driver's seat of the old Nissan pickup he'd borrowed from a friend. He'd been dreaming of eating a big juicy hamburger with fries and a chocolate milkshake.

"C'mon, let's go," Sutcliff shouted. "We can't lose them."

"He's pulling a giant trailer. My guess is we'll catch him no problem. Say, are you hungry?"

"What? No! Who can think of food right now? We have some animals to save."

Spearman, who almost said "I can" but thought better of it, put the truck in gear and headed for the freeway on-ramp and sped up to catch the "cat trailer," as his zealous girlfriend called it, in the sweltering afternoon heat.

Sutcliff and Spearman caught up with the truck and trailer near the little town of George and stayed comfortably behind as it drove along. They got close enough to see the Florida plates on the trailer, which confirmed they were following the right truck. She had figured the rig would be going by sometime in the afternoon based on messages she had received from some Facebook friends in Colorado and Idaho. They'd been scouting for her and had successfully tracked the big black pickup and trailer as it motored across the west.

"So, what are we going to do now?" Spearman asked.

He didn't really know Sutcliff's master plan. She'd rattled on about so many different ideas for setting the cats free, he couldn't remember which one she had landed on. Frankly, Spearman wasn't wild about any of the plans he'd heard. Most of them revolved around him climbing into the enclosed trailer and cutting the door locks to let the cats out. It seemed to him that that was an excellent way of ending up as lunch for a lion or a treat for a tiger.

"We'll wait for him to stop for the night, and we'll go from there," Sutcliff said.

Spearman felt like saying that didn't sound like much of a plan, but he decided to not rock the boat. He enjoyed Sutcliff's spunk, which carried over into their romps between the sheets. Speaking of wildcats, she definitely was one. She loved making love to him and did so often. He'd wait to see how things panned out before he made a fast exit if it looked like he could be in danger. No chick, no matter how hot or how great she was in the sack, was worth getting mauled to death over.

When the black truck towing the long white trailer pulled into Ellensburg, they followed it off the highway. And when the rig pulled into the parking lot of a motel, they parked across the street at a mini-mart.

"Looks like he's going to check in here," Sutcliff said. "It'll be perfect. We'll heist the truck and trailer in the middle of the night when no one is around to see what we're doing."

Spearman just sat and peered through the buggy windshield.

"You said you've hotwired a bunch of rigs – you think you can do that one?" Sutcliff asked as she nodded her head in the direction of the truck and trailer.

"Yeah, it shouldn't be too tough. The main thing is getting the car alarm off as quickly as possible. Most people ignore those things anymore, but if it has a unique-sounding alarm, the guy might hear it and come to see what's going on."

"Okay, well, let's hope we can get it done quickly. I hate the thought of those beautiful cats being jailed for one more minute."

"You don't want to let them out here, do you?"

"No, we're going to take them into the mountains, where they have a chance to live like they were always supposed to. There are lots of deer and rabbits and stuff up there for them to eat."

"Do you think they know how to catch a deer?" Spearman asked.

Sutcliff poo-pooed his skepticism. "They are wild cats deep down. Mother Nature will take over, and they'll soon learn how to hunt and fend for themselves."

"Speaking of fending for themselves, since we're going to be waiting here for a while, I think I'll wander over to that Dairy Queen. I'm starved."

The tall blond with the tattooed muscles got out of the little truck, stretched, and wandered up the sidewalk to the fast-food restaurant. He ordered a double burger with cheese and two salads, hold anything that resembles meat.

When the meals came, Spearman wolfed down the burger in three bites, grabbed the bags with the salads, and headed back to the Nissan where his hot, crazy girlfriend sat watching the cat trailer.

CHAPTER 3

Based on his appearance, some people thought of Carson Dobbs as dimwitted. In actuality, the man was a genius. His IQ, the last time it was checked, was pushing 150. The problem was he had schizophrenia and occasional bouts of depression. He'd also been diagnosed with bi-polar disorder, but he didn't believe it. Some days he just wanted to blow up the world, and others he wanted to have people leave him alone to do his reading and writing.

One day, as the whine of more dirt bikes cut through the forest, traveled into the open window of his shack, through his ear canals and inside his brain, Dobbs began devising a plan to keep the riders away from his territory. He knew if he was ever going to have some peace and quiet, he was going to have to kill someone. Maybe he'd have to kill more than one. He had to put the fear of Jesus into these idiots. It needed to be something that would make them go away and stay away.

At first, he thought about having a mysterious creature like Sasquatch attack a rider or two, but after giving it more thought he decided that might bring even more idiots into the woods looking for the mythical creature. No, the killing needed to be done by a predator that lived in these mountains. A grizzly bear would be good, but the big bears hadn't been seen in the Central Cascades for decades. Black bears were not known for attacking people, so that was out. And while he had seen two different wolves in the area since he moved in, the authorities didn't believe the big canines were in this part of the state yet so no one would believe a pack of wolves had attacked a person.

The logical choice, one that would be believable, would be for a cougar to kill a rider or two.

Once he had settled on the killer species, he had to figure out how to make it look like a mountain lion was doing the killing. First order of business was to get his hands on one of the big cats, preferably a dead one. In the three years he'd been living in the shack deep in the Cascades, he'd seen many tracks that he assumed were cougars, and he'd caught a glimpse of one a couple times, moving through the trees like a silent tan ghost. But he had no clue where exactly to look for one.

Dobbs knew mountain lions fed mostly on deer, although he assumed they would also take a young or injured elk and wouldn't pass up snacking on a hare or grouse. There had been fewer and fewer mule deer near the shack. He believed it was because many of the deer he saw had something that was causing them to lose all their hair. No hair meant no protection against the freezing temperatures in the winter. When Dobbs went out looking for mushrooms last spring, he had found the remains of several deer that had not made it through the winter.

But there were quite a few elk around. He would shoot one every couple of months or so. He preferred the taste of the elk over the deer, so he was glad they were more plentiful. This time of year, the elk were high in the mountains. Or at least most of them were. He'd see or hear elk almost every day. The bulls were starting with their eerie mating calls, so Dobbs could keep a pretty good track of where the animals were most any time.

He decided a young elk, left out for the scavengers, would be a good way to get the cougar he needed. The big cats, he knew, would always take a free meal when they could. The tracks he'd seen were mostly around the carcasses of the deer and elk he had killed and left in the woods.

Dobbs knew he would have to be patient, but what the hell, he had nothing but time. He would take his rifle, an older .308 Winchester he had purchased at a pawn shop soon after he had moved up into the Cascades, and head out first thing in the morning. He would follow the sounds of the elk, move in, shoot a young one, and stake the carcass down in a spot where he could watch it.

It was something he had done often over the past few years, but this time he would leave the bulk of the meat on the elk, hopefully for a cougar to find.

*

After talking with the owner of the traveling big cat show, McCain had a much better idea what he was looking for, not that it was his job. Like he'd told Sam Banister, there were all kinds of police watching for the truck and trailer, including the State Patrol who most likely would spot it on one of the highways.

McCain's bigger concern was the cats' safety and what might happen if someone were to release the animals into the wild. That would create some real concerns, and many of them would land in his lap if the cats were released in Region 3.

When he got back to his truck after chatting with Banister and Deputy Hernandez, McCain was struck by the inviting temperature inside the vehicle. It was nice and cool, after having the AC running for fifteen minutes. Jack barely lifted his head when McCain got into the truck. The dog was enjoying his afternoon nap in the cool temperature of the back seat.

"Don't get up," McCain said sarcastically to the yellow dog. "Go ahead and sleep. You might need your rest if we have to track some exotic cats."

McCain sat in the cool air and checked the notes he'd taken during his talk with Banister. He knew what a tiger and female lion looked like. And he'd seen dozens of bobcats in the wild. But he didn't know if he could identify a caracal or an ocelot. So, he opened up his phone and googled each of the cats.

A caracal, according to the photo he was looking at, resembled a small cougar in color and facial features but had longer ears with long black tufts at the point. The information accompanying the photo said adult caracals, which were native to Africa, Asia, and India, weighed about twenty-five pounds, so they were maybe three times the size of a house cat.

The ocelot's face looked much more like a house cat's while its coat featured stripes and spots, similar to a leopard. A full-grown ocelot could be over forty pounds, so definitely bigger than a bobcat and more the size of a young cougar.

With the exotic cat photos fresh in his mind, McCain put the F-150 into gear and headed back out to the freeway. He headed toward the Thorpe exit, which would allow him to climb up into the area of the national forest west of Cle Elum, commonly referred to as the Taneum, to do some more looking around. He figured the State Patrol and Kittitas County Sheriff's Office had I-90 and the other main roads covered. He'd go hit the backroads leading up into the mountains to do what he was paid to do, and, if he happened to see the stolen pickup and trailer parked someplace, or an ocelot wandering around, all the better.

Unfortunately, while he saw a few black pickups, including one towing a white cargo trailer, it wasn't the outfit everyone was looking for. And the only feline he saw was a black cat that ran across the road in front of him. He tried not to think about the old wives' tale. Still, he couldn't help but remember his grandpa telling him that a black cat crossing your path was an omen of bad luck, and possibly death.

Chapter 4

It would be a stretch to say that Dobbs' plan to attract a cougar worked perfectly. The first elk he shot got eaten by coyotes before a cougar even had a chance to feed on the carcass. He was amazed at how quickly the small pack of coyotes had devoured the meat he had left on the animal.

The young elk wasn't big, but it was big enough that Dobbs had trouble moving it to the spot he had picked out for his cougar ambush. To lighten the load, and help his larder, he had taken the backstraps from the animal for himself. It was his favorite part of the elk, and he figured a cougar wouldn't miss them. With the innards still in the elk and all the other meat on the hindquarters, he figured there would be plenty remaining to attract a big cat.

When Dobbs had returned to the animal the next morning, there wasn't much meat left. Two golden eagles were feeding on what was left, with a small group of ravens sneaking in for a bite once in a while when the eagles were preoccupied. Dobbs didn't mind the birds. In fact, he figured the chattering of the ravens, crows, and magpies might actually attract a cougar.

With the next elk Dobbs shot, he staked the carcass out but spent the night guarding it. The coyotes again came for the free meal, but, in the red filter of Dobbs' powerful flashlight he'd strapped to his Winchester with duct tape, he started shooting the wild canines. He would kill one, and the others would run off. The chance for such a tasty meal, however, was too much, and the others would return. That happened two more times before the last two coyotes tucked their tails and ran off, never to return.

Whether it was the squawking of the birds or the smell of the now-decaying venison, a cougar finally appeared on the third day. Dobbs caught a slight movement up on the ridge above the little trickle of a creek where he'd staked the elk. After watching for a few moments, he caught the movement again, and this time he saw the long tail of the cat which told him immediately it was a cougar.

The big cat moved without a sound, its big, padded feet deadening any noise as it moved. The cougar stayed low to the ground, taking one step and slinking slightly forward, looking all around as its nose searched for any unnatural scents.

Dobbs waited until the cougar's head was behind a tree about a hundred and twenty yards away, and he raised his rifle. When the cat slowly cleared the tree, Dobbs put the crosshairs of his rifle's scope right behind the animal's shoulders and slowly squeezed the trigger.

At the shot, the mountain lion jumped straight up, turned as it flew through the air, and ran up the slope of the hill, back the way it had come. Dobbs watched as the cougar ran away and saw it crash dead into a pile of brush, just short of the top of the ridge.

When he got to the dead cat, Dobbs felt a little remorse. He didn't mind killing the elk and deer and turkeys and grouse that fed him throughout the year, but this was different. He didn't need the meat, but as he thought about it, he did need the cougar's hide and paws. He stopped feeling remorseful and went to work getting the parts he required to rid his world of the incessant noise-makers.

*

Spearman and Sutcliff waited until four o'clock in the morning to make their move. They figured it was the perfect time, late enough that everyone – even the barflies – would be sound asleep, yet early enough to beat the crowd that had to be at work at six. As promised, Spearman was able to quickly hotwire the pickup. After unlocking the truck door with a Slim Jim, the pickup's alarm started blaring. But Spearman knew exactly where to go to pull and cut the wires under the dash to stop it quickly. In a matter of two minutes, Spearman had the truck running, and with Sutcliff following in the Nissan pickup, they headed out of town.

On I-90 westbound near Snoqualmie Pass, Sutcliff passed the truck and trailer and took the lead. She had told Spearman she knew exactly where she wanted to release the cats, so he dutifully followed her as they gained elevation, passed through South Cle Elum, and headed for one of the Forest Service roads that would take them high into the Okanogan-Wenatchee National Forest.

Once they got up the Forest Service road a few miles, Sutcliff pulled off in a wide spot, got out, and walked back to the truck Spearman was driving.

"We'll go as far as we can up this road," she said to Spearman through his rolled-down window. "I want to get as high as we can into the mountains."

They drove slowly but steadily uphill along a spur road. A couple switchbacks were such tight turns that Spearman thought the long trailer wouldn't make it. Fortunately for him and the cats, he was able to negotiate the turns. Next, they took an even smaller two-track road, and when that road finally petered out, Sutcliff pulled to the side to allow the bigger truck through.

"How the hell are we gonna get this thing turned around to get outta here?" Spearman asked as he climbed out of the truck. The tiny road ahead of him ended in nothing but brush and trees.

"We'll just back it out," Sutcliff said as she walked to the back of the trailer. "There was a turnaround a ways back."

Spearman felt like asking who "we" was, knowing full well it would be him trying to back that giant trailer down the road, but he figured the last thing he needed right now was to get into a tiff.

"Grab those bolt cutters," Sutcliff ordered. "I think we can cut this lock."

Spearman got the bolt cutters up and tried three different times to cut through the shackle – the steel bar that enters the top of the lock. With one last burst of strength, the cutters clipped through the bar.

"Damn, they really don't want anyone getting in there," he said as he pulled the now-useless lock off the door bar.

It was just getting light as they opened the door to the trailer. Cat eyes stared out at them from within. The closest cat was the Bengal tiger, in the largest enclosure in the trailer. The tiger paced back and forth as it looked at Sutcliff and Spearman.

"We're going to have to get the tiger out first," Sutcliff said.

Once again, Spearman almost asked, "who is we," but again he thought better of it. He knew he would be the one in there with the cutters, trying to open the steel-barred doors. As he looked at the tiger, he started having some serious second thoughts. The cat was huge, much bigger than he had imagined. The feline's paws were as big as catcher's mitts. He started to wonder what they would do to a human being if they ever got a hold of one.

"Are you positive we really want to do this?" he asked. "How are these things going to survive out here?"

He'd asked the question before, and she gave him the same answer. "They're wild animals deep down, and their natural instincts will take over, especially if they're hungry."

Spearman could tell there was no dissuading her, so he grabbed the bolt cutters and moved closer to the door of the tiger cage.

*

As he drove, McCain listened closely to his radio for any calls about the trailer. But none came. He spent all day driving the back roads up in the Manastash and then cut over the hill to Bald

Mountain and spent a little time looking around there, although he didn't believe the cat burglars would have gotten this far from Ellensburg. He finally called it a day and headed back to Lower Naches where he lived with his wife, Sara.

When he pulled into the driveway of the house, Sara's big black sedan wasn't there, so McCain sat in the truck and gave her a call. His wife, who kept her maiden name, Sinclair, was the FBI agent stationed out of the Yakima office. Sara stayed extremely busy, mostly working with tribal police on the Yakama Indian Reservation. She occasionally got involved in some federal drug cases and had been vital in tracking and catching a serial killer two years prior.

McCain pressed the send button on his phone and waited. He tried not to call her when she was working, but he'd been out of phone service for much of the day and just wanted to connect with her. More than anything, he was curious what she might want for dinner. The couple had a deal: the first one home was in charge of dinner, whether it was cooking or going to get some take out, usually Chinese or Mexican.

McCain listened to the phone ring five times before it went to Sara's voicemail.

"Hey there," McCain said. "Just checking in. I've had kind of a weird day, but Jack and I are home. Anything special you want for dinner?"

He clicked off and turned to Jack. "I know what you want for dinner," he said to the dog, now standing in the back seat of the truck, tail thumping hard. The yellow dog had learned what the word "dinner" meant at an early age. It was his favorite word in the whole world.

If McCain didn't move quickly enough at dinner time, which was almost always the case, Jack would start barking to let his human partner know that he wasn't just hungry, he was famished.

"Okay, okay," McCain said as he opened the truck door to let Jack out. "Let's go eat."

Jack barked with happiness all the way to the front door.

After feeding Jack, McCain took a shower and then headed to the kitchen to see what he might find to make for dinner. He found a couple boneless chicken breasts in the refrigerator and decided to throw them on the grill. But he'd wait a bit to see if Sara called, so he'd know when to have it ready.

He was just checking his phone for any missed calls when he heard a knock at the door.

McCain opened the door and said, "Hi Austin. What's up?"

Austin Meyers was the kid who lived across the street. After Austin's father divorced his mom and left for California several years earlier, McCain had become a bit of a father figure for the young man. He'd taught the boy how to fish and took him on his first hunting trips, and now McCain was teaching the teenager how to drive.

"Any chance we could go driving again tonight?" Austin asked. "Mom's out with Charlie, and I can use her car."

Charlie was Austin's mom's new boyfriend. McCain had only met the man a couple of times and while he seemed like a nice enough guy, McCain still didn't know enough to decide whether he would be good for Jessie and Austin.

"I think we can manage that," McCain said. "But I have to figure out dinner for Sara and me first. How 'bout I give you a shout when we're all done."

"Sounds good. Thanks, Luke."

As McCain was closing the door, his phone rang. He looked at the screen then said, "So, what do you think about grilled chicken for dinner?"

McCain and his wife Sara had been married just nine months, so they were still new to the world of marital bliss. But as far as he was concerned, it was the perfect marriage and she was the perfect girl for him.

At five-foot-ten inches tall, with a slim, athletic build, black hair, and a beautiful smile, Sara was way out of his league. Or that's the way he always felt. She never made him feel that way though and always told him how much she loved him and appreciated having him in her life.

The two had worked together with other law enforcement agencies on the case of the Cascade Killer, a serial killer who was murdering women and dropping their bodies in the Cascade Mountains. With Sara and Jack's help, McCain was able to track down and catch the murderer.

"Chicken sounds great," Sara said. "But I'm going to be another half hour or so."

"That's fine. I'll have dinner ready when you get here."

McCain clicked off and called Austin.

"How about if we go do some driving about eight?" McCain asked, knowing that Austin would be happy to go at any hour of the day or night.

"That'd be great! See you then."

Over their dinner of grilled chicken, fresh fruit, and baked beans, Luke and Sara talked about their days at work. They actually liked discussing their days and the things they were working on, as it sometimes helped to consider things from a different angle. Three or four times over the past several months, Luke had said something that helped Sara with one of her cases and vice versa.

After Luke told his wife about the missing truck and trailer full of exotic cats, Sara thought about it for a while and then said, "My bet is this isn't a random deal. I think the person who stole the trailer knew what was in it, and they intend to do something with the cats."

"I thought about that," McCain said. "But there wasn't one word on the trailer that would indicate what was inside. How would anyone know?"

"Everything's on the internet now. I'm sure the Wild Cats of the World has a website and a social media presence. Maybe both. And if anyone has any hacking skills or knows someone who can get into Florida's licensing agency, they'd have no trouble getting a license plate for both the truck and trailer."

"That's true, but how would they know when they're coming through this area?"

"The fair starts this weekend, right? I'm sure they've been

promoting the cat show as part of their attractions this year. It doesn't take much to figure out they'd be driving by on the interstate sometime soon."

"Yeah, I guess," McCain replied. "But it could also be someone who just was hoping there would be some equipment or something else of value in that trailer."

"That's possible, but it seems like too big of a coincidence to me. What will happen to those cats if they get turned loose someplace in the mountains?"

"No clue, but I doubt they've ever learned to hunt for themselves. They've been in captivity most of their lives. I don't think it would turn out well."

They talked a bit more about the cats, and about Sara's day, which was pretty routine and filled with meetings.

"I'm doing another drive with Austin at eight," McCain said as they were finishing up the dishes. "We're taking Jessie's car. She's out with Charlie."

"I get some strange vibes from Charlie," Sara said. "Maybe it's because of my little situation a couple years ago, but the first time I met him, he kinda gave me the willies."

"I've been thinking the same thing, but I think we should give it a little time. Jessie seems to like him. And he seems to treat Austin okay."

"I guess," she said. "There's just something about him. I like Jessie too much to see her get hurt. I'm going to keep my eye on him."

"You're the FBI agent," McCain said with a shrug as he headed for the door to meet up with Austin.

Chapter 5

"SLOW DOWN!" McCain yelled as Austin drove the Honda Passport about twenty miles an hour too fast through a left-hand turn. At that second, McCain wished he had one of the brake pedals on the passenger side of the car like some of the driver's training vehicles. If he'd had one, he would have been stomping it through the floorboard.

Austin applied the brakes quickly and slowed the SUV enough to not run off the road. They'd had a similar issue on their first driving adventure, but even after McCain explained why you need to really slow down on a sharp turn, Austin either missed it or decided he'd try to scare McCain enough to scream like a child.

Once again, McCain explained centrifugal force and the consequences of speed and turns.

"Okay, okay, I get it now," Austin said.

McCain hoped Austin really did understand as they continued down State Route 12 toward Yakima.

"So, how are things going with Charlie?" McCain asked.

"What do you mean?" Austin asked.

"You know. Do you like him? Is he nice to your mom? How does he treat Bear?"

Bear was Austin's two-year-old yellow Lab. McCain figured you could tell a great deal about a person by the way they treated animals.

"He's okay. He seems to like Bear, but I'm not too sure Bear likes him. He pretty much shies away from him when Charlie tries to pet him."

"Hmmm," McCain muttered. He knew that dogs have a real sense about people, and if they don't like a person, there is most likely a reason why. "Well, give Bear time. I'm sure he'll come around."

Austin said his mom really liked Charlie. He said she'd been depressed for a long time after his dad left, and the young man liked seeing his mother happy.

"What does he do for a job?" McCain asked.

"I'm not sure," Austin said. "He seems to be rich. He always has money and gives me ten bucks every day for lunch. I spend less than five and put the rest in my truck fund."

"Oh, what's that?" McCain asked.

"Mom said she would help me buy a car when I turn sixteen, but I need to come up with most of the money. I've saved a bunch from my summer job bucking hay and changing sprinklers for Mr. Wilson, but the extra lunch money from Charlie is helping too."

"Good thinking," McCain said. "As long as you're eating semi-healthy things for lunch. So, Charlie's never said what he does for a living, huh?"

"My mom said he's in some kind of import/export business," Austin said. "But when I asked her what he imports and exports, she said she didn't know. I can try to find out more if you want."

"Nah, that's okay," McCain said. "I was just curious. Let's head back home."

*

The tiger emitted a low, throaty growl as Cory Spearman moved close to the door of the largest steel cage.

"It doesn't sound very friendly," Spearman said to Sutcliff. "And I really don't like the way the thing is looking at me."

"You'll be fine. Once we get the door open, it'll be finally headed to freedom. I think it knows we mean no harm and we're setting it free."

There was that "we" thing again, Spearman thought. And by the looks of the tiger, he didn't believe for one second the huge cat understood their good intentions.

Against his better judgment, he moved forward slowly to get the bolt cutters on the lock. The tiger stepped as far back into its enclosure as it could while continuing the low growl and a look that, if Spearman had to describe it, was the proverbial one that kills.

Clunk! As soon as he had the lock cut, Spearman turned and exited the trailer, figuring any second the huge tiger would be on his back, sinking his large fangs into his neck or skull. But the rush of the cat never came.

"What's it doing?" Sutcliff asked from her hiding spot behind a large pine tree.

Spearman slowly peeked around the trailer door, back toward the steel cage.

"Nothing," he said. "It's just standing there. But the door isn't actually open. The lock is cut, but the door is still closed."

"Well, you better go open it."

"I cut the lock. Maybe you should go open it," he said irritably.

When Spearman heard no response from Sutcliff, he turned and looked at her. Talk about looks that could kill. He saw something in her eyes that actually scared him worse than the tiger. He immediately started back into the trailer.

This time, he went in without the bolt cutters. When he saw that the tiger was still pressed up against the back of its cage, Spearman slowly lifted the keeper on the gate. And as he backed away, he let the gate swing open.

Again, as he turned to exit the trailer, he thought he might feel the tiger's claws sink into his back, but again, nothing happened. Another peek around the door showed the tiger still standing at the back of the enclosure, even though the gate was wide open.

"What's happening?" Sutcliff asked.

Spearman felt like telling her to get her ass up here and look for herself. Instead, he remembered the look he'd just seen and said, "It's just standing in the back of the cage. Maybe we should just back off and let it come out when it's ready."

"I wish we had some meat," Sutcliff said. "I bet that would coax it out. We're never going to get those other cats out with the tiger blocking the way."

The couple chatted about it for a couple minutes and decided that Sutcliff would stay in the black pickup and watch to see if the tiger came out while Spearman took the Nissan pickup back to the nearest store to buy some meat.

"I think the last store we saw of any size was in Cle Elum," he said as he was climbing into the small truck. "It's probably going to take a couple hours for me to get there and back."

"That's okay," Sutcliff said. "Get going and get back as quickly as you can."

She then climbed into the back seat of the truck to wait.

As Spearman drove down the bumpy Forest Service road, he again started thinking about taking his leave of all this craziness. He knew that if they didn't get eaten by the tiger or the lion, there was a decent possibility they were going to get caught. Surely, they would do some jail time for hijacking a traveling cat show and setting the exotic cats free.

He did like the sex with Sutcliff. It was the best he'd ever had. But was great sex worth dying for? Was it worth spending time in prison? And that look in her eyes had been pure evil. He knew if he left her up there in the woods, he might have to change his name and move to some small town in Wyoming or something to avoid her wrath.

The drive to Cle Elum took almost forty minutes. The whole

time he was waffling. Leave Cassidy up there on her own with the cats or get the meat and get back up there to see what happens next?

In the end, he decided that the sex really was worth risking his life and possible time in incarceration. As he drove back up the hill, he justified his decision. He could bail pretty much anytime. And as crazy as Sutcliff was, she was also very smart. All they had to do was let the cats out, pull the truck and trailer to some other location far from where the animals were set free, then get in the Nissan and they'd be home in no time. So long as a lion didn't dine on them.

*

It took Carson Dobbs the better part of a day to skin the mountain lion. He had purchased a book on taxidermy, and it showed step-by-step photos on how to skin a cat. The photos were of a person skinning a bobcat, but the text said that the process would also work on a cougar, or any other cat for that matter.

He carefully and painstakingly worked the skin off the carcass of the big cat. When he got to the feet, the book said to just cut them off at what would be the ankle bone. So that's what he did.

Dobbs finished the job by skinning the head. He "turned the ears," a procedure where you actually turn the ears inside out. Then he carefully removed the hide from around the eyes using an X-Acto knife. When the hide was totally removed, he spread it out and tediously removed even the tiniest pieces of flesh from the inside of the pelt.

The next step was to stretch the hide and salt it down. He had purchased several pounds of salt on his last trip to civilization and had plenty for the cougar hide. He got an old sheet of plywood, laid it on the ground and stretched the hide as best he could, tacking it and extending the legs out. Then he sprinkled it down with salt.

Dobbs followed the other instructions the best he could with the limited supplies he had. After several days of letting the salt do its thing, he thoroughly washed the hide in saltwater. As he did, he began working it and stretching it in an effort to keep it malleable and soft. He wasn't doing this to make a life-size mount. It didn't need to be perfect. He just needed the hide to be pliable so that it wouldn't encumber his movements.

The cougar's feet were going to be the tricky part. He needed the claws to extend when he attacked the unfortunate motorcycle rider, but he knew by looking at the cougar tracks he'd seen in the mud and snow over the past few years that when the cats walked the long, sharp claws were not exposed. If he was going to sell his ruse of a cougar killing a motorcyclist or two, he needed to make it look as real as possible.

When it was all said and done, he configured two of the cougar's feet with the claws fully extended and the other two with the claws pulled into the toes. It would take a while for the feet to dry enough to be usable, but he had nothing but time. He set them out in the sunshine and continued to work on the hide.

Off in the distance, he heard the high-pitched whine of a motorcycle riding one of the trails down the mountain. Dobbs now wished he had started his scheme a few months earlier. If he'd done so, he would be putting an end to the noise right now.

"Just wait," he mumbled to himself as he went back into his shack.

Chapter 6

"How did the driving lesson go?" Sara asked her husband as he came through the front door.

"It was fine," McCain answered. "It got better after he almost rolled the car taking a turn on the Old Naches Highway. I think he's getting it figured out."

"Well, it's good of you to go with him. Did he tell you how it's going with Jessie's new boyfriend?"

"Yeah, he said the guy was nice and gives him more than enough money to buy lunch every day. Says he's rich. Some kind of an import/export guy."

"Hmmm. Well, I hope he's good for Jessie and Austin."

"Austin said he's putting the lunch money and his summer savings toward buying a car. He's pretty excited about getting his license."

"I remember those days."

"So do I. It gave me the freedom to go fishing and hunting when I wanted, and no more dances with a parent driving us to and fro."

"I hated it when my dad drove us," Sara said. "He would embarrass me to no end, asking my date questions. So, what you got going tomorrow?"

"Jack and I are going to head back up to Kittitas County. I haven't heard if they've found those exotic cats, but if they haven't, maybe we can help."

The yellow dog was lying on the cool linoleum in the kitchen, and when he heard his name, his tail started thumping the floor.

"That trailer full of cats could be down in California by now," Sara said. "And what are you going to do with it if you find it? The last thing we need is for you and Jack to be wrangling lions and tigers."

Thump, thump, thump.

"Oh, I've got the owner's phone number on speed dial. He'd be getting a call from me to come deal with the cats. But if they've somehow gotten out somewhere, well, we might just have to go looking for them."

"I don't like that at all. I worry enough about the cougars and bears out there getting a hold of Jack."

Thump, thump, thump.

"Hey, what about me?"

"You have a gun. I think you can protect yourself just fine. Promise me you'll keep Jack out of harm's way."

Thump, thump, thump.

"I promise. Now, if we're done with all this, how about we go to bed and do a little snuggling?"

When Jack heard that, he got up and headed to the bedroom.

"Oh no," McCain said. "Not you. You've got your own bed out here."

*

When Spearman arrived back at the truck and trailer, he could see the back door to the trailer was still open, just like he had left it, and the tiger was still in its cage. The big feline was lying down with its head up, watching as the Nissan went past.

As he got past the trailer, he could see the truck. Sutcliff's head popped up from the back seat, her hair all tussled.

He parked the little pickup, double checked the trailer to see if anything was moving behind it, and then climbed out. He walked over to the GMC and opened the passenger door.

"Looks like you got a nice little nap," he said.

"Yeah, I was so tired. Is the tiger still in the trailer?"

"Yep, just as happy as can be, lying there like a princess."

"You got some meat?" she asked.

"The cheapest cuts I could find. I even asked the butcher for some old meat. Told him I was making my own dog food. He got me some roasts that he'd just taken off the shelf."

"Good, let's put it out there to see if the tiger will come out."

"I was thinking about that," Spearman said. "I think we shouldn't put all the meat out. We need to make sure we can get the lion and those other ones out too."

"You're smarter than you look," Sutcliff said. "Good idea. Now, I'll stay here while you go throw some of that meat out behind the trailer. You might even put a piece in the door of the tiger's cage, just so it knows what we're giving it."

This was going to get him killed, Spearman thought. Why didn't he just keep on driving to Wyoming?

Spearman listened as he quietly approached the back of the trailer. Nothing moved. He peeked around the back and into the trailer. The tiger immediately saw him and emitted a low growl.

"It's okay," Spearman said softly to the big orange and black cat. "We don't want to hurt you. We just want to give you something to eat."

Then he took a piece of flank steak and tossed it at the back of the trailer inside the edge of the open door.

"There you go," he said. "Eat up."

The tiger didn't move.

Spearman took another piece of flank meat and tossed it up farther into the cage, right in front of the tiger. Still the big cat didn't move. It didn't even look or sniff at the meat. It just stared at the man throwing the meat and kept growling.

After watching the tiger for another minute, Spearman walked back to the pickup.

"What happened?" Sutcliff asked as Spearman climbed in next to her.

"Nothing. It just laid there, staring at me."

"Well, hell. How are you going to get those things outta there?"

"I think we just need to be patient. Sooner or later, it will come out to eat that meat."

Spearman was right. Unfortunately, it was later rather than sooner. During the four-hour wait, Spearman took a little nap, and then the couple discussed what their next move might be.

"We can't just leave the trailer here with the cats in it," Sutcliff said. "They'll starve to death. The whole purpose of this was to let those cats finally live their life like they are supposed to, wild and free."

Spearman thought about pointing out that this couldn't be more different than their native habitat, and since they were raised in captivity, they had never had to hunt for their meals. Instead, he held his tongue.

"Well, we have to get that tiger out first," he said. "Then we can try to get the others out."

As he said that, he began to worry that this was going to be a much bigger process than simply opening the doors to a bird cage and watching all the birds just fly away.

*

McCain had been giving the stolen trailer full of exotic cats a lot of thought. He had gone to sleep thinking about it, and he started thinking more about it the minute he woke up.

"I believe you're right," he said to Sara as she was getting ready for work. "I think the trailer was targeted. But unless you had the facilities and knowledge to care for those animals, and planned to keep them for yourself, what else would you do with them?"

"There might be a market for the cats," she answered. "Dead

or alive, I don't know. I'll do a little asking around when I get to work."

"Or, someone might want to just turn them loose," he said. "But where? If they're so radical to think that the animals should be living outside of cages, they'd want to turn them loose in the wilderness where their contact with people would be minimal."

"That would be the logical answer," Sara said. "But someone who knowingly steals a trailer full of exotic cats probably isn't thinking very logically. So, what are you going to do?"

"Well, the early archery elk season starts tomorrow, so Jack and I are going to go make sure none of the bow hunters have opened the season early. If we get a chance to do some looking around for the truck and trailer, we will."

"Okay, but promise me: If you do find the trailer, be extra careful."

McCain assured his wife he'd be safe, kissed her on the cheek, called Jack, and headed out to his WDFW police truck. Jack ran to the back door of the truck and bounced up and down, anxiously wanting to jump in.

"Here you go, boy," McCain said as he opened the door and watched the dog fly into the truck.

He drove up I-82 to I-90 and headed west along the interstate. When he got to Cle Elum, McCain pulled in and stopped at the popular meat shop on the town's main street.

He ran into the shop and asked the man behind the counter, "Has anyone been in in the past twenty-four hours asking to buy a large amount of raw meat?"

The man thought about it a second and said, "No, sir."

McCain thanked the man, jumped back in the truck, and ran up the road to the Safeway grocery, went into the back where the meat was cut, packaged, and displayed, and asked the butcher there the same question. He got the same answer.

If the cats were being held somewhere in the area, he figured they would need to be fed sometime soon, and unless the cat-nabber had planned ahead and had brought some meat with him, he would have to buy some nearby.

At the first little store he stopped at in Roslyn, he got an interesting answer to his question.

"Yeah, there was a young guy in here earlier today, bought up probably sixty pounds of raw meat, mostly beef," the man in a white apron said. "Said he was making his own dog food. Took a bunch of flank meat and some roasts that I'd just taken out of the case."

"Does that happen often?" McCain asked.

"No, but occasionally if someone is having a big shindig or wants to smoke up some jerky or something, I'll sell a big quantity. But sixty pounds, that's a lot."

"What did the guy look like?"

"He was probably late twenties or early thirties. Long blond hair. Kinda looked like one of those surfer guys you see on TV. He was wearing a jacket but he looked pretty buff. Like you. Well-built. Wasn't quite as tall as you, though."

"Would someone be buying meat to make dog food?"

"Yeah, I guess. Some of the folks around here have sled dogs and run in races when the snow hits. I'm guessing they might do something like that."

McCain thought about it for a few seconds and asked, "Did you see what he was driving?"

"Sure did. I helped haul the meat out to his truck. It was an older, smaller pickup. Grey colored. Maybe a Nissan or Mazda."

"How'd he pay?"

"He had a pocket full of cash. That always works for me."

McCain thanked the man and headed back to his truck.

"Well, that gives us something else to look for," McCain said to Jack who had no clue what he was talking about. But the dog was happy to see McCain, so he stood in the back seat wagging his tail.

"Let's go see what we can see."

He put the truck in gear and headed across the freeway and up into the Cascades.

Chapter 7

The tiger took its sweet time eating the raw meat. Occasionally, it would look around at the couple sitting in the back seat of the truck watching it eat. Spearman thought it was staring right at him every time.

"I wish that thing would wander off," he said to Sutcliff. "The way it looks at me gives me the creeps."

"I do too," she said. "I really want to release the other cats so we can be out of here. The longer we're here, the more likely some hiker or hunter is going to stumble into all of this."

"What if it doesn't move?" Spearman asked. "Or worse yet, what if it goes back into its cage?"

"It's not going to do that," Sutcliff said, like she was some kind of tiger mind reader. "It's finally free. It's going to wander off into the woods, not back into the trailer."

"How about if that tiger is still just lying there an hour from now, we pull the trailer out of here and go someplace else to let the others out?" he bargained.

She thought about that for a moment and said, "Okay, that sounds like a good idea. But I think it's going to go off on its own."

An hour later, the tiger was in the exact spot, directly behind the trailer. It had gone over to a tree and urinated. Neither Sutcliff nor Spearman had ever seen a tiger pee and they were amazed at the amount of liquid that came out of the tiger's behind and how far it went.

"Jeez, I wouldn't want to be hit by that," Spearman said with a chuckle. "It was like a tiger fire hose."

But, after relieving itself, the tiger plopped back down and just stared at the two people in the back seat of the black truck.

"I don't know if it's the power of suggestion, but I really have to pee now," Sutcliff said.

"How are you going to get out and do that with the tiger watching our every move?" Spearman asked.

"I could get into the bed of the truck and pee over the side."

"Good luck with that. That tiger can probably leap over this truck in a single bound. Two jumps and it would be all over you."

Sutcliff cringed.

"But I really gotta go."

"Let's drag the trailer away from here like we planned. We'll get down the road and pull over, close up the trailer door, and you can pee. Then we'll find another spot to let the rest of the cats out."

Which is what they did. Spearman drove the GMC pulling the trailer, and Sutcliff drove the smaller Nissan pickup. It took a little maneuvering for Spearman to get the truck and trailer turned around. As he did, the tiger got up and loped twenty yards off to the side.

After they'd driven down the road a mile or so, they stopped, closed the trailer door, and relieved their bladders. Then they headed down the hill, looking for another road that would again take them into the high country.

*

Archery elk season was not nearly as popular as the general modern rifle season that started in late October, but the early season for bow hunters still attracted a good number of participants. And many would be hunting out of camps with wall tents. Some would be camping in travel trailers or even motorhomes.

In his experience, McCain found that about ninety-nine-point-nine percent of the archery hunters adhered to the rules. Sometimes, however, an over-anxious archer would see an opportunity to arrow an elk just before the season opened. Those hunters figured that if they got checked in the early days of the season, it would be too hard to tell when the animal was shot.

Then there was the rare bow hunter who, either out of frustration or inability, would bring out a high-powered rifle and shoot one. Then they would shoot an arrow at point-blank range into the bullet hole to make it look like it was the arrow that had killed the animal.

McCain had run across both situations a couple times over the years. Today, as he and Jack drove up into the Taneum, they were looking for the hunter who just couldn't wait until tomorrow. But mostly, he wanted to talk to some of the people in the camps to see if they may have seen the black GMC pulling a long white cargo trailer.

At the first camp he came to, McCain pulled off the little two-rack road and stopped behind a gun-metal gray Dodge pickup. As he climbed out, two men in camouflage clothing stepped out of a large white canvas wall tent.

"Hey, officer," the first man said. "What's up?"

"Hi, guys," McCain said. He left Jack in the running truck. "Just checking to see if you may have seen a newer model black GMC pickup pulling a fairly large white cargo trailer?"

The men looked at each other and shook their heads.

"No, sir. I haven't seen anything like that recently," the older, first man out of the tent said.

"There's been a few travel trailers headed up the road today, but no cargo trailers," the second, younger man said.

"Okay, thanks," McCain said. "Let me give you my card, and if you happen to see an outfit that matches that description, would you give me a call?"

Both men agreed. McCain wished them good luck with their hunt and jumped back into the truck.

He checked hunters at three other camps. None had seen the pickup or trailer. He left his card with them all. It never hurt to have extra eyes out there watching for the trailer full of exotic cats.

At the fifth and what would be the day's final camp, McCain's appearance wasn't met with open arms. There were four men in the camp, all big men, two maybe in their mid-forties, the other two in their twenties. McCain guessed they were probably from the same family, and they were not happy to see him. He knew not to take it too personally. They would have been just as disgruntled if any other game warden had happened into their camp, let alone a sheriff's deputy or police officer.

McCain had seen the look before and could feel the group's uneasiness.

"Hi, fellas," he said. "How's your day going?"

"Good, until now," a man with a glistening bald head and a brushy, burnt-orange mustache grunted. He wore a camo shirt with the sleeves ripped off. They were most likely ripped off because his thigh-sized biceps hadn't fit them. On the upper arms, circling the muscles, were about seven strands of barbed wire tattooed into the skin.

McCain quickly took in all four men and noticed the two younger men had red stains on the knees of their camo pants and specks of blood on their arms. One even had some blood specks on his face.

"Been seeing any elk?" McCain asked.

"Haven't been looking," said a second man, this one with the sleeves still attached to his camo shirt. "It ain't hunting season yet."

The man had thick, dark black stubble on top of his head, and even more black stubble covering three-quarters of his face, indicating a potential contest-winning beard in the making. McCain figured if he was there for more than a few minutes, he might actually see the man's facial hair growing.

"I understand that," McCain said. "Just wondered if you'd seen any animals in your travels today."

"Nope," red mustache said. "Is that all?"

"I'd like to see your hunting licenses and tags if I could," McCain said. He knew this request wasn't going to land well.

"You could see them if we was hunting, but we ain't," black beard said as he crossed his thick arms across his big chest. "So, why don't you go bother someone else?"

The other three men all crossed their arms and stared at McCain. If Russell Wilson had this group for his offensive line, McCain thought, he'd never get sacked.

He could push the situation, but McCain decided to attack this little problem from another direction. He just nodded at the men, turned, and headed for his truck. When he was in the truck, he quickly looked at the license plate of the closer of the two trucks sitting there and memorized the tag numbers.

He then backed out and headed down the hill. As he drove, he grabbed his radio mic and said, "Wildlife 148 calling for Wildlife 135."

He knew his fellow WDFW officer Stan Hargraves was working just over the hill and hoped to get him to come help with his situation.

"Wildlife 135, go ahead 148," the radio crackled.

"What's your location?" McCain asked.

"Manastash," Hargraves said.

"Any chance you can get over here? I have a need for more manpower."

After Hargraves told him he was on his way, McCain provided his exact location and told him what he thought he had stumbled into.

"I'm positive they killed something based on the blood on their clothes and skin," he explained. "I have Jack with me, so I think we can find the animal if we can keep the men under control."

The radio crackled again.

"Wildlife 148, this is KCS Deputy Hernandez," a female voice said. "I'm about thirty minutes from you. I can come assist if needed."

"That would be great, thanks," McCain said. "See you soon."

He then turned to the computer in his truck, opened the Department of Licensing site and typed in the license plate number that he had memorized. The little circle in the computer screen whirled away, and in a minute the information on the license popped up. The dark blue Chevy 1500 pickup was owned by a Victor Osborn, address in Fircrest, Washington.

McCain then put Osborn's name and address into the WDFW website. Within a couple minutes, all the information he needed was on the screen. It showed the man did have a current hunting license with an archery endorsement. But he also had a couple previous violations on his record. One was for hunting out of season, and another for not tagging an animal at the time of the kill. McCain wondered which one of the men was Osborn, so he entered his information into another part of the DOL website. A half minute later, a copy of the man's driver's license popped up on the screen. Osborn was the one with the bald head and orange mustache.

As he sat and waited for Hernandez and Hargraves, McCain thought about how to approach the men in the camp. Straightforward would be the most professional. Go in, talk to the men with the blood on their clothes, and see if he could get an honest answer.

But being straightforward could incite more anger from the gruff crew. Instead, McCain thought about sneaking in on the camp from behind. He'd done that before with good success. And, with this group of men, it might work better at preempting any possible altercations. He'd talk to the other two officers when they arrived.

Chapter 8

The plan the three came up with was a combination of the two ideas McCain had been mulling over. They decided that Hargraves and Hernandez would circle around the camp and come in quietly from behind while McCain approached them head-on, man to men. If he could get the answers he needed from the men, great. If they got confrontational, then the other two officers would come in. And they would be armed with shotguns.

McCain waited for fifteen minutes to let Hargraves and Hernandez get into place and then he drove back down the two-track into the camp. This time, the men were in a big green canvas tent. They filed out the front door one at a time when they heard McCain's truck pull in.

"What do you want now?" black beard said. "We told you we wasn't hunting."

"You know," McCain said. "I'd like to believe you, but I need to ask a few more questions."

McCain pointed to black beard and Osborn.

"You two can go stand over by the fire pit. I need to talk to these two gentlemen," he said, pointing to the two younger men with blood on their pants. They'd cleaned the blood off their skin, McCain noticed.

The two younger men seemed nervous and looked at the older men for help.

"Waddaya want with them?" black beard said. "They done nothin' wrong."

"I didn't say they did," McCain said. "I just want to ask them some questions. Now, you two, go to the fire pit please."

"I don't think we're going to do that," Osborn said. "In fact, I think we're gonna ask you one more time to leave."

"I'm not leaving without talking to you two first," McCain said, directing his gaze at the two younger men.

"Then we'll just make you leave," black beard said.

From behind the men, Hernandez and Hargraves stepped out of the brush and worked the actions of their shotguns, jacking shells into the chamber. The sound was crisp and clear in the mountain air, and it made the two younger men jump. Three of the men turned and looked at the two newly arrived officers. Black beard just stood staring at McCain, with the tiniest of grins on his face.

"I don't believe you'll be making anyone do anything," McCain said, staring right in the eyes of the man with the black flat top. "In fact, to make sure of it, I want all four of you face down on the ground, hands behind your backs."

Slowly, the two younger men complied. But the two older men just stood there.

"There's an easy way of doing this and a hard way of doing this," McCain said. "Your choice."

"This is bullshit," Osborn said. "You have no right."

"I have probable cause," McCain said. "That means I have enough evidence to believe at least two of you were involved in killing an animal out of season today, and we're going to get to the bottom of it."

That shut the men up, and the two older men went down onto the ground. While Hargraves stood by with his shotgun, Hernandez and McCain handcuffed all four men. They sat the two older men up and then helped the two younger men to their feet.

"This way, fellas," McCain said as he walked them over to his truck. When he got to the truck, he opened the back door and let Jack out. As soon as the yellow dog hit the ground, McCain told him to sit. Jack dutifully obeyed.

"I want you boys to meet Jack," McCain said. "I don't know if you read about it a while back, but this is the dog that tracked down the serial killer who was killing women and dumping their bodies up here in these woods. He can find anything given a little time. Now, before you say anything, I have a pretty good idea you opened elk season just a little early, and the meat and other body parts are stashed around here someplace. You can tell me the truth right now and we'll get this straightened out right here and now. Or you can lie to me and I can send Jack out to do his thing. Then we'll be doing a bunch of paperwork and processing at the Kittitas jail when he finds the meat. How would you like to handle it?"

As it turned out, the men confessed that one of the two younger men had, in fact, killed a cow elk earlier that morning. They had hoped to tag it when the season opened the next day. They pointed out where the meat was stashed, and while Hargraves started writing roughly six hundred dollars in tickets to the man who shot the elk and a two-hundred-and-sixty-dollar ticket to the man who assisted in the butchering, McCain and Jack went out to retrieve the meat.

It took four trips, packing elk quarters and backstraps. Hernandez put the meat in the back of her air-conditioned SUV and left to deliver it to a butcher in Ellensburg who would cut the meat for donation to a local homeless shelter. The elk would make several very tasty meals.

The man with the black beard was Osborn's brother, Ken, and after checking him out on the computer, McCain found that he too had a couple past dealings and citations with Fish and Wildlife officers.

"You two have a record for doing this very thing," McCain said to the Osborns. "You'd think you'd learn your lesson."

The men just sneered at him, one through a bushy burnt orange mustache and the other through a black beard that McCain swore was a quarter inch longer than it had been earlier in the day.

"Now, I can guarantee I'll be back to check on you tomorrow, and the next day, and the day after that, so let's play by the rules, okay?"

McCain's little speech was met with more sneering from the two older men. The younger men nodded their heads in agreement.

The Bengal tiger, having never seen a coniferous forest before, had no idea what to do with her newfound freedom. She was thirsty and sleepy. First a drink, and then a nap. But where would she find water? There was always water in the giant trough in her enclosure. There was no such thing here. An internal urge told her to start walking. So, off she went into the trees and up over the hill.

Spearman, who was leading the way in the black pickup pulling the cat trailer, hit the main Forest Service road and turned to the west. He figured going up that road would get them to another spur road where they could get off the beaten path and try again to release the cats.

They drove up the road, gaining altitude as they went, mile after bumpy mile. After a half hour, Spearman saw a side road and decided to take it. He figured the narrower roads were not traveled as often as the main roads and felt this would get them to a spot where they could let the cats go.

The road he had chosen went for about a mile along a side hill and ended up at an old log landing. That gave him plenty of room to circle around, but because the hillside had been logged in the not-too-distant past, there weren't many mature trees around. It wasn't a clearcut because there were still some fir trees standing here and there, but it was pretty wide open.

"What do you think about here?" he asked Sutcliff through his rolled down driver's window.

"Looks good to me," she said. "I'm getting anxious about all of this. I'd really like to get the cats out of the trailer, dump this stuff, and get on our way."

"Okay," Spearman said. "Hopefully, the other cats will be more anxious to get out of the trailer."

He turned off the truck, grabbed the giant lock cutters, walked to the back of the trailer, and opened the door. As the door swung open, the daylight poured into the bowels of the trailer, and he could see cat eyes looking at him from several places.

"Wonder which one of these things is going to kill me," he said under his breath.

The trailer was set up with a narrow walkway that went past the tiger enclosure to the lion's cage. Instead of opening the lion's door, he decided to open the smaller cats' enclosures first and hope they would scurry out of there.

The smaller cats weren't as intimidating as the tiger, but he knew if one wanted to attack, they could certainly do some damage. To keep a bit of distance from them, he cut the door locks for the three smaller cats and undid the latches but waited to open the doors until he was back toward the rear door. He had found a long, stout rake in the trailer – probably for cleaning the different cages – and used it to swing each of the doors open.

None of the cats came out as their doors opened, so Spearman backed out and returned to the trucks. He told Sutcliff what he'd done, and they watched the back of the truck with anticipation.

"Maybe we should try to entice them with the meat, like we did with the tiger," she said.

"Let's wait just a bit," he said. "Then we can try it."

"We need to get them out of there," Sutcliff said. "The longer we stay out here, the more we risk getting caught. Maybe you can take that rake and kind of shoo them out."

Spearman didn't have any experience dealing with caged exotic cats, but he did grow up with some house cats. His sister had a couple as pets, and he was around them enough to know you don't "shoo" cats anywhere. That bobcat and the one with the long black tufts on its ears would likely run right up that rake handle and into his face if he started poking at them.

"I don't think that's a good idea. Let's just sit here and watch for a bit. If one goes, maybe they'll all go."

About five minutes later, the bobcat walked out the back of the trailer, looked around for about three seconds, and ran off down the road.

"There's one," Spearman said. "Come on, where's the others?"

The others were content to stay right where they were. Even the raw meat wasn't enough to get them to move. After sitting there for almost an hour, Sutcliff was about ready to admit defeat.

"Let's try to get the lion out," she said. "If we can get that one out, we'll just leave all the doors open for the others and get the hell out of here."

"Okay," Spearman said. He was dreading this one. The smaller cats had a look of fear in their eyes, but not the lion. A couple times as Spearman had walked by its enclosure, it had snarled and raised a paw like it wanted to grab him by the throat and shake him until he was dead.

Again, he entered the trailer with his lock cutters and went to work on the lion's cage door. He was looking at the lock as he strained to cut it, not really watching the lion, when the thing charged at him.

"HEY!" Spearman yelled as he jumped back. One of the lion's paws had shot out between the bars and had caught the tail of his shirt. Luckily, the shirt ripped, and he was able to keep moving back.

"Holy shit," Spearman said as he backed out of the trailer.

"What happened?" Sutcliff asked, a smile on her face.

Spearman saw the grin and realized she actually thought it was funny. Well, if she wanted that lion out of the trailer, she was going to have to do it herself. He was done.

"That tiger was a pussycat compared to the lion," Spearman

said. "I'm not going back in there with that thing. It wants to kill me. Let's get in the little truck and get the hell out of here."

"Now slow down," Sutcliff said. "What exactly happened?"

He told her the whole story, and she started to smile at the part where the lion raised its paw. By the time he told her about the lion charging the door and ripping his shirt, she was laughing so hard tears were streaming down her cheek.

"It's not funny," Spearman said. "If that thing would have caught me, who knows what it would have done."

Sutcliff couldn't stop laughing. Him telling her that it wasn't funny, in such a serious manner, holding the tattered tail of his shirt in a shaking hand, just made it all the more humorous to her.

When she finally stopped laughing, wiping tears from her face, he said, "I'm serious. I'm done." And that started her laughing all over again.

"I'm taking Scott's truck and heading back to Seattle," he said as he walked toward the Nissan. "If you want to stay and deal with these cats, fine. But I'm through."

He was walking to the truck when she ran up and grabbed his arm.

"I'm sorry – you're right. Let's leave all the meat at the back of the trailer, throw some in for the lion, and we'll go. Hopefully, the smaller cats will get out. We'll make an anonymous call to the cops and let them know where the trailer is so they can come care for the lion and any of the ones that won't get out."

Spearman took a couple of the roasts and pitched them into the lion's cage. The big cat just stared at him with contempt and hatred. Then he dumped the rest of the meat in the grass and dirt at the back of the trailer.

As they drove away from the truck and trailer, Sutcliff was pissed. She really wanted to liberate those poor wild animals from captivity, but she had mostly failed.

"We should have planned this out better," she said to Spearman as they bounced down the Forest Service road. "Next time, I'm going to do something different. Those cats were depending on me to succeed, and I failed them."

Spearman wondered just what his girlfriend was contemplating when she had said "next time." The last thing he wanted to do again was try to steal some exotic animals living in captivity.

"You really want to try this again?" he asked.

"Don't you?" she asked. "I'm more determined than ever. There are thousands of animals living in cages that need to be freed."

She really was a little bit crazy, Spearman thought. But she was incredible in bed. He wondered again if the desire for great sex was actually going to kill him. He believed it very well could. And if that lion had gotten a hold of him, it might have been that very day.

Chapter 9

It was the opening day of archery elk season and McCain, along with the other wildlife police officers in the region, would have a busy day. He liked the archery season because normally there were very few, if any, issues with the hunters. He enjoyed meeting people and talking to them. Being an ambassador for the Department of Fish and Wildlife was a big part of the job, and he took it seriously.

McCain had shared the information about the young guy coming into Roslyn to buy bulk meat with his fellow WDFW officers and the Kittitas County Sheriff's Office. He wasn't sure it was anything, but it could be, so they all added the older gray Nissan or Mazda pickup to their watch list. He also kept an eye out for the newer black GMC truck, either pulling a trailer or not. Though that model truck was much more common, when he spotted one later that day, McCain thought maybe he'd hit pay dirt.

The pickup was parked on a narrow spur road just off the main Forest Service road heading up Cabin Creek in Kittitas County.

McCain wanted to do some patrolling up this way because he thought there was a chance the cat burglars might have headed to the hills with the truck and trailer versus heading to Seattle or some other populated areas. If the catnappers were environmental activists, then the mountains seemed to McCain like a likely destination for them.

As McCain pulled up behind the truck, he saw the license plates were from Washington and not Florida. But he knew car thieves often switch plates as soon as they have a hot vehicle on their hands, so he decided to investigate. McCain walked up alongside the truck and looked through the driver's side window. A man with long blond hair and head-to-toe camo was sound asleep. He hated waking the guy, but McCain went ahead and tapped on the window.

The man jumped awake and started grabbing for something. McCain put his hand on his service revolver until he saw that the man was reaching for his keys sitting next to him in the center console. He got the keys, put them in the ignition, turned it a quarter turn, and then rolled down the electric window.

"Sorry about that," McCain said.

"Man, I was dead out," the guy said. "I woke up at 2:30 to get up here, and as I was waiting for daylight, I decided I would just close my eyes for a few minutes. "

McCain apologized again and asked the man for his hunting and driver's licenses. The man dug into his back pocket, pulled out his wallet, and extracted a Washington State driver's license and a hunting license. His name was Nolan Kerr, and he said he worked at the Les Schwab tire store in Ephrata.

"So, Mr. Kerr, I assume you are up here archery hunting elk?"

"Yes, sir. Or at least that was my intention. Didn't mean to sleep half the morning away. I guess I was more tired than I thought."

"Is this your truck?" McCain asked.

"Yes, sir."

"Can I see the registration?"

Kerr tilted the visor in front of him and pulled out the

registration. As he was looking at the paperwork, which appeared to be in order, McCain explained why he had asked for all his information.

"We're looking for a truck the same model and color as yours, last seen pulling a big, white cargo trailer."

Kerr thought about it for a few seconds and said, "I think I might have seen the outfit you're looking for."

"Oh yeah?"

"Yesterday, when I was scouting. I noticed it because the truck looked very similar to mine. I thought they might be hunters pulling a big trailer full of horses."

"Where did you see it?"

"It was on the Nelson Siding Road, just off I-90 between Cle Elum and Easton, heading west."

"About what time?

"Let's see . . . it was early, like at five or somewhere around then."

"Okay, thanks. It might be the rig we're looking for or, like you said, just some hunters wanting to set up a horse camp. Thanks, and again, sorry to wake you."

About that time, a bull elk bugled in the distance. Kerr perked up.

"I'm awake now, and I hear them calling."

As McCain backed out, Kerr was putting on a pack and grabbing his compound bow. He gave McCain a quick wave and started walking up the trail toward the bugling elk.

*

About five miles to the west, a gray Nissan drove down a Forest Service road until it hit I-90 in Easton, merged into westbound traffic, and disappeared among the thousands of vehicles heading over Snoqualmie Pass. When Spearman and Sutcliff got to North Bend, they pulled off the interstate and followed the road into a cluster of mini-marts and fast-food restaurants.

"Look for a pay phone," Sutcliff said. "There has to be one here."

"I haven't seen a pay phone in like fifteen years," Spearman said. "No one uses those things anymore."

"We're going to use one as soon as we find one. Now LOOK!"

They came across one outside of an older gas station. Spearman pulled in next to it, Sutcliff jumped out, dropped a quarter into the phone, and dialed 911.

"Nine-one-one, what's your emergency?"

"The authorities are looking for a stolen trailer full of exotic cats. I know where it is. Get a pen and listen carefully."

She told the operator exactly which Forest Service road they had been on and approximately how far up the road they were when they turned off on the side road.

"What's your name?" the operator asked.

"You don't need my name. What you need to know is those cats might starve or cook inside that trailer if someone doesn't get there fast." Sutcliff hung up and jumped back into the gray pickup. "They should find them unless they all got out. I sure hope they did. They deserve to live the rest of their lives as free animals."

Spearman bit his tongue. No sense telling her again that the animals probably had no chance on their own out there in the wilderness. She'd never believe it.

As they drove away, the pay phone began to ring. The kid working inside the gas station heard the phone ringing and came out to answer.

"Hello?" the kid said into the phone.

"Yes, this is the North Bend police. Did you see who just placed a call on this phone?"

"I sure did. She was hot. I mean, really good looking."

"Can you describe her, please?"

"I just did," the kid said. "I mean, like, she was smoking hot. Almost nasty."

"Can you give me a description of her as in color of hair, height, weight, those types of things?" the officer asked.

"She had dark hair, tall, skinny, like those *Sports Illustrated* swimsuit models. Well, like most of those *Sports Illustrated* models.

I think they are allowing some not-so-skinny models in there now. They're all hot, though. Man, she was like an eleven."

The police officer decided to shift gears.

"What was she driving?" she asked.

"She wasn't driving anything," he said.

"You mean she was walking?"

"No, she climbed into a POS gray pickup with some surfer dude."

"POS?" the officer asked.

"You know, a piece of shit. It was older, and the paint was faded. I would take it though. It's a better POS than my POS. I got a 1994 Chevy Cavalier and . . ."

"Did you happen to get a license plate number?" the officer interrupted.

"Um, no. Why would I want to do that? They didn't do nothing besides make a phone call. Is that against the law now?"

"No, it's not," the officer said.

She took the kid's name and cell phone number and told him that he might be needed at some point to make an identification on the woman who made the phone call.

"Happily," the kid said. "I'll see her in my dreams. She was a sparkler."

"Sparkler?"

"You know. Twelve hundred degrees hot."

With that, the police officer hung up and put out an alert for local, county, and state police to be looking out for an older gray pickup. She decided not to pass on the description of the truck as being a POS driven by a surfer dude with a sparkler riding next to him.

*

McCain was heading west on the Nelson Siding Road between Cle Elum and Easton when he received a call from Kittitas County dispatch.

"All officers in the vicinity, we have a possible ten-twenty on the stolen truck and trailer with the exotic cats. Unidentified female caller said the trailer is located on FR 41 out of Easton. Said it is off the main road about eleven miles up the hill."

"Wildlife 148, copy," McCain said. "I'm in the area and will check it out."

"Copy," the dispatcher said.

"Have you called the owner of the truck and trailer?" McCain asked.

"Yes, KVS is transporting him that way."

"Okay, I will report if I find anything."

McCain clicked off the radio and headed to Easton and Forest Service Road 41.

Chapter 10

The tiger found water in the next draw where there was a spring-fed creek. She drank enough of the cool, clear water to quench her thirst. Then, with her primary needs met for the time being, the tiger wandered down the creek, taking in the new aromas and sights. When she found a spot in the shade under a young Douglas fir, the big cat turned a couple circles and lay down for a much-needed nap.

*

The cougar paws with the claws extended were not exactly how Carson Dobbs had wanted them to turn out, but they would do the job. Held just right and swung with enough force, they certainly would make some deep and gruesome cuts on a person. They might not be exactly how a live mountain lion would do it, but the result would be close enough.

To try his newly constructed weapons out, he decided he needed to build a training dummy. He would try to make it as human-like as he could out here in the wilderness.

Dobbs had once shot a black bear when he was low on meat. It had amazed him how much the animal, once it was rid of its thick furry hide, looked like a human body. Hung in a tree, the carcass with arms and legs still attached was almost eerie to look at.

As he thought about how to test his cougar paws, his mind went back to the one time, the only time, he had taken a bear for food. As he thought about it, he remembered how the bear had tasted. Although a person could certainly eat the oily meat, he much preferred deer, and especially elk over the bear. At the time, he told himself no more bears, but now, with the need for a test dummy, he believed a bear carcass might just be exactly what he needed.

Occasionally, a bear would wander by his shack, but you couldn't count on one coming by with any regularity, so Dobbs figured he would have to go out to find one. He had read that bear hunters sometimes baited the bruins by putting out meat scraps, fruit, and baked goods. Unfortunately, he had none of that.

Then he remembered the honey tree he had found a mile from his cabin. Dobbs liked honey but never wanted to risk a bee attack to get some. He had seen bear scat near the old tree and claw marks on its trunk where a bear had climbed up to steal some of the sweet nectar.

As with the cougar, Dobbs decided to stake out the honeycombed bait and wait for a bear. It took him much longer than he would have liked, but Dobbs was extremely patient. He had to sit at the tree for four days before a black bear came by. Whether the bear was coming for the honey or was just wandering by, Dobbs didn't know, but the bruin was definitely close enough to shoot with his rifle.

It only took one well-placed shot to put the bear down. Dobbs did not want to spend a lot of time tracking a potentially wounded bear, so he waited until the animal turned its head at him and shot it right between the eyes. At the report of the rifle, the bear collapsed in a heap.

Skinning the bear was not a difficult job. Dobbs had the

innards removed and the hide off in less than twenty-five minutes. The bigger chore was going to be getting the whole carcass up the hill and back to his cabin. Even with the entrails, hide, head and paws removed, the body weighed a hundred and twenty pounds.

At first, he tried to transport the carcass over his shoulder in a fireman's carry. He made it about fifteen yards up the hill before he realized that wasn't going to work. Dobbs had brought a ten-by-ten tarp and a length of rope with him, so he decided to try wrapping the carcass in the tarp and pulling it up the hill. It wasn't perfect, but it worked better than trying to carry it. Slowly but surely, he pulled the bear's carcass up the hill. Occasionally, it would get hung up on brush or a downed log or limb, but after three hours of pulling and resting, he got the carcass to the tree near his shack.

He threw the rope up over a thick branch and ran it under the bear's front legs and then through holes he had cut just below the top rib on each side of the carcass. With the assistance of a come along he had nailed to the tree, Dobbs inched the carcass off the ground and eventually got it just high enough that the back legs were barely above the dirt and pine needles. The bear was now positioned perfectly and stood about five feet tall. It was just the right height to mimic a person, Dobbs thought.

Next, he grabbed some old clothes he'd purchased from random Goodwill stores here and there, dressing the bear carcass in items that were either too big or too small for him. Using a hank of rope, he tied the britches around the bear's middle and put an old flannel shirt over the bear's front leg, wrapped around the back of the animal, and through the other front leg. It now looked even more like a human standing there – a headless human, but human nonetheless.

The light of day was fading as he finished dressing his test dummy, so Dobbs decided he would put off his practice attacks until morning, when he could see what his cougar paws would do to actual flesh.

*

McCain turned up Forest Service Road 41 but resisted the urge to get up the hill quickly. If whoever stole the truck and trailer was intent on releasing the cats into the wild, there was a chance he might see one of them as he drove, so he took it slowly.

"I don't know what we are getting into here," McCain said to Jack, who was sitting in the passenger seat, watching out the window.

The dog could always sense when McCain was excited or worried, and it always brought him to attention. Most of the time he would be lying in the back seat, napping, but now he was watching ahead, as if he knew what McCain was thinking.

They drove slowly up the hill. McCain kept an eye on his odometer. When he was about nine miles up the hill, he slowed even more. Every time he saw a road of any consequence that led off the main road, he would take it. Four different roads went to nothing but old log landings or dead ends.

The fifth side road was different. McCain noticed fresh vehicle tracks in the dirt, so he drove very slowly as he moved up gradually through the trees and around a bend. He caught a glimpse of the trailer through the trees and as he finished the gradual turn, there it was, with its back door open. A black pickup sat in front of the trailer.

"This is it, boy," McCain said to Jack. The dog was looking intently at the trailer, transfixed by some movement inside.

"Wildlife 148," McCain said into the microphone. "I've found the trailer."

"Copy," the dispatcher's voice came back. "Any cats?"

"I haven't looked yet. Stand by."

"Copy."

McCain grabbed the twelve-gauge shotgun from the rack in the center of his truck, made sure it was loaded, and opened the driver's side door. As he did, he scanned the trees and brush for any tiger or lion.

"You stay here for a minute," he said to Jack.

The dog knew what that meant and obediently sat down. He

watched as McCain slowly walked in front of his police pickup and moved gradually to the back of the trailer.

As McCain drew closer, he could see a female lion lying in a big middle cage and two smaller cats in smaller enclosures toward the front of the trailer. The doors to all the cages were open. Based on their coloration and ears, he could tell the two smaller cats were the caracal and the ocelot.

"Shit," he said under his breath when he realized the Bengal tiger was not in the trailer. The other missing cat was the bobcat, but McCain was less concerned by that.

The remaining cats seemed relaxed, although they were all panting. McCain figured that meant they hadn't had water, and since the day was warm, they definitely needed to drink. Before he turned to walk back to his truck to report his findings, he did another thorough inspection of his surroundings. He had seen a Bengal tiger at the local fair in Yakima and knew that a fully grown one would be nothing to mess with.

McCain moved back to his truck and climbed in.

"Wildlife 148," McCain said. "Total of three cats in the trailer. The lion, caracal, and ocelot. No Bengal tiger or bobcat."

"Copy," the dispatcher answered.

"What's the ETA of Mr. Banister?" McCain asked.

"This is KCSO. We're about twenty minutes out," replied a deputy who'd been following the conversation.

"Copy. I'll go out to FR 41 and tie some orange flagging at the turn to the side road. Then I'll come back in and watch to make sure none of the remaining cats get out."

"Copy. We'll be there shortly."

McCain started the pickup and backed up all the way out to the main Forest Service road. Again, before opening his door to get the flagging tape from his truck bed, he searched the surrounding area. Seeing nothing out of place, he jumped out, grabbed the orange tape from the truck's utility box, and put several pieces of the flagging material on the branches of trees just ahead of the turn to the side road.

With that done, he returned to where he had a good view of

the trailer and stopped. As he and Jack looked into the back of the trailer, McCain started thinking about the situation. If he'd stolen the trailer full of cats with the intent of releasing them, would he leave the truck and trailer at the spot of the release? If they had any brains at all, McCain figured they would most likely try to set the cats free and then move the truck and trailer someplace else. There was one way of telling if the cats had been released here. There would be tracks left by the released tiger and bobcat walking away from the trailer.

McCain looked around for any sign of the orange and black tiger and then opened the door, shotgun in hand. He left the truck running with the AC on for Jack and climbed out. He moved out of view of the back of the trailer and drew closer to it. As he did, he looked for fresh cat tracks in the soft dirt of the two-track road. When he got about halfway to the back of the trailer, he found his first track. It was definitely a cat track, and it was fresh.

In all the time McCain had spent in the woods, growing up hiking and hunting as a young man, and then in his capacity as a wildlife police officer, he had seen many, many cat tracks. He'd seen plenty of cougar tracks and enough bobcat tracks to know that these were the latter. He'd never seen a tiger track, but knowing the size of the live tigers he'd seen at the fair, he knew their paw prints had to be much larger than a cougar's. But, as he searched around the trailer, always keeping an eye on the back of rig for any exiting cats, he couldn't locate any other cat prints.

Fresh people prints, on the other hand, were plentiful. Most were a man's boot tracks – size eleven was McCain's guess. And, close to the black truck, he found a couple smaller shoe tracks, either a young man or a woman. Since the call that had come in about the truck and trailer was a woman's voice, he figured the smaller tracks were hers.

Chapter 11

McCain was kneeling and looking at the bobcat tracks when he heard a vehicle approaching. It was a Kittitas County Sheriff's SUV, driven by Deputy Alivia Hernandez. A very anxious-looking Sam Banister was sitting in the passenger seat.

The SUV was still rolling to a stop when Banister opened the passenger door and flew out.

"Thank God you found them," he said to McCain as he walked right by to the back of the trailer. "They have to be petrified."

As soon as Banister was in the back of the truck, the three cats all moved forward. The man closed the doors to the different cages and then turned and asked McCain to close the back door.

"You going to be okay in there?" McCain asked.

"Yes," Banister said. "I just want to fire up the air conditioner and get them some water. I'll only be a minute."

A few seconds later, McCain heard a motor at the front of the trailer fire up and start purring along. Five minutes later, a side-hatch that was almost totally invisible popped open, and Banister climbed out.

"Well, they seem to be just fine," he said to McCain. "But now I'm really worried about Timba. She's never been in the wild alone, and I have no idea how she'll survive."

"I don't believe the tiger was released here," McCain said. "But the bobcat was."

"How do you know that?" Hernandez asked.

"No tiger tracks anywhere around this area. I looked pretty closely. The bobcat, on the other hand, took off right here," he said pointing at the cat tracks and then pointing in the direction they went into the woods.

"Oh, man," Banister said. "That's not good. How in the world will we know where she is?"

"The tiger or the bobcat?" Hernandez asked.

"Timba," Banister said. "The tiger. Frankly, I'm not worried about the bobcat. It had been rehabilitated after being hit by a car a year or so ago. It knows how to survive out here. I was going to turn it loose somewhere in this area when I was done with the show."

After discussing alternatives with Banister, it was decided he would take the truck and trailer and go on to Puyallup, where he still could participate in the twenty-one-day fair. He had only missed one day of his commitment and even though he was two cats short, he figured he could at least salvage some of his appearance fee. The man was visibly worried about the tiger and how she was going to survive, but as McCain explained to him, there was really no way of knowing where the big cat might be in the hundreds of thousands of acres of National Forest in the region.

"We'll get you all the paperwork via email for releasing the stolen truck and trailer," Hernandez said. "And if we happen to find the tiger, or if there is a sighting, we'll need you to come right away."

"Of course," Banister said. "I really feel like I should stay. I don't know how she's going to make it out here on her own."

After more discussion, with assurances from McCain and Hernandez that Banister would be the first one called if the tiger was spotted, he reluctantly headed to the black GMC pickup. Before he pulled around to leave, he got out and double-checked the three cats left in the Wild Cats of the World traveling show. As he drove by, he shot a nervous smile at the two officers, waved meekly, and took off.

"Any idea where to look for a Bengal tiger around here?" Hernandez asked as they watched the back end of the trailer disappear.

"Not a clue," McCain said. "But I'm definitely going to be on the lookout."

McCain told Hernandez to do the same, wished her a good day, and they both headed to their rigs.

Before he left, McCain let Jack out to pee and stretch his legs a little. After Jack relieved himself, he immediately went over to where McCain had seen the bobcat tracks and started sniffing around.

"Whatcha got there, boy?" McCain asked.

Jack kept his nose to the ground and started working the tracks toward the trees. McCain followed. When the dog got to moving too fast, McCain would talk to him to slow him down. They followed the tracks over a small hogback ridge and into a draw where a trickle of water ran. As they approached the water, Jack slowed and really worked the green grass. McCain figured the bobcat had spent a bit of time there getting a drink. Then the dog took off up the other side of the draw.

Jack, with McCain following close behind, tracked the bobcat for over a mile. Finally, when it looked like Jack was never going to stop, McCain called the yellow dog back. Banister had said the bobcat would most likely be able to fend for itself, and by the way it was covering ground, it looked to McCain like he was right.

"Come on, boy," McCain said to Jack as he turned back toward the truck. "I think we're tracking a cat that has no intention of being caught."

Jack looked McCain right in the eyes, trying to figure out what he was saying.

"And besides, what would we do with the thing if we caught up to it?"

*

The tiger had tried to nap, but being in such a new and strange place, with so many new smells and sounds, made sleep impossible. She got up and walked back to where she had left the trailer. That trailer had been home during many trips – it was where she ate and drank. But when she got back to where the trailer had been, it was gone, and although the smell of the raw meat still clung to the grass, that had also vanished.

She lay down in the grass, near where she had eaten the meat. Soon, hunger would push her to go looking for something to eat. But for now, she rested.

*

With a vicious swipe, Dobbs slashed at the bear carcass with the dried cougar paw. To his satisfaction, the extended claws ripped through the old clothes and into the flesh. He swiped again and again, tearing the shirt to shreds and cutting the meat with deep slashes. Dobbs tried each of the paws to make sure they were both convincing. A cougar would use both paws, and to make the attack look natural and real, Dobbs would have to do the same.

When he was convinced the cougar paws would stop a rider or two, and hopefully keep the noisy motorcycles and four-wheelers from disturbing his peace and quiet, he cut the carcass down. Afterward, he burned the clothes in his fire pit and then took the carcass back down the hill. Dragging it was much easier with gravity's assistance. When he got to where he had removed the bear's entrails, he found that some coyotes had come in and eaten them. What tiny scraps they had left, the ravens and jays had devoured.

Dobbs pulled the carcass to the spot where the gut pile had

been, untied his dragging rope, and headed back up the hill. He was confident that within days, maybe even hours, the scavengers would reduce the bear carcass to a bunch of bones.

Satisfied with his attack paws, Dobbs also wanted to make sure the other two paws, the ones without the claws extended, would work in making pawprints. This would further sell the idea that a cougar was attacking riders.

While the feet of the mountain lion were drying, he had also continued tanning the hide into a semi-flexible state, so he could wear it over his body. When he had it in a form that he thought was usable, Dobbs took it and placed it over his shoulders. The cougar hide was not long enough to cover his legs, but he wasn't worried about that. He just had to create the illusion that it was a live cougar, not a man, attacking the riders.

Frankly, he planned to kill the first rider or two, so nobody would really need to think about what they had seen. If for some reason, however, one of the riders did live, they needed to believe it was a mountain lion that had jumped them.

For the next several mornings, Dobbs donned the cougar skin, grabbed the paws, and practiced running through the woods. He stopped in spots and practiced placing the non-claw paws on the ground to emulate a cougar walking through the woods. And he practiced placing the paws in a believable pattern, as if the big cat were running too.

Dobbs had studied the various cougar tracks he'd seen during his time living in the wilderness. Now, as he looked at the prints he'd placed in the dried dirt and grass, he believed he had it down. Nobody would know the difference.

The last thing he needed to do was to remove all signs of his own tracks. He had sewn a pair of moccasins from a deer hide and now wore those along with his cougar suit. The deer-hide slippers left an impression in the dirt and grass, but there were no tread patterns that would commonly be left by boots or shoes.

Dobbs practiced stepping on rocks and downed logs. When he did have to walk in the dirt, he used a broom he'd fashioned out of a fir tree limb and some dried grass. A quick sweep with his broom, and the moccasin tracks disappeared in the dust.

With a little more practice, Dobbs felt he would be ready to make his first, and hopefully last, fake cougar attack. And then, finally, he would be able to get back to the quiet of his woods, where he could write and think in peace.

Chapter 12

McCain spent the remainder of the day patrolling the Forest Service roads in the area where the trailer had been located. He thought whoever had stolen the trailer probably released the tiger somewhere up in these mountains but not close to where the truck and trailer had been left. The cat burglars might have transferred the tiger into another trailer and were now transporting it far away for some other purpose. But he thought the chances of that were slim.

As he drove, McCain kept a vigilant eye on the woods, often stopping to use his binoculars to glass areas that piqued his interest. He saw several elk and a few deer but nothing that even slightly resembled a Bengal tiger.

Throughout the day, McCain checked a few archery hunters, either in camps or walking down the roads. He would look at their licenses and archery tags and then, without trying to scare them, he would inform them about the tiger.

"You're kidding me, right?" a husky, younger man all decked out in camouflage said after McCain told him about the tiger.

"What are we supposed to do if we see the thing?"

"We'd appreciate it if you'd call 911," McCain said.

"What are the laws about shooting a tiger?" the man asked.

"I don't believe there are any laws about that," McCain said. "But I would advise against it."

"Yeah, well, if the thing looks like it's going to do me harm, I'll shoot it in a second."

"I understand. But you better make sure of your shot. The last thing anyone needs is a wounded tiger on the prowl. This one's been raised in captivity, so it's been around people its whole life. The owner said it shouldn't attack, but who knows what it'll do if cornered or threatened."

McCain thanked the young man, wished him luck on his hunt, and continued down the road. He was halfway down the hill, headed back into Cle Elum for gas and a snack, when he got a call on his cell phone. He pushed the button on his steering wheel, allowing the Bluetooth to take over, then said, "McCain."

"This is Hargraves. I just got a call from an NBC reporter who wanted to know about the tiger running around near Cle Elum."

"Wow, that didn't take long," McCain said.

"He'd like to talk to someone. Since you're the one who found the trailer, you think you can talk to the guy?"

"I guess. Give me his phone number, and I'll make contact."

"Ten-four. And if you're out of the truck, keep your head on a swivel."

"Yeah, thanks," McCain said and clicked off.

McCain called the reporter – a youthful-sounding kid named Stewart Edson – and gave him the basics of what he knew. Edson wanted to talk to McCain on camera, and they agreed to meet in Cle Elum at the Dairy Queen.

Before the reporter arrived, McCain gassed up his truck and ran into the DQ to grab a chicken strip basket and a chocolate milkshake. He came back out to the truck and was greeted with a cold nose in his neck – Jack was making it apparent that he would like McCain to share.

"You're not a Labrador," McCain said. "You're a chow hound."

Jack watched as McCain took a bite of chicken, dipped in white gravy, and then ate a French fry. Wherever McCain's hand moved, Jack's gaze followed. After a couple bites for himself, he gave Jack the last piece of his chicken strip. The dog gobbled it up without even chewing.

"Oh, come on!" McCain said to the dog. "I paid good money for that, and you didn't even taste it."

Jack ignored the admonishment and stared at the next chicken strip in McCain's hand.

McCain was just slurping the dregs of his milkshake when the NBC News van pulled up next to his WDFW truck. The reporter, who looked like he'd graduated from college about fifteen minutes ago, ran over to McCain's truck, eager to get on what could be the hottest story of his young career.

"Officer McCain," the kid said. "I'm Stewart Edson. Thanks for meeting me."

"Sure," McCain said. "So how do you want to do this?"

"Can we run back up into the hills where you found the trailer?"

"I guess so, if it's important. Although it looks like a hundred other spots up that way."

"I'd like it to be authentic. Do you think we'll see the tiger?"

"No, I don't," McCain said as he started his truck. "Let's go."

For the second time that day, McCain and Jack drove up Forest Service Road 41 to where they'd found the trailer. He'd barely come to a stop and turned the truck's engine off before Edson was standing next to his door.

"Okay, this is great!" Edson said. "Let me get my camera and tripod, and I'll ask you a few questions."

When the young reporter returned, he set up the camera and tripod and helped McCain place a wireless microphone under the top button of his shirt.

"Okay, I think we're ready," Edson said. "Please say and spell your last name for me."

McCain did as he was asked and then answered about thirty

questions from Edson about locating the trailer, how they knew the trailer with the cats was stolen, and where McCain thought the tiger might be located.

"We have no clue where the tiger might be," McCain explained. "It might be in another truck or trailer headed to Canada for all we know. But it also might have been let loose out here in the woods. As is always the case when people are recreating outdoors, they just need to be aware of their surroundings."

"And remind everyone what the tiger looks like," Edson said.

"It looks like a tiger," McCain said, thinking back to the radio conversation he'd listened to between the dispatcher and the sheriff's deputy the day before. "Just like the tigers in the picture books."

"Yes, of course," Edson said seriously.

Just for the fun of it, McCain started glancing over the reporter's shoulder every now and again as he asked questions. Then he said, "Don't move!"

Edson froze with a look of panic in his eyes that McCain wished the TV audience could see.

"Sorry," McCain said. "There was a wasp about to land on your head."

That sent the reporter ducking and spinning around. McCain wondered what part of "don't move" the kid didn't understand.

"Oh man," Edson said. "I thought you saw the tiger. And I hate bees."

The reporter finally ran out of questions. Still, he asked if McCain could wait for a few minutes while he took some footage of the trees and mountains in the distance. It was obvious the kid did not want to be out here by himself.

With the interview complete and Edson back on the road to Yakima to file his story, McCain headed back down the hill again. As was the case with these kinds of stories, word would spread quickly about the tiger. If he was a betting man, McCain figured he, or someone, would be talking to reporters from all over the place come tomorrow.

Chapter 13

When he arrived home at a little before six, Sara was already there. She had seen the report of the tiger on the five o'clock news. McCain had called her at work and told her about finding the trailer, and about the reporter running him down near Cle Elum.

"You looked good on TV," Sara said in greeting. "Very handsome. And evidently, you're an expert on tigers."

"Great," McCain said. "Can we go grab something for dinner? Jack ate half of my chicken strips at lunch, and I'm starved."

Sara laughed then said, "Sure. You go change, and I'll feed Jack."

Hearing that, the yellow dog started barking and led Sara to his dish.

"Settle down," Sara said to Jack. "I'm sure you can make it two more minutes without dying of starvation."

"Don't count on it," McCain said as he came down the hall,

pulling on a Washington State University T-shirt. "So where do you want to go eat?"

"I've got a hankering for fish and chips."

"How about Gold Creek?"

"Perfect. Unless you don't want to spend any more time in the mountains."

"Actually, that sounds really good to me."

After Jack was done eating, they loaded him into the back seat of McCain's Toyota Tundra and the three of them headed up SR 410 to the little restaurant next to the two-lane highway near Chinook Pass. As they drove, McCain told Sara more about the call that came in from an anonymous woman on where to look for the trailer, and how he'd found it.

"So, the guy who owns the cats has no idea who might have wanted to steal the trailer and the animals?" Sara asked. The FBI agent in her was kicking in, and she was talking to her husband as an investigator.

"No clue," McCain said. "He's from Florida and couldn't figure out how anyone would even identify his trailer as having exotic cats in it."

"Did the North Bend cops follow up on where the call came from?" she asked.

"Good question," McCain said. "I don't know."

With that, Sinclair opened her phone and looked up the number for the North Bend police. When she had the number, she punched it into the phone's keypad, put it on speaker, and waited for an answer.

On the second ring, a male voice came on the line. "North Bend Police Department. Officer Haskins speaking."

"Yes, Officer Haskins, this is Agent Sinclair with the FBI. I'm following up on the call your department received this morning about the abandoned exotic cat trailer in Kittitas County."

"Yes, ma'am."

"I understand it was a woman caller. Did you follow up on where the call originated?"

"I didn't take the call, ma'am. But as I understand it, we did, and found out the call came from a gas station near Interstate 90."

"Any chance someone saw the caller?"

"As a matter of fact, the kid working in the gas station saw the caller, but he wasn't overly helpful with a description."

McCain didn't mean to, but he started laughing when the officer told of the kid describing the woman caller as sexy-hot.

"She was with a young guy who looked like a surfer, and they were driving an older, gray, smaller-sized pickup."

McCain interrupted. "That's the same description I got from the butcher in Roslyn yesterday."

"Okay," Sinclair said. "Any chance there are security cameras at the gas station or any businesses nearby?"

"I'm sure there are some in the vicinity," the North Bend officer said. "I can check around and see if the gray truck pops up at about the time the call came into the station here."

"That would be great, Officer Haskins. If you find anything, can you please give me a call?"

Sinclair gave the officer her FBI office phone number and her cell number, thanked him, and ended the call.

"Well, there you go," McCain said. "We might have the perps by dinner tomorrow. Then we can figure out where they dropped the tiger, if they did."

"Yeah, if they'll tell you," Sinclair said. "That is, if they know."

Jack slept in the back seat of the pickup while McCain and Sinclair had the restaurant's famous fish and chips. They enjoyed the meal, and Sara caught Luke up on everything she was working on in her office.

On the ride back down to Lower Naches, Sinclair watched out the window for wildlife. "Do you think the tiger could have made it over the mountain into this area?" she asked.

Most people didn't realize that, as the crow flies, the area west of Cle Elum and Ellensburg was fairly close to Chinook Pass and SR 410. Wildlife biologists had radio-tagged numerous deer, elk, cougars, bears, and even a few turkeys that started on the I-90 side of the hill and ended up on the SR 410 side and vice versa.

"Probably not yet," McCain said. "Unless something was chasing it. It sounds like the tiger is relatively docile and has no real experience living in the wild. My guess is if we can find out where it was dropped, it will stay in that same area, at least for a few days."

"Would you try to track it with Jack?"

When Jack heard his name, his tail started thumping the back seat.

"Oh, maybe, but I'm guessing the thing has big enough paws that I should be able to track it."

"Good," she said. "I don't know what I'd do if Jack got mauled by a tiger."

McCain just stared at his wife.

"Oh, and you too," she said with a grin. "I don't want you to get mauled either. But you'd have a rifle to protect yourself, right?"

Then she started laughing. When she looked over at McCain, he was giving her his hurt baby face. She laughed even harder.

Sara was still giggling when McCain's phone started chirping.

"McCain," he said into his Bluetooth.

"Officer McCain, dis is Simon Erickson from KAPP-TV. I understand you found da trailer wid da exotic cats, and you think dare might be a chance dat da tiger is still in da mountains up dare?"

Every time McCain talked to the energetic reporter, he wondered how he had chosen the field of television news reporting with a bit of a speech impediment. But, to his credit, it didn't slow the young reporter down any.

McCain answered his questions and agreed to meet with Erickson the next morning for an interview. Like the NBC reporter, Erickson wanted to meet him where the trailer had been found, which suited McCain just fine. He wanted to keep looking around that area for signs of the tiger.

After he hung up the phone, Sinclair said to him, "I'm guessing this is just the beginning. I bet you'll be talking to Seattle reporters tomorrow and maybe even some from farther away than that."

"I don't even want to think about it," McCain said. "Let's get home and shut our phones off."

"Can we stop at the store first?" Sara asked. "I need to pick up a couple things for my lunch tomorrow."

They pulled into the grocery store in Naches. Sara jumped out and ran in for the items she needed while McCain stayed in the truck with Jack. As he was sitting there, a familiar truck pulled up alongside. It was the vintage Chevy of Jim Kingsbury, a retired gentleman who was often seen around Naches.

McCain often ran into Kingsbury here and there, including up in the mountains fishing at one of the many lakes sprinkled around the region. Kingsbury almost always wore a *Crocodile Dundee*-style hat and a shirt with some humorous or political saying. McCain was always amazed by the shirts because of all the times he'd seen the man, he had never seen the same shirt twice.

Kingsbury didn't see him sitting there in his personal truck. McCain considered letting the man pass, but he decided it might be entertaining to talk to him for a minute while he waited for Sara.

McCain rolled down his window and said, "Hey, Jim!"

Kingsbury turned to come have a chat. The man's shirt today was black with bold white lettering that read, SURELY NOT EVERYBODY WAS KUNG FU FIGHTING!

"Hey, Luke. I saw you on the news tonight. That's something about that tiger. I can't imagine the thing running around up there in the hills. Especially during archery elk season. I bet those guys will all be packing pistols along with their bows tomorrow."

"Probably," McCain said.

"Or they'll quit hunting altogether," Kingsbury said.

"My guess is the hunters are too dedicated to their sport," McCain said. "They'll just move to a different unit if they're that concerned."

"I guess. So, what's the plan? You and that famous dog of yours going to be up there tracking the tiger?"

"We'll be up there looking around, for sure. But we have no idea where to start, or even if the tiger was set loose up there. It might be in a truck headed for Texas or someplace for all we know."

"Well, if anyone can find it, it will be you and Jack."

Hearing his name, Jack sat up and wagged his tail.

"Hey, there's the famous Jack now," Kingsbury said. "And what about that beautiful wife of yours?"

"She's right here," Sara said, walking up behind Kingsbury. She gave the man a hug, stood back to read his shirt, and laughed.

"Well, I wish you luck finding that tiger," Kingsbury said. "The last thing we need is some exotic creature up there hunting down our deer and elk."

"Hey, tigers have to eat too," Sara said. "As long as they don't eat yellow dogs or men with badges."

Kingsbury bid the couple farewell and headed into the store. McCain backed the truck out of the parking spot and turned east on SR 12, headed toward home.

"Do you think he makes those shirts up himself?" Sara asked as they headed down the highway.

"He must. I have no other explanation for where he gets them."

"I'm guessing he's independently wealthy. How else could you afford a different shirt every day of the year?"

"Maybe he's had them for years and when he moved here from wherever it is he moved from, he just brought them back out for a whole new audience."

"Could be. Someday it would be fun to learn the whole story."

McCain's phone only rang twice more before they got home.

"You're going to have a fun day tomorrow," Sara said after McCain had shut off his phone and they had gotten into bed.

"Jeez, thanks for reminding me," McCain said.

"Maybe I can do something to take your mind off of it," Sara said as she rolled over and kissed him, melting into his arms.

"It'd sure be worth a try," he said and shut off the light.

Chapter 14

His day started off how the previous one ended. McCain's phone lit up the second he turned it on. He had voicemails from two other local TV reporters and a reporter from the *Yakima Herald-Republic*. All wanted interviews, and the *Herald* wanted to set up a photo shoot.

The next call that popped up on the phone was from area code 206.

"You're right," McCain said to Sinclair, who was just finishing some scrambled eggs at the kitchen table. "Seattle is calling."

"How'd they get your phone number?" she asked.

"Maybe the kid I talked with yesterday passed it on. The stations are all owned by the same companies."

McCain answered the call and chatted with the cheery reporter from the NBC affiliate in Seattle for a few minutes. When he hung up, his wife looked up from her breakfast plate.

"Are they coming over for an interview?" Sara asked.

"Doesn't sound like it, unless we find the tiger. Then they'd like to be here for that. She'd like for me to call if that happens."

"Will you?"

"News coverage is not my highest priority right now. As a matter of fact, this isn't really my case. Kittitas County has jurisdiction and responsibility, so I think I'll just pass all this media stuff on to them. They must have a public information officer."

"Good luck with that. You're the one who found the trailer, so you're who they'll want to talk with."

"Jack and I are going to disappear right after we finish with the local press. I've got them all coming to the same place so I can get this over with and go back to doing what I'm paid to do."

McCain grabbed his gear, whistled for Jack, and headed for the front door.

"Hey! No kiss goodbye?" Sara asked.

"Sorry," McCain said as he walked back and gave her a kiss.

"Be careful," she said. "And keep an eye on Jack."

As he was driving back up to Kittitas County and FR 41, McCain called the Kittitas County Sheriff's Office and chatted with Deputy Hernandez. She told him their public information officer, or PIO, was not in, but she would be happy to give him the message that McCain was going to turn all tiger calls over to him.

"Oh, he'll love that," Hernandez said after McCain asked if he could handle the calls.

McCain couldn't tell if she was being sarcastic or not and said so.

"No, he'll definitely love it," the deputy said. "He's like a moth to a light when it comes to TV cameras. He'll take every call you send his way."

"Perfect," McCain said. "Thanks, Alivia."

He pressed the "end" button on the steering wheel and drove along, feeling better that the media were now someone else's problem. Well, all the other media that was. He still had to do several interviews with the Yakima news people.

McCain arrived at the spot up on FR 41 about the same time as Erickson. The young reporter set up his camera, put the wireless microphone on McCain, and in a minute, they were into the interview. Erickson asked many of the same questions he'd asked last night, so the interview went fairly smoothly. After the reporter was done with McCain, he set himself up in front of the camera and talked right into the lens.

"Officials aren't positive dare is a tiger up here in dees woods, but dey are warning everyone to be extra careful if dey are planning to be in diss area for any reason. For da five o'clock news, I'm Simon Erickson."

Just as Erickson finished up, two other TV cars drove in. They were from the CBS and NBC stations in Yakima. The NBC reporter was Stewart Edson from the day before, but the CBS reporter was a young lady McCain didn't recognize. The second she climbed out of the car, McCain knew there was going to be trouble. She had a look on her face like she'd just stepped in a steaming pile of cow shit.

The reporter, who was about five-foot-nine with wild blonde hair framing her pretty face, marched right over to McCain in four-inch-high heels. As she blew by him, she almost knocked poor Simon Erickson to the ground. To McCain, she said, "I was led to believe this was an exclusive interview!"

McCain just stared at her.

"I can't believe this," she barked. "We'll all have the same story, recounted by the same nobody. My news director is going to be livid."

Erickson and Edson moved over by the NBC car and chuckled at the histrionics of their fellow reporter.

McCain stood, watched, and waited as the young lady huffed and fumed. She was talking to herself. "What am I going to do?"

"Listen," McCain finally said to the woman. "Miss?"

"Scott," she said. "April Scott."

"Listen, Miss Scott. I have no idea where you come from or where you think you are, but this isn't New York or Los Angeles. This is Yakima. Now, I know I'm just a nobody, but if you want to do an interview, let's get on with it. Otherwise, I have a tiger to find."

April Scott huffed and fumed some more.

"Mr. Edson, let's do this thing!" McCain hollered over to the men at the cars.

Edson brought his camera over and set up for his interview. April Scott walked back to her car to make a call, almost turning her ankle when her foot toppled in the high heel.

While Edson readied his equipment, McCain watched Scott flail her arms about as she spoke loudly into the phone.

"She's pissed," Edson said to McCain as he was attaching the wireless microphone.

"Yeah, well, the sooner she realizes where she is, the sooner she'll get over it," McCain said.

McCain answered pretty much the same questions that Edson had asked him the previous day. But what the reporter really wanted were updates. Basically, McCain couldn't give him any.

As Edson was dismantling his camera and tripod, Scott approached again and said, "I apologize for getting upset, Officer McCain. I was under the impression this was going to be different."

She didn't say a word about calling him a nobody.

McCain just stood there and waited for her to make the next move.

"If you still have time, I'd like to do the interview," Scott said.

"That's fine," McCain said. "But let's move it along. I really do need to get going."

Once she had her camera set up and the microphone attached to McCain's collar, she asked her first question.

"So, where is this tiger from?"

"I believe this one is from Florida."

"I didn't know they had tigers in Florida. I thought they were from India or someplace."

McCain didn't know if she was kidding or serious. He looked at her for a second. Behind all the makeup, dyed blonde hair, and unnaturally white teeth, there was a person who might actually think tigers were running free in Florida.

McCain just stared at the reporter and then said, "Tigers are native to India and other parts of Asia, but there are hundreds of captive tigers in the United States and elsewhere. This one happens to be from Florida."

"Oh, how interesting," Scott said, turning and flashing a blinding white smile at the camera.

"What do they eat?" she asked.

"They eat any small animals they can get their paws on," McCain said.

At that the reporter gasped and looked very concerned.

"You mean like dogs and cats?"

"I guess if they can find one in the jungles of India, then yes."

"So would the one that is running loose around here attack a dog or cat?"

"If it gets hungry enough, I'm sure it would."

"Oh my," Scott said, turning again to look at the camera. "There you have it. A wild cat has been set free in the Cascade Mountains, and officials are warning everyone to keep household pets indoors until the lion is captured."

"Tiger," McCain said.

McCain took the microphone off his shirt, handed it to Scott, and walked to his truck. The two other reporters were standing nearby. They'd heard the entire interview.

"Dat was someteen," Erickson said.

"Yes, it was, but I don't know what," McCain said as he jumped in his truck. "See you fellas later."

As McCain drove down the dirt road, he looked at Jack and said, "Where do they get some of these reporters?"

The yellow dog just stared at him.

"Exactly," McCain said.

McCain had decided to work some of the country west of Cle Elum and Roslyn, at a little lower elevation than where he'd found the cat trailer. If the guy who looked like a surfer had purchased the meat in Roslyn, they might have had the pickup and trailer up in the Taneum. It would be like finding the proverbial needle if he was lucky enough to spot the tiger tracks, or even better, the tiger itself somewhere up in that country. Still, it was worth a try. And he could rationalize looking around there because he would be able to both search and check on the area's archery elk hunters.

The morning was spent driving the different Forest Service roads, checking all the side roads and two tracks. He often stopped and looked at tracks in the dirt, but none came close to matching what he believed would be the very large paw prints of a Bengal tiger. McCain figured it would be like hearing a rattlesnake for the first time. When he saw the tiger print, he would know it.

He talked with several archery hunters throughout the morning. None of the hunters had any idea there might be a tiger running loose in the mountains, but most seemed unconcerned once he informed them.

"Just don't tell my wife," one hunter said with a laugh. "If she knew I was hunting where a tiger might be, I'd be stuck sitting on the couch, or worse, back at work."

"Yeah, my wife wasn't too wild about me and Jack coming up here," McCain said, pointing at the dog. Jack was circling a big pine tree, looking for a chipmunk that had scurried over there. "But the owner of the tiger said she'd been raised in captivity and spent hours and hours at fairs and sportsmen shows, so he wasn't too concerned about the cat attacking."

"If we see the thing, you want us to call you?" the hunter asked.

"No, just dial 911, and the sheriff's office will take the information."

McCain gave the same information to each of the dozen or so hunters he chatted with throughout the morning.

It was getting close to noon, so McCain decided he'd drive into Cle Elum for lunch. He was just pulling into the small town when his phone lit up. He looked at the screen and saw that Sara was calling.

"No, we haven't been eaten by a tiger," he said by way of answering the call.

"Well, that's good to know. But that's not why I'm calling. I heard from Officer Haskins from North Bend. They did some checking, and they think they have a photo of the gray pickup after it left the gas station."

"Good news. Are they sending you the photo?"

"Yep, and as soon as I get it, I'll see if we can get a license plate number. And maybe, if we're lucky, a decent look at the people in the truck."

"Of course, it might not be the same truck," McCain reminded her. "But it's our best lead so far. Will you share this with Kittitas County too, please?"

"Already talked to them. I spoke to their PIO. A guy named Ronald McDonald."

"Jeez, I bet he got nothing but grief in school."

"Yeah, I asked him if he went by Ron, and he said nope, he liked using his full name."

"Okay by me," McCain said.

They talked for a few more minutes, McCain telling her about his interviews, including talking with April Scott.

"Are they not teaching anything to these kids in school nowadays?" Sinclair asked.

"I think they are. It just isn't landing with some," McCain said. "We'll probably see her on the national news in a few years."

Sinclair laughed at that, wished him luck on his afternoon patrol, and clicked off.

"Now, what do you want to eat?" McCain said to Jack as he headed down the main drag of Cle Elum, looking for someplace to get a sandwich.

Chapter 15

The cougar tracks looked almost perfect. Or at least Dobbs thought they did. He had practiced placing them in the dirt around his cabin, and then, using his handmade broom, he would brush them away.

He practiced doing the same thing with his own moccasin prints. He'd walk for a hundred yards, over dirt, grass, and rocks, and then he'd backtrack, trying to place his feet in the same spot walking backward. It was almost like he was moonwalking. And as he went, he'd brush at the tracks until they disappeared. On the grass he wasn't as particular, as he believed the green shoots would pop back up on their own over a short period of time.

After several days of working with the paws, the ones that would do the killing and the ones that would do the walking, Dobbs believed he was getting very close to his first attack. The next thing he needed to do was scout for the perfect place. He needed to make the attack far enough away from his shack so that authorities wouldn't be nosing around, but it needed to be close enough that it would scare the riders away from the area. After all, that was the ultimate goal.

Over the next four days, Dobbs walked every one of the trails set aside for the motorbike riders. A couple times as he was walking the trails, he heard a rider coming. When this happened, he would step a ways off the trail and hide behind a big tree. Never once did the riders notice him. Afterwards, he told himself that this was going to be easier than he first thought.

When Dobbs had covered the trails within a three-mile radius of his cabin, he felt like he had three good possibilities for the attack. His next step was to sit at each of the spots and wait to see how the riders rode the trail. He needed to make the attack swift, and he had to do so without risking serious injury to himself.

After another week of watching the three locations, he was able to observe riders at each of them multiple times. At each spot he watched, the riders had to slow way down to make a hairpin turn. The second time he watched, he moved close to the trail and sat close enough to pounce. Again, all riders seemed oblivious to him sitting just feet away behind a rock or some bushes.

Finally, after all his analysis, Dobbs picked what he thought was the perfect location for his attack. His plan was coming together. Soon he'd make his move.

*

Timba the tiger lay under the low branches of a medium-sized Douglas fir, not far from where she had been coaxed out of the trailer the morning before. She was starting to get hungry, and this was the last place she knew food had been. Again, instincts took over, and like she had done when thirst drove her to seek water, the growing need for food got her moving. What she was looking for, she did not know. But the tens of thousands of years in her genes told her to start searching.

*

After lunch, which consisted of a club sandwich cut in fourths and a healthy heaping of fries, McCain was ready for a nap.

Not that he could take one. When he got back to the truck, he was greeted by a very needy yellow dog looking for any scraps McCain might have saved for him. When McCain magically pulled one of the sandwich quarters out of his pocket, Jack started bouncing up and down on his front feet.

"Oh, for crying out loud," McCain said. "You're acting like you haven't eaten in a week."

He parceled out the layers of the small quarter, and Jack gobbled up the bacon, turkey, and cheese in quick gulps.

"Someday you're going to choke to death from eating so fast," McCain said.

Jack wasn't listening. He was sniffing around for another possible bite.

About that time, McCain's phone rang again. It was the 206 phone number from earlier that morning.

"This is McCain," he said into the phone.

"Yes, this is Sandra Kim," the friendly female voice said. "The reporter from KOMO-TV in Seattle who called earlier."

"Sure," McCain said. "How can I help you, Miss Kim?"

"I talked with the NBC reporter in Yakima, a Stewart Edson, and he has sent the video of his interview with you this morning. We want to air part of it in a story for tonight's news about the stolen cat trailer, and the possibility of a tiger running free in the central Cascades."

"So, what would you like from me?" McCain asked.

"Well, without scaring people, we'd like to know how likely it is that a tiger is actually running around up there?"

"I'd say the odds are better than fifty-fifty," McCain said. "I know for a fact that a bobcat was set free at the location where we found the trailer. But there were no tiger tracks. So it wasn't set free there. All I can say is if people are coming this way to recreate in the National Forest, they should keep their eyes open."

*

Cassidy Sutcliff and Cory Spearman had just returned to their

Seattle apartment after their shift at the restaurant. Spearman clicked on the TV and saw a reporter talking to the camera, an inset tiger video playing next to her. Spearman turned up the sound.

"Officials report there is a good chance the tiger has been released in the central Cascades, in the mountains west of Cle Elum," the woman reporter said.

Spearman pushed the pause button on the remote so that Sutcliff could come see the story.

"Hey babe, you better come watch this."

Sutcliff, who was in the middle of changing out of her work clothes, came into the room topless. For a second, Spearman forgot why he'd called her in.

"Watch what?" she asked.

"The TV news has a story about the tiger we set free."

He rewound and let Sutcliff see the short segment he'd just watched.

The news story continued.

"We talked with the owner of the tiger, a star of the Wild Cats of the World show, an attraction at the Washington State Fair in Puyallup. He told us the tiger is really very docile and is used to being around humans," Sandra Kim said.

They cut to a concerned-looking Sam Banister who basically said word for word what Kim had just said. Then he added, "The tiger has never spent a day in the wild, so it has no idea how to hunt for food."

"That's bullshit," Sutcliff said. "Those cats are all wild in some form. That tiger is probably hunting down its dinner right now."

Unlike the young Yakima TV reporters, Sandra Kim had actually done a little investigating on her own. She had discovered, by talking to a Kittitas County deputy sheriff named Ronald McDonald, that the North Bend police might have video footage of the vehicle used by the suspects.

"And we have it on good authority that the FBI is now involved in the investigation," Kim said.

"Oh shit!" Spearman said, finally taking his eyes off his

girlfriend's nakedness. "The FBI! We really don't need that. What do you think we should do?"

Sutcliff was thinking.

"First, we need to go talk to that idiot, Scott," she said after a minute. "We need to take his truck and dump it someplace. He needs to tell anyone who asks that his truck was stolen three days ago. That way, they can't connect it to us."

"I'm not sure he'll do that," Spearman said.

"Then you need to convince him. Tell him his insurance will get him a new truck. Make him understand how important it is to you."

"Jeez, I don't know," Spearman said. "Maybe we should just pack up and head back to Australia or somewhere else far away from all of this."

"Or," Sutcliff said. "I was thinking about sneaking into that fair and seeing what we can do about letting the other cats loose. Wouldn't that be fun?"

Spearman saw his girlfriend had that look in her eyes, and once again the idea of getting mauled by a lion started creeping into his mind. But he'd quickly forget it.

"Come on," Sutcliff said as she walked down the hall to the bedroom. "Enough scheming for now. We need a bit of exercise to balance us out."

*

The rest of McCain's afternoon was spent checking more side roads, looking for tiger prints, and talking with elk hunters. After talking with one final elk hunter, McCain decided to get back to Yakima and see what Sinclair might have on the security camera photo of the gray truck in North Bend.

He was dropping down the last hill into the Yakima Valley on I-82 when his phone rang. It was Stan Hargraves.

"Yeah, Stan," McCain said into his Bluetooth. "What's up?"

"Can you take a break from your tiger hunt to help me with an investigation I have going?"

"Sure, what you got?"

"I took a call late yesterday afternoon about a group of guys fishing for sturgeon below Priest Rapids Dam. The caller said the men are keeping the big sturgeon, and he believes they're selling the eggs for caviar."

"Did you check 'em out?"

"Yeah, I was down there today and watched them for a while, then went and checked on them. They were all legal with licenses and had no fish. They said they were just fun fishing, catching the big sturgeon and then releasing them."

"So, no cause for concern."

"No, but they're up to something. I could just feel it."

"What do you want to do?"

"I'm going to talk more with the guy who called in the tip. But I was thinking that, since the men have seen me, maybe you could go and fish somewhere nearby, doing the same thing they claim to be doing, and keep an eye on them."

"I have no equipment and very little knowledge about catching sturgeon, but I know a guy. In fact, his fishing buddies call him the Sturgeon General. Let me call him and see if he'll come fish with me. If we can catch a big seven-footer, we could play dumb and ask the caviar guys about what to do with the fish."

"That sounds like a really good plan. If we can't make it happen tomorrow, then maybe the next day or two?"

"I'll call him and let you know."

Hargraves thanked McCain and hung up.

When McCain got to Sinclair's office in downtown Yakima, her big black Chrysler sedan was sitting out front, so he went in. Her assistant said Sinclair was on a Zoom meeting with the Portland office, but she'd already been on for almost an hour and should be finished soon.

While he waited, McCain stepped outside to make a call. He scrolled through the contacts on his phone until he came to Jay Janderick, the Sturgeon General. McCain clicked on the name, and two seconds later, Janderick answered.

"Yeah, this is JJ."

"Hey JJ, this is Luke McCain. How you been?"

"Pretty good. I hope this isn't an official call."

"Well, actually it sort of is," McCain said and then took him through the plan to try to catch the sturgeon poachers. "You think you could help us? I have no gear and not much experience in how to catch a sturgeon."

"I have to work tomorrow but could help you the day after."

After deciding when and where to meet, McCain thanked Janderick, clicked off, and went back in to see if Sinclair had time to show him the truck photos. His wife was just walking out of her office when he came back through the front door.

"Let me guess," Sinclair said. "You want to see the truck photos from North Bend?"

"You are the smartest FBI agent I have ever met," McCain said. "Yes, please."

McCain followed her into the office and stepped behind her as she sat in her desk chair and started punching keys on the keyboard. In fifteen seconds, she had the photo of an older Nissan pickup on a road, presumably in North Bend, up on her monitor.

"I've played with the photo a little, and can see the license plate a bit, but the angle of the shot makes it almost impossible to read."

McCain was looking at the passenger in the truck. He couldn't tell for sure, because the person was wearing a hat and sunglasses and there was a reflection in the window, but it looked to him that the passenger was a woman.

"I'm not sure image enhancement will help us any. The photo's resolution looks really low," Sinclair said. "But I have an FBI friend who I can ask to double-check. I'll see what she can do."

"That's gotta be the cat burglars," McCain said. "Can I have a copy of the photo so I can show it to the butcher in Roslyn?"

Sinclair pushed the print button, and a second later an eight-by-ten print of the security photo slid into the printer tray.

"Perfect. Thanks," McCain said. "See you at home."

Chapter 16

Carson Dobbs believed he had the perfect plan for the perfect crime. He could kill a person, maybe even two or three, and an animal would take the blame. It couldn't get any better than that.

He'd decided to make his attempt late on the upcoming Friday afternoon. Dobbs figured there would likely be some riders in the mountains, but not nearly as many as there would be on the weekend. Most weekends in the summer, the motorbike and four-wheeler noise was nonstop. And sometimes it would go into the night.

Dobbs thought about making his cougar attack in the dark but opted to do it just before then, when he could still see well enough to hit his mark. On Friday evening, just before dark, there should be a rider or two. His plan was to take a lone rider if he or she came along. If there was a pair or small group of riders, he'd take the last one coming down the trail. A lone rider was Dobbs' preference, since there would be no one else around to see what was happening.

The three-day Labor Day weekend had just ended, and he knew, as the days and weeks went by, and the temperatures in the mountains dropped, there would be fewer and fewer riders. The upcoming Friday would be the day.

*

After a lengthy negotiation with Scott Cramer, the co-worker who had lent Spearman his truck, it was agreed that Spearman would take Cramer's truck to Portland and leave it, with the keys in the ignition, on a back street someplace. Sutcliff and Spearman agreed they would pay whatever the deductible was on Cramer's insurance when he reported it stolen. And Cramer agreed to say the truck was stolen two days before the couple had driven it to Eastern Washington to steal the cat trailer.

"Once you leave it in Portland, walk to the bus station and get back here to Seattle," Sutcliff instructed. "Then we'll figure out what to do with the cats at the fair."

As Spearman drove Cramer's pickup south on Interstate-5, he again started thinking about not coming back. Maybe he would drive right on through Oregon and down to Southern California. There were a lot of hot chicks in L.A. Surely, he could find one who wasn't as off-kilter as Sutcliff.

Sutcliff's new idea of breaking into the fair and releasing the cats was even crazier than stealing the truck and trailer. Even if they were successful, what good would it do? The cats would most likely stay on the fairgrounds and be rounded up in hours. Why risk getting arrested, or worse, harmed, just to have the animals captured again within hours? Spearman gave it a lot of thought on the three-hour drive to Portland.

When he reached Oregon, he was torn: keep driving to Southern California or go back to Seattle and continue this wild ride with Sutcliff? He decided he would drive into Portland and scope out a place to ditch the pickup. If things didn't look right, he would head back to the freeway and keep rolling south.

As it turned out, he didn't have to leave the truck in some seedy part of town. He stopped at a 7-11 in one of the industrial areas close to the Willamette River, and left the keys in the ignition while he went in and bought a Slurpee. When he returned to the parking lot, the gray Nissan was peeling out, exhaust billowing from its tailpipe.

"That answers that," Spearman said to himself as he slurped his frozen drink. He looked around at the city and then started walking toward the high-rise buildings to find the Greyhound station.

*

Word of the Bengal tiger running free in the Cascade Mountains was now national news. Somehow, the bigger TV stations in Portland, Los Angeles, Chicago, and New York all got McCain's phone number, and his cell buzzed constantly.

At first, he'd answer and tell the callers to contact the Kittitas County Sheriff's Office and ask for Ronald McDonald. Most of the reporters thought he was joking. One even said, "Yeah, right. And if he's not there, do I ask for the Hamburglar?" Eventually, he would convince them that the deputy sheriff with the famous hamburger clown name was the person to speak with on all things Bengal tigers in Washington State. It didn't take long for McCain to start screening his calls – he stopped answering ones from any number he didn't recognize.

"How did they get your number anyway?" Sara asked as his phone buzzed away at breakfast the next morning.

"Again, I'm guessing they contacted one of the local reporters, and they passed it on, probably thinking they were doing a big favor to someone who might help advance their career."

"I'd think they would want to learn a few things here first, before they worried about making it to the big time."

"Don't get me started," McCain said.

"So, are you going with Stan to try to catch the sturgeon poachers today?"

"No, my guy has to work, so we'll try tomorrow. I'm going to take Jack back up into the Taneum to see if I can find those tiger tracks."

"Okay. I got the truck photo to my friend, and she said she'd try to have something back to me today. If we have any luck with the license plate, I'll run the numbers and see what I can find out. I'll let you know if we get anything."

Sinclair kissed McCain on the cheek and gave Jack, who was sitting by McCain hoping for a bite of sausage, a pat on the side before heading out.

"Have a good day," McCain said as he opened the newspaper to catch up on the Mariners and Seahawks.

With two big brown eyes staring up at him, McCain found it hard to concentrate on his reading. Finally, he took a bite of his sausage and slipped the other half to Jack.

"There. Now go lie down. We'll be leaving in a minute."

The yellow dog reluctantly obeyed.

McCain looked at his phone again as it buzzed for the ninth time that morning. He didn't recognize the number. In fact, the number looked too long, with a couple extra digits and dashes in the front. Under the number, it read, "London, England."

He almost answered it just to say he talked to some news person in England, but then he thought better of it. He put his phone in his pocket, grabbed his hat, and headed for the door.

"Cheerio! We're off," McCain said to Jack in a horrendous British accent. The dog jumped up and led the way out the door to the tan WDFW truck.

On the way up to the Kittitas Valley, McCain called Hargraves and told him about Jay Janderick. They made a plan to meet early the next morning.

"Good luck finding Tony the Tiger," Hargraves said.

"That's Timba," McCain said with a laugh. "And we're going to need it."

*

Timba the tiger had meandered throughout the night. She had

seen a few deer and a whole herd of elk as she wandered through the trees, along a creek, and up over one ridge, then another. The animals were all fleeing from her – not at the sight of the big cat, but at her smell. Even though they'd never smelled a tiger before, they knew to run for their lives. She didn't try to chase them but did slowly follow a couple of the deer for a mile or so. Even though she couldn't see or hear them, she knew where they were by their scent. It was very enticing.

At one point, a snowshoe hare jumped from the brush close to where she was walking. It startled her, and she crouched, ready to move quickly if needed. The hare bounced left and right and disappeared into the darkness.

Throughout the night, the big cat continued through the forest, gaining elevation, looking for the meat she'd been fed all her life.

*

McCain decided he'd start his day by driving to Roslyn and talking to the butcher who had helped load the sixty pounds of raw meat into the gray pickup. When he arrived, the butcher recognized McCain from a few days earlier and said, "Hey, officer. Did you find the guy in the gray pickup?"

"No, not yet, but we might have a photo of the truck that was here. Do you mind taking a look at it for me?"

"Sure," the butcher said. "This doesn't happen to have anything to do with the tiger that was set loose around here, does it?"

"Actually, you're right," McCain said. "We're still not positive the tiger was released around here, but we are going on that assumption for the time being. We think the man who came in here and bought the meat from you may be involved."

The butcher looked at the truck and started nodding his head. "Yep, I think that's the same truck. At least it sure looks like it." He looked a little closer at the blurry image of the person in the passenger seat and said, "But that's not the dude who came and bought the meat."

McCain thanked the butcher, gave him his card, and asked

him to call if the man returned to buy any more quantities of meat.

"Will do," the butcher said. "I hope you find that tiger. My wife is scared to even walk out to the car. And now she won't even let the kids out to play. Half the town is panicked."

"We're working on it. We think the tiger is way up in the higher elevations, so there's probably no reason to worry."

"You try telling that to my wife," the butcher said, giving McCain a wave.

As he left Roslyn, McCain thought about what the butcher had said. He hadn't thought much about the ramifications of what a tiger on the loose might mean to the people who lived in the mountains. Of course, some of them would be scared, and maybe for good reason.

"We better figure out where that cat is, and fast," he said to Jack, who was sound asleep in the back seat. He looked back at the dog and said, "A lot of help you are."

McCain jumped back onto I-90 and headed east. He exited at Thorpe and took the Taneum Road up the mountain where he spent several hours searching along the various roads in the Okanogan-Wenatchee National Forest. Every little spur road, jeep trail, or two-track, McCain took, looking carefully for any tracks that might indicate the tiger had been there. On his search, he saw plenty of coyote tracks, deer tracks, elk tracks, and even a couple sets of bear and cougar tracks. But no tiger tracks.

If nothing else, McCain felt like he was eliminating possible locations where the big cat might have been let loose. But the more McCain looked, the more he questioned whether the tiger actually had been released in these mountains.

Along the way, McCain would stop and chat with an elk hunter or an ATV driver. The word of the tiger was getting out, and a few people asked him about it. But others had not heard of the possibility of a tiger running around in the mountains.

"Do you think we're in danger?" one ATV rider asked, looking around like the tiger might be lurking nearby.

McCain gave his pat answer. No, he really didn't think people were in danger, but they should always proceed with caution in the woods, and not just because there might be a tiger wandering around.

"There are plenty of things to watch out for," McCain said to the ATV rider. "Rattlesnakes, cougars, bears. They could all potentially cause problems for someone. But that likelihood is very remote, just like it is with the tiger, in my opinion."

That seemed to appease the young man for the time being. McCain told him to call 911 if he did happen to see the tiger.

After six hours, McCain decided to give it up and head for Yakima. He still had some coordinating to do with Jay Janderick and Stan Hargraves ahead of their sturgeon fishing trip on the Columbia.

Chapter 17

The plan was to meet at the old K-Mart store, now a big U-Haul Center right off I-82, at five-thirty a.m. Janderick would have all the fishing gear and bait, and they would ride in his truck. Hargraves would follow them down to the river and set up several hundred yards back, up on a hill where he could watch with a spotting scope and binoculars.

McCain had left Jack at home, as he was unsure of just where the dog would ride in Janderick's pickup. Plus, he felt the dog would most likely not be needed today.

When they all arrived at the meeting place, they briefly went over the plan again. McCain and Hargraves would have radios but wouldn't use them unless something happened.

"If we catch a sturgeon," McCain said. "We'll keep it in the water and either walk it up the river to where the caviar guys are or call them down."

Janderick and McCain knew that sturgeon are hardy fish. Keeping one in the water for a few minutes before releasing it is rarely fatal. McCain had once seen a sturgeon in the back of a pickup in Yakima. It was still alive at least forty-five minutes after being caught. The fish seemed like you could have thrown it in a swimming pool and it would have been just fine.

After their short meeting, the men took SR 24 east through Moxee and to the Columbia River. They crossed the river at Vernita and then turned toward Priest Rapids Dam. Hargraves had pinpointed where he had talked to the men two days before, and as Janderick and McCain drove down an extremely bumpy and primitive road to the river, they looked for the men.

They were watching for an older white Chevy Suburban, and as they crested the last little rise before the river, they saw the SUV parked up ahead. Three men were standing near the rig, smoking cigarettes, and talking. McCain could see three stout fishing rods about fifteen feet apart, sticking out of large metal rod holders that had been pounded into the rocks on the shoreline. Lines stretched from the tips of the rods out into the fast-flowing river.

"They're early risers," McCain said. "I wonder if they were fishing at night."

"It all depends on what they're doing with the dam," Janderick said. "The water here can fluctuate drastically and in a hurry. Early morning is usually a good time to fish because they aren't dumping a bunch of water through the turbines to generate electricity. So, now's the time to fish."

"Let's go downriver from them a hundred yards or so and set up," McCain said.

They drove downriver, parked, and started unloading their gear. They looked just like a couple of sturgeon fishermen looking for a good time, hoping to fight one of the prehistoric giants.

Janderick already had their rods rigged and ready to fish. All he had to do was put some bait on the large circle hooks and add about sixteen ounces of lead to get the bait to the bottom of the river where the fish could find it. Once he had one rod baited and rigged with the weight, Janderick made a long, arcing cast out into the dark waters of the Columbia. He handed the rod to McCain and went about rigging the next one.

McCain had been watching the men in the white Suburban out of the corner of his eye, and all three seemed to be pretty interested in what he and Janderick were doing. With a second rod rigged, Janderick moved upriver a few yards and made another long, looping cast into the river, holding the rod until the lead weight caught in the rocks on the river's bottom.

Instead of putting their fishing rods in rod holders like the men upriver, McCain and Janderick continued to hold theirs, waiting for the telltale tap, tap, tap that a sturgeon had picked up the bait.

"What is that bait?" McCain asked as they waited.

"Rotting chicken innards," Janderick said. "Smells good, huh? If there's a sturgeon anywhere downstream, they'll come looking for it."

As they chatted, McCain noticed one of the men from upstream walking down to them. As the man got closer, he said, "Morning, guys."

"Good morning," McCain said. "Any luck yet?"

"Naw, we just got set up before you guys got here. Never seen you before. Fish here often?"

"Well, we're kind of newbies," Janderick said. "I borrowed this gear from a friend of mine who told me how to use it. We've always wanted to catch a big sturgeon, so we decided to give it a try."

"It looks like you have the right setup," the man said. "What are you using for bait?"

"Chicken guts," McCain said. "You could probably smell the stuff from up at your rig. It stinks."

"Never tried that, but who knows – it might work. Good luck," the guy said as he turned back toward the Suburban.

"Good luck to you too," Janderick said.

After about ten minutes, McCain's fishing rod tip start tapping.

"Here's a bite," he said to Janderick. "Should I let him eat it?"

Janderick was staring intently at the tip of the rod. He didn't say a thing for almost a minute, and then he yelled, "Set the hook!"

McCain had done a good deal of drift fishing for steelhead

and salmon, so he knew what to do. When he reared back on the stiff, heavy rod, he felt the weight of a fish on the other end, and the battle was on. The sturgeon went straight out into the heavy current, and then started running downstream.

"Better follow it," Janderick said, as he quickly reeled in his bait.

McCain took off down the river, reeling when the fish would come and letting the line peel off the big level wind reel when the sturgeon ran. A couple times, he glanced up the river and saw that all three men at the Suburban were watching him do battle with the big fish.

It took the better part of an hour for McCain to finally bring the big sturgeon close enough to the shoreline for Janderick to wade out, grab the fish by its mouth, and roll it over. Sturgeon are big and powerful, but when rolled on their back, they become almost comatose.

When Janderick finally had the fish subdued, McCain gave out a big whooping holler.

"YAAAHOOOO!"

He looked up, and two of the guys from upstream were walking down to them.

"Whoa, that's a nice one," the guy who had come down earlier said. He was about forty, five-foot-ten, and wore a stained, gray pullover sweatshirt and a greasy Lamiglas hat. His face was covered in a four-day, reddish-brown beard, and a half-burned cigarette was hanging out of his mouth.

The other guy, about the same age and a little taller, wore a red-checkered flannel shirt and tan Carhartt britches. He said, "Looks like a six-footer. What are you going to do with it?"

McCain gave the man a puzzled look. "Well, you can't keep them, right?"

The two men looked at each other and smiled.

"Well, no. You're supposed to let them go, but if you're willing to part ways with that fish, we'd give you twenty bucks. If anyone asks, we'd tell them we caught it."

"I don't know," McCain said. "You guys really like to eat sturgeon that much?"

The second man looked around to make sure no one else was there, smiled at his buddy, and said, "Listen, what we do with the fish is our business. You want to sell it or not?"

"No thanks," McCain said. "Let's let it go, J.J."

Janderick withdrew pliers to pull the big hook out of the sturgeon's vacuum cleaner mouth, when the shorter of the two men said, "I wouldn't do that."

McCain and Janderick turned around and saw that the man in the greasy Lamiglas cap had pulled a pistol out from behind his back and was pointing it at them.

"Go get that fish, Jep," he said to his buddy.

McCain wondered if Hargraves was seeing all this.

"Okay. No need for guns," McCain said. "If you want the fish that bad, you can have it."

Janderick pulled the fish closer to shore for the taller man to come take. The man grabbed the fish, pulled it up onto the rocks, and then began dragging it back toward the Suburban. The shorter man gave McCain and Janderick a smile, showing yellow, cigarette-stained teeth, and said, "Nice doin' business with you boys. Catch another one, and we'll be glad to take it off yer hands, too."

When the two men had the fish back at their rig, McCain hid himself behind Janderick's pickup and pulled out his radio.

"Did you catch all that?" McCain asked.

"Ten-four. How do you want to proceed?" Hargraves asked.

"I say we stay here and keep fishing. We'll not bait our hooks so we won't catch any more, but maybe those three will, and we'll get them for a few more violations, although we don't really need any more. Assault with a deadly weapon will do just fine."

"Roger that. I'll stay here and continue to watch. Keep your radio handy. I really don't want to lose these guys now."

"Ten-four."

It didn't take long before they needed to make their move. The guy in the red-checkered shirt suddenly set the hook and was soon fighting a fish.

"They have a fish on," Hargraves said. "Let's wait until they get it in and see what they do with it. I'm going to get closer and will stay just out of sight along the road."

"Roger. We'll drive up that way and watch them. Seeing as we're all buddies now."

McCain had put his service revolver and badge in a small backpack on the floor of Janderick's truck. He now pulled out the badge and pistol. He clipped both the badge and pistol in its holster to his belt.

As was the case every day he worked, either undercover or in uniform, McCain was also wearing his protective vest under his sweatshirt. After having the pistol pulled on them, he was glad to have it.

"When we get up there and start to deal with these guys, you just stay in the truck. And if that guy pulls that pistol again, you get down," McCain said to Janderick.

The two men pulled in their gear and threw everything in the back of the truck. Then, as they watched the guy fight the fish, getting it closer to shore, Janderick put the truck in gear and slowly moved up the rocky road.

As they got a little closer, they watched as two of the men waded out, grabbed the sturgeon, and slid it up onto the rocks. Lamiglas hat pulled a folding hunting knife from his pocket, flipped the blade out, and in one quick blow, stuck the knife in the sturgeon's head. Five seconds later, he was running the knife up the belly of the fish, extracting a long string of brownish-red eggs from the fish's insides.

"Come on in now!" McCain said into the radio. "We got 'em."

McCain jumped out of the truck, drew his pistol, and walked toward the men. They were so engaged in collecting the roe from the sturgeon, they paid him no attention.

"Freeze!" McCain yelled. "You're all under arrest!"

The men immediately looked up and saw McCain holding his badge in his left hand and a pistol in his right.

Two of the men looked surprised and a little worried. Lamiglas just smiled a yellow-toothed grin. McCain saw that the man still had the hunting knife in his right hand, and McCain knew if the guy was going to go for his pistol, he'd have to drop the knife.

"Put your hands up in the air where I can see them," McCain ordered. He could hear Hargraves' truck quickly approaching. "And drop that hog-sticker."

Lamiglas just kept smiling. He didn't drop the knife and he didn't raise his hands.

"You know what, mister?" McCain said to the man with the yellow grin. "If you saw my scores from the pistol range last week, you'd be doing exactly as I say. I can place my shot wherever I want. Forehead. Eyeball. Testicles. Not a problem. So make one little move, and we'll see where this ol' forty-five expanding bullet goes."

At that, McCain moved the front end of the pistol down so it pointed at the man's crotch. A half-second later, the man raised his hands.

"Easy," McCain said. "You don't want me jumpy."

Lamiglas dropped the knife before very slowly raising his hands. His yellow teeth disappeared behind tight lips as the grin melted away.

Hargraves was walking down the rocky bank just in time to hear the end of McCain's little speech. His pistol was out as well. He walked to the men, reached behind Lamiglas's back, and pulled out the revolver. Then he checked the other two men who only had pocketknives. He threw the knives into the rocks, and then told each of the men to turn around and put their hands behind their backs. Hargraves cuffed two of the men with the handcuffs he had in his utility belt, and McCain tossed him his pair for the third man.

Once the men were all cuffed and sitting down on the riverbank, Hargraves said to McCain, "What was all that BS about you being a crack shot? You can't hit a bull in the butt with a banjo."

McCain looked at Lamiglas who stared back at him with an ugly look, even without the yellow teeth. "Yeah, but he didn't know that. I figured he wasn't willing to chance it."

Janderick helped collect the fish carcasses and the eggs and put them in big evidence bags that Hargraves had in his truck. The men had killed and gutted the fish they'd taken from McCain too, and so there was plenty of evidence against them.

After calling for assistance from the Grant County Sheriff's Office, McCain told Janderick he could head home.

"Once we get these guys transported to jail, I'll catch a ride back with Stan," McCain said. "Thanks so much for your help, J.J. We couldn't have done it without you."

After Janderick was gone, Hargraves asked, "So, anything new on the tiger deal?"

"Not much," McCain said. "Sara's colleague is trying to get a photo enhanced that might give us the plates of the truck the cat thieves were in. I've looked all over the mountains and haven't found one tiger print. I've talked to fifty elk hunters, and none of them have seen anything. I don't know. I'm sure someone will see something, but right now we're not making much headway."

"Well, hopefully something will break soon," Hargraves said.

Chapter 18

Six days had passed since the stolen cat trailer had been located. Now, just about everyone in the State of Washington believed the tiger had been released in the woods west of Cle Elum.

The whole country knew about the missing tiger, and it was becoming a storyline the big networks and news stations were following daily. CNN and NBC had huge trucks parked in Cle Elum with camera people, technicians, and reporters running about.

Ronald McDonald was becoming a TV star. You couldn't change the channel without seeing his smiling face on the news. In reality, McDonald knew very little about the situation, but he was ever present and offered hope that the tiger would be found soon. McDonald reminded anyone who might be out enjoying the great outdoors to stay vigilant and extra careful.

One of the stations had started a "Timba Talk" segment that appeared every evening. The same reporter would talk to anyone who might give insight into the tiger's prospective activities in the wilds of the Pacific Northwest. The installments covered how it might be feeding itself and where, ultimately, it might end up.

On the most recent edition of "Timba Talk," Doctor Jonah Taylor, a tiger expert at the St. Louis Zoo, said the tiger might roam for a hundred miles or more. He noted it could very well end up in a larger city where the tiger might find it easier to prey on dogs and cats than the Cascades' inhabitants such as moose and caribou.

"Even though Timba was raised in captivity," Taylor said, looking very seriously into the camera while talking to the reporter over Zoom, "she most assuredly will revert back to a wild animal, hunting for her food, doing whatever she needs to do to stay alive."

Another talking head, a zoology professor from Cal-Berkley who specialized in the study of big cats of the world, was on the opposite side of the argument. She believed Timba might be in the early stages of starvation at this point.

"She has been hand-fed her whole life," the professor said. "She has no knowledge of how to hunt for herself. It is a learned skill, passed down from mother to kitten. Most assuredly, she is wandering around just looking for meat that has been thrown her way. If she doesn't find any, she will die a slow death of starvation."

McCain watched some of the news stories and just shook his head. The sudden boom in media attention was making his job all the more difficult. The day before, as he patrolled the woods trying to check on hunters and look for possible signs of the tiger, road traffic was triple the norm. Cars full of people, all hoping for a sighting of the now famous Timba, were driving up and down the Forest Service roads from daylight to dark.

"And it's only going to get worse," McCain said to Sara as they ate a quick breakfast before each headed to work. "I feel really bad for the elk hunters. The commotion of all the people driving around has really made a mess of their season."

"Well, I heard back from my friend. She was able to get a partial read on that grainy photo I sent her. Now that we at least have some of the numbers from the license plate on the Nissan pickup, we can start narrowing down who the owner might be," Sara said. "I've got a little time today and will see what I can find."

"That'd be great," McCain said, and then called for Jack. "We're headed back up that way."

"Have fun. And be careful. I'll call when I get the truck owner information."

McCain was almost dreading the day. He opened the back door for Jack, who literally flew into the seat, and then hit the road. Before he headed west back into the Taneum, McCain stopped in Ellensburg for gas. Just off the interstate, there was a group of what looked to McCain to be college students, waving signs and yelling at the cars going by. The signs read "Save Timba," and they were singing "Save that Tiger," a song McCain had heard before but couldn't remember where from.

Just off the main road into Ellensburg, a big green van had parked. It had a vinyl sign stretched across the side that read "Timba Toys." McCain could see a giant stuffed tiger perched atop the van, with dozens of other tigers of various sizes placed all around. A guy in a floppy blue sun hat, sunglasses, and a tan safari vest sat in a folding lawn chair amongst the fake tigers, looking at his phone.

As gas was pumping into his pickup, McCain called Sara.

"We really need to find the owner of that gray truck," McCain said after explaining to her what he'd just seen. "It's starting to get crazy."

"I'm already working on it. I've found a few possibilities, and I'll let you know soon."

"Okay, thanks. Jack and I are heading up into the mountains. I'll check with you later when I get cell service."

Sinclair did, in fact, have some possibilities. Of the license plates that started with the same letter-number sequence they were able to positively identify in the enhanced photo, nineteen belonged to Nissan, Mazda, and Toyota pickups. Of those pickups, nine were gray or silver in color. And only three of those were older model vehicles.

One Nissan was located in Spokane, another in Seattle, and there was a gray Mazda in Wenatchee. Sinclair pulled up the names and addresses for the owners of each and tracked down their phone numbers. She called each of them.

The woman who owned the Nissan in Spokane said that her truck hadn't been driven in eight months, since right before someone had T-boned her in an intersection while driving home from work.

The young man who owned the gray Mazda in Wenatchee said he had just arrived back home two days ago. He and a buddy had taken the truck to Billings, Montana to do some fly fishing on the Yellowstone River. Unfortunately, they'd had engine trouble, and the truck was still sitting in a shop in Billings. They'd ridden the bus back to Wenatchee.

She then called Scott Cramer in Seattle about the third gray truck.

"Mr. Cramer, this is Agent Sinclair with the FBI in Yakima. Do you have a minute to help me out?"

She heard the man gulp, literally, as she said those three simple letters, "F-B-I." It was not uncommon to get that response from people, but this guy seemed extra nervous.

"Yes, ma'am," Cramer said in a shaky voice.

"Do you own a 1992 grey Nissan pickup?"

"Yes, ma'am. Er . . . well, I did. It was stolen late last week."

"I see. And what day was it stolen?"

"Well, I'm not sure on that," Cramer said. "I don't drive it often, and it sits in the parking lot of my apartment complex. I take the bus to work and . . . let's see . . . I guess it was Monday I noticed it missing."

"But you think it was stolen late last week?"

"Well, yeah. But I guess I really don't know."

"Did you report it stolen?"

"Yes, ma'am. On Monday, when I saw it was gone."

"And did you let your insurance company know it was stolen?"

"Yes, ma'am."

"I see," Sinclair said and paused for a bit. "Mr. Cramer, do you happen to have a photo of your truck you could email to me?"

"I sent a photo to the insurance lady. I could send that one to you, too."

"That would be great."

She gave Cramer her email address and thanked him for the information.

"Okay then," Cramer said, hurrying to end the conversation.

"Mr. Cramer, just one more thing. We believe your truck, or a truck very similar to yours, was used in a case where a trailer full of exotic cats was stolen. Maybe you've heard about it or have seen the reports on TV."

"Yes, ma'am. I mean, no ma'am. I wasn't involved in anything like that."

"That's good, because if you were, or had any knowledge of who might have committed the crime, you could be in serious trouble."

"Yes, ma'am," Cramer said once more, this time with an even shakier voice. "I'll email you the photo right away." And he was gone.

Sinclair placed her phone back into the receiver on her desk and sat there for a minute. Mr. Cramer, she believed, knew more than he was telling her.

While she waited for the photo of the gray truck to appear in her email, Sinclair decided she'd help McCain out a little. She had some comp time sitting on the books. It was Friday, and she didn't have any meetings scheduled. Maybe she would just shoot over the hill and visit Mr. Cramer in person.

*

The zoology professor in California had been closer in her estimation than the doctor in St. Louis. Timba had wandered around looking for meat, passing up chances at hare and young deer. She was getting hungrier with each passing day. Then, on the third day away from the trailer, she came upon the carcass of a half-eaten elk calf. A cougar had killed the elk the day before and had buried the carcass under some leaves and brush, where it would remain until the cougar returned.

The tiger had smelled the dead elk from a good distance away and located it quickly in the debris. She uncovered the hind quarters of the elk and soon began tearing into the flesh.

She had eaten several pounds of meat when she caught some motion in the trees. The cougar was returning to feed on its kill and was ready to run off anything, like a coyote or a badger, that might have discovered the carcass. The cougar came in quickly when it saw the tiger on its kill, but it stopped short of attacking. The strange cat was bigger than any predator the cougar had ever seen. The cougar put its ears back and gave a loud snarl. The tiger looked at the cougar, pulled another large chunk of meat off the elk, and carried it into the trees.

*

McCain continued his patrol. As he was heading back into the high mountains, a pickup truck full of six men came roaring around the corner. When he saw that the three men standing in the bed were holding rifles, McCain quickly pulled into the center of the road to block it.

The pickup, an older Ford F-250, came to an abrupt stop, and a couple of the guys quickly opened the bolt actions and pulled clips out of their rifles. In Washington State, having loaded shotguns and rifles in vehicles is not allowed, and it was obvious the guys knew it.

McCain rolled down the back windows but told Jack to stay. Then he climbed out and walked toward the blue Ford.

"What are you fellas up to?" McCain asked as he got close to the truck.

"We're going tiger hunting," said one of the young men in the back of the truck.

"You are, huh?" McCain said. "Can I see your rifle?"

The man, who looked to be in his late teens or early twenties, reluctantly handed it over. The bolt on the rifle was open, but there were still cartridges in the magazine.

As McCain was looking at the rifle, he could see the man on the passenger side of the pickup fidgeting. He was slowly trying to eject the clip from the rifle he had against his leg, pointed into the wheel well.

"Don't move," McCain said as he turned and looked at another young twenty-something man.

The young man froze.

"Listen," McCain said. "Here's what we are going to do. Turn off the truck, and then I want all of you to get out and stand here next to it. Leave your rifles right where they are. You guys in the back, lay them down in the bed."

"Crap," the guy sitting in the passenger seat said. "I told you guys this was stupid."

"Nobody told you to load your rifle, Cam," the driver said. "I didn't load mine."

"Shut up, Chip," the passenger said.

McCain watched carefully as the six men all climbed out and lined up. He then checked four rifles, three of which had cartridges in the magazines. A couple cartridges were lying in the back of the truck.

"So, you're going to shoot that tiger if you see it?" McCain asked after he got their driver's licenses and sorted out who belonged to each of the rifles.

"Well, we thought it would be fun to look," Chip the driver said. "We didn't figure we'd see it. Even if we did, I'm not sure any of us would actually shoot the thing. From what I've heard, it's about half tame."

"There are actually no laws against you doing that," McCain said. "But there are laws against driving around with loaded weapons. I'm going to write tickets to the three of you with loaded rifles. I know you know better."

McCain pulled out his ticket book and started filling out the paperwork. As he did, he spoke to the young men.

"Listen, you all seem like good guys, just out having fun. I get that. But you might think seriously about shooting the tiger if you see it. And that's a big if. I've been up here almost a week and I can't even find a track. Frankly, I'm still not positive it got released up here."

"Cam there couldn't hit it if he did see it," one of the guys from the back of the truck said. "He couldn't hit an elephant."

"Shut up, Nick!" the guy from the passenger seat said. "Like you're a crack shot."

They went back and forth for a few seconds and then Chip chimed in. "Frankly, officer, none of these guys are much of a shot. And I wouldn't shoot at a tiger, unless it was charging me."

"Okay, fellas," McCain said, handing the tickets to Cam, Nick, and one other young man named Eli. "The problem is, if you did happen to wound it, then it becomes my problem, and the last thing I want to do is have to run down a wounded tiger."

The guys listened, most with their heads down as they kicked the dirt.

"So, be smart. Have fun. And keep those rifles unloaded until you get out of the vehicle."

"Yes, sir," they said in unison.

The young men all climbed into the truck. McCain walked over to the driver and handed him his card.

"If you do happen to see the tiger, would you please call me or 911? My cell number is on the card."

"We will," said Chip.

"Not me," said Nick from the back of the truck. "I'm going to shoot me a tiger."

"Aw, you couldn't hit a school bus at fifty yards," Cam said out the passenger window.

"Shut up, Cam," Nick said. "You missed that spike standing broadside at thirty yards last year."

Chip looked at McCain and just shook his head. Then he put the truck in reverse and started backing down the road. McCain walked to his truck and also headed down the road. When he got around the corner, the blue Ford was backed into a two-track, and McCain could hear the young men still bickering.

Chapter 19

It took Sinclair two hours and twenty minutes to get over Snoqualmie Pass and to the large apartment complex in Renton where Scott Cramer lived. Sinclair parked, wandered around until she found apartment 429, and knocked on the door. There was no answer. She was just about to turn and walk back to her car when the door next to Cramer's opened.

"You looking for Scott?" a guy with messed-up, just-got-outta-bed hair said. He was barefoot and wore a tank-top undershirt and sweatpants.

"Yes, I am," Sinclair said. "Any chance you know where he works?"

"Yeah, he works at Archipelago. It's a highfalutin restaurant downtown. I couldn't afford a dinner salad there," the rumpled man said. "Whatcha need Scott for?"

"We're trying to help him find his stolen truck."

"His truck was stolen? When?"

"He said late last week."

The guy leaned against the doorjamb and ran his hand through his wild hair as he thought.

"I'm pretty sure I saw it here Monday morning," he said. "But I might be wrong."

"When does Scott usually return from work?" Sinclair asked.

"He works through the dinner shift, I think. Usually gets home by about eleven-thirty."

Sinclair thanked the man and started to walk away.

"Are you a cop or something?" he asked as she walked down the sidewalk.

"Or something," she said.

When she got back into her car, Sinclair tried to call McCain again. She'd left him a voicemail as she was leaving Yakima. Again, he didn't answer. This time she hung up without leaving a message.

She punched the address for Archipelago into her Maps app and headed into downtown Seattle. Finding a parking spot someplace near the restaurant was the next challenge. She didn't like doing it, but she finally found a spot that was marked as a loading zone, parked there, and put an official FBI sign on the dash.

As she walked into the restaurant, she was greeted by a very friendly manager. The man, in a dark blue suit and tie, asked if she had reservations.

"No, I'm not planning on dining today," Sinclair said. "I'm hoping to chat with Scott Cramer for two minutes."

The man frowned slightly. "Can I tell him who is asking for him?"

"You can say it's about his stolen truck."

"Oh, I hadn't heard his truck was stolen. Just one minute."

The manager turned and walked through a maze of tables and chairs, most filled with people enjoying their late lunch or early dinner.

Sinclair looked around at the waiters and waitresses. She first spotted a good-looking man in his thirties with long blond hair, delivering food to a table toward the back of the restaurant. A minute later, a tall and strikingly beautiful waitress, also in her thirties, walked over to a table near Sinclair and chatted with some guests. Sinclair remembered McCain telling her that the kid who saw the woman make the call to the police in North Bend had said she was super-hot. This woman certainly fit that description.

Scott Cramer and the manager soon emerged from the back of the restaurant and approached Sinclair. As she reached out to shake his hand, Sinclair glanced over his shoulder and caught the eye of the young woman. She was definitely paying attention.

"You have some information on my truck?" Cramer asked.

"Possibly," Sinclair said. "I'm Agent Sinclair with the FBI. I talked to you this morning on the phone."

Sinclair saw Cramer's Adam's apple bob as he gulped. He seemed incapable of speaking for several seconds.

"Did you get the photo I sent of my truck?" he asked nervously.

"Actually, no. I did not. Did you send it?"

"I think I did," Cramer said, his voice shaking.

Sinclair noticed the pretty, tall waitress wait until she got the attention of the man with the long blond hair, and then the waitress nodded subtly toward the back of the seating area. He headed that way.

"Listen, Mr. Cramer. We believe it was your truck that the suspects in the stolen exotic cat case were driving, and we think you might know who stole or used your truck to do so."

Cramer was shaking his head as if to say no, that Sinclair was wrong.

Sinclair turned to the manager and said, "Can you tell me who the two wait staff personnel are that just left the room? One is a tall, attractive woman and the other a nice-looking man with longish blond hair."

"Oh, that's Cassidy and Cory. I think they're dating."

"Could you ask them to come up front please?"

"What is this?" the manager asked. "Do I need to go get the owner?"

"If that's what it takes to talk to those two, yes. And give him this," Sinclair said as she handed him a business card.

The manager took the card, looked at it for a second, got a worried look on his face, and marched to the back of the dining area.

"So, did you find my truck?" Cramer asked meekly.

"No, not yet. But I think you already knew that. In fact, it's my guess you knew you would never see it again. You can keep yourself out of a lot of trouble if you'll tell me if Cassidy and Cory borrowed your truck for a few days last week."

Cramer's head dropped, which told Sinclair everything she needed to know.

"Where's the rear entrance to this place?" she asked him.

"Straight back through the parking lot on this side," Cramer pointed to the right.

Sinclair went out the front door, turned, and ran to the back. She got there just as Spearman was coming out the door. Sinclair pulled her pistol and said, "Your shift over early?"

Spearman looked at Sinclair and her pistol, then raised his hands.

"Where's Cassidy?" Sinclair asked.

"She boogied a few minutes ago," Spearman said. "I wanted to grab my tips."

"You might just need them," Sinclair said. "We need to talk."

Sinclair collared Spearman and made a quick call to 911. She identified herself as FBI Special Agent Sara Sinclair, gave her badge number, and asked for assistance from Seattle PD. The dispatcher said there would be an SPD unit there in two minutes. Sinclair then walked Spearman to her car, where they waited impatiently for the local police to arrive.

When the SPD cruiser pulled in next to Sutcliff's car, she pulled her badge and identified herself.

"What's FBI from Yakima doing over here in our neck of the woods?" one of the officers asked.

"Helping on the case of the exotic cats that were stolen over in Kittitas County. You heard of it?"

"Heard of it?" the other SPD officer said. "It's been all over the news here. It's like the time that sea lion got hurt. The media named him, and they did a story on him every day for a month. We got people dying in the streets of drug overdoses, and thousands of homeless people living under bridges, and all the newsmongers care about is a tiger loose in the mountains."

"Well, I believe this is the guy who stole the trailer full of cats, and I need to chat with him about where he turned the tiger loose so we can try to find it."

"Yes, ma'am," the first officer said. "What can we do to help?"

"Mostly, I need you to just be here so that he doesn't run on me. I'm going to show him some maps. Can you just hang here for a few minutes?"

Sinclair had Spearman lean against the back of her vehicle while they talked.

"Listen," Sinclair said gently. "Your girlfriend ditched you. Your friend is about to fess up to loaning you his pickup. You didn't even get a chance to collect your tip money! Everyone is prepared to leave you high and dry. That is, unless you help this investigation and yourself. Just tell me what happened."

Spearman paused, looked at Sinclair ruefully, and slouched deeper into his stance against the bumper.

"I knew we would get caught sooner or later," Spearman said finally. "At least I didn't get eaten by that lion."

Sinclair chuckled. "Did you think that was a possibility?"

"Yeah, you should have seen how that thing looked at me. And it took a swipe at me as I was trying to cut the lock from its cage."

She chuckled again.

"We can get into the details later, but what I really want to know is if you released the tiger in the mountains near Cle Elum. And if so, where? We have a real issue developing."

"We saw the news that it's creating," Spearman said. "It got Cassidy all jacked up. She's ready to start hitting zoos, to let all the animals go."

"So, you released the tiger?"

"Yes, ma'am. But not where we left the truck and trailer."

"If I showed you a map, could you point out where it was?"

"I might be able to, but we weren't looking at maps. I just drove, looking for a remote road off one of the main Forest Service roads."

Sinclair grabbed her iPad and opened it, pulling up a U.S Forest Service map of Okanogan-Wenatchee National Forest. Then she zoomed into the mountains west of Roslyn and showed it to Spearman.

He looked at it and pointed at the map.

"I got the meat at the butcher shop here," he said, pointing at Roslyn. Then he traced the line along some roads. He followed it for quite a way and then said, "It should be right in here."

Sinclair zoomed in on the map a bit more and then converted the map to lines that showed longitude and latitude. She tried McCain one more time on her phone. Still no answer. She left him a quick voicemail, telling him she'd caught one of the suspects and gave him the approximate coordinates to where the tiger was released. She told him she'd be headed back to Yakima as soon as possible and clicked off.

"Now, what to do with you, Mr. Spearman?" Sinclair asked rhetorically.

"You could just let me go," he said, giving her his most charming smile. "I promise never to do anything like this again."

"Yeah, I wish I could," Sinclair said. "Because I almost believe you."

Sinclair talked to the SPD officers for a couple minutes, and they offered to take Spearman to the city lockup to hold until charges could be filed by Kittitas County.

CHAPTER 20

The sun was starting to drop in the west as Carson Dobbs collected all the items he was going to use in his attack. He mentally went through the checklist. He had his cougar feet (front ones with claws, back ones without), the cougar hide, his moccasins, his broom, a headlight, some water, a few granola bars, and a coat. He'd be hiking back to his shack at night, and it would be dark and possibly cold.

When he had everything collected, he put them in an old, aluminum-framed backpack, stuck his arms through the straps, hefted the pack onto his back, and started hiking the three miles down the hill to the spot he had chosen.

Throughout the day, he had done some reading and writing in his manifesto, listening as the occasional ATV or motorcycle buzzed around on the trails below. Every time he heard one, he would smile. Today may very well be the last day he'd have to put up with them.

Dobbs took his time working his way down to his predetermined ambush spot. It wasn't a straight descent by any means. He would drop into one draw, side-hill across to another, and then work his way down another. Sometimes he even had to climb up over a small ridge to get to the next draw.

For the first couple miles he stayed in his boots, but as he got close to where he wanted to be by dusk, he took off the boots and put on the moccasins. Then he brought out his handmade broom and started brushing his tracks. After he'd come across a side hill, walking on a game trail, Dobbs turned around and looked at where he had just walked. There was nothing. Not a trace of a human track. He was pleased.

The last mile down the hill took nearly an hour. He didn't want to make a mistake, so he took it slow. Once, when he was about a quarter mile from his spot, Dobbs heard a motorcycle roaring up the bike trail. He stopped and ducked behind a tree, even though he couldn't see the trail.

The sound of the motorcycle got his heart racing. He had thought long and hard about what he was going to do. He was not concerned about taking someone's life. He knew he would feel no remorse about that. But he really didn't want to be caught. He had much work to do, and finally having some quiet time to work on things would make all this worth it.

Mentally, he knew it wouldn't be difficult, but physically, it could be tough. Slashing at the bear carcass hung from the tree was one thing. Tearing into a human being, who could possibly fight back, would be another.

His plan was to go for the throat. He'd done some research and knew there were two main carotid arteries in the neck that carried the blood from the heart to the brain. They were large arteries, and if one, or hopefully both, were slashed, the person should bleed out in short order.

Dobbs envisioned his attack as he worked his way down the last little part of the hill. There, he climbed onto the rock, surrounded by brush, that he had chosen as the spot for his surprise assault.

There were still about twenty minutes of daylight left when he was finished setting up. He had used his cougar tracks, mounted on stiff rods he'd made from pine branches, to make tracks to the rock. Then, with the clawed paws securely affixed to a couple of short, stout pieces of wood, Dobbs donned the cougar hide and sat in wait, just like a real cougar.

Patience was a mountain lion's true advantage as they stalked their prey and waited to pounce. Dobbs wasn't quite as patient. In fact, he started to fidget after about fifteen minutes, and all of a sudden, he had the incredible urge to urinate.

The last thing he wanted to do was pee himself, so after listening closely for any riders coming along the trail, he got up, and with the clawless cougar feet on their sticks and the broom in this mouth, he walked over to a small group of pine trees and peed. He brushed away the human tracks and left the cougar tracks in the dirt, walking back to the rock.

Just then he heard a motorcycle coming. He couldn't be sure, but he believed it to be a lone rider. Again, his heart started to race.

The annoying buzz of the motorcycle engine got closer and closer. Dobbs grabbed his two short-handled claw paws and waited.

Five seconds later, he saw the light of the motorbike bouncing through the trees and then it was there, ten yards from him, slowing to make the hairpin turn. Dobbs could see the rider, but the rider had not seen him. When the man on the bike was about three feet below him, Dobbs jumped.

His bodyweight hit the rider squarely and knocked him off the motorcycle. Stunned, the man landed on his stomach. He wanted to see who or what had hit him, so he rolled over. As soon as the two men were face-to-face, Dobbs swung his cougar-claw paws with amazing speed and accuracy.

The problem was – and Dobbs hadn't considered this – the man was wearing a helmet. The strong nylon strap that kept his helmet secured was blocking much of his throat. On the first strike, the claws ripped some flesh, but it didn't do the damage Dobbs intended. So, he struck again and again. The man had lifted his arms to try to fend off the strikes. His forearms were quickly shredded by the claws.

The other thing Dobbs hadn't anticipated was that, although the cougar claws were sharp as razor blades, they also acted like fishhooks. In a real-life cougar attack, the cat would use its front claws to grab and hold the animal while its back paws raked the animal's belly to disembowel it. As Dobbs continued striking the man, the claws stuck to his jacket. Finally, on a blow to the man's arms, the claw sunk into his wrist, puncturing the radial artery. As Dobbs pulled the claw free, blood spurted everywhere.

Dobbs continued swinging the paws like a madman, but already he was tiring. This was not going as he had anticipated. The portion of the man's face sticking out of the helmet was sliced in several places, and there were deep slashes on his upper throat, but the carotid arteries had not been hit.

Dobbs struck from the left side and the right, one slashing blow after another. Finally, mostly due to the loss of blood from the wound in his wrist, the motorcyclist lost the energy to fight. Dobbs quickly undid the man's helmet straps and gave one quick slash across his throat. Blood poured from the wound and within another half minute, the man was dead.

During the attack, the motorcycle kept running. Dobbs thought about turning it off but decided to let it run. That's what would happen in a real cougar attack. The bike would run until it burned all the fuel or the gas leaked out of the tank.

He had just enough daylight to double-check his tracks. There were heavy footprints and knee prints around the dead man, so Dobbs brushed those away. Then he placed clawless paw prints around in the dirt, pushing some deeper than others to make it look like the cat had strained hard to fight the man. Dobbs avoided looking at the dead man too much. Still, he knew his victim appeared like he'd been attacked by something wild.

He quickly rounded up his stuff, took off the cougar hide, placed everything in his backpack, shouldered the pack, and then moved parallel to the trail before starting back up the hill. As he walked, he brushed away the moccasin prints and placed the cougar tracks at the appropriate intervals. Once he hit some grass, Dobbs took less effort to cover his tracks and moved quickly through that area.

As he approached a shale rockslide on the hillside above him, Dobbs figured that would be the perfect place to change back into his boots. He walked thirty feet up into the rocks, sat down, placed the cougar paws in his pack, changed into his boots, and moved slowly up through scree. Out of the shale slide, Dobbs side-hilled much of the rest of the way, cutting back and forth as he gained elevation, working through draws and over small hogbacks as he went.

Dobbs had stopped occasionally on his hike back, both to catch his breath and to listen for other motorcycles. He didn't hear one at all until he was almost to his cabin. It would be the first of many he would hear during the night.

When he got to the shack, Dobbs stripped off his clothing. He was surprised by how much blood had gotten on him. He had it on his face, neck, shirt, pants, and moccasins. The only clean part of his shirt was the portion that had been covered by the cougar hide. He pulled it out of his backpack and saw that it, too, was covered in the biker's blood.

He would need to burn everything, but Dobbs decided to do that the next day. And he would do it several miles from his shack, just in case someone noticed the smoke.

When he finally went to bed, several hours later, Dobbs wondered if he would have to attack another rider. He hoped not. None of it had played out like he envisioned, and he really did not want to have to do it again.

As he was finally drifting off to sleep, he thought he heard an unfamiliar guttural growl. If he'd gotten up and looked, he would have seen a Bengal tiger sniffing around his bloody pile of clothes on the trail just outside his tiny cabin.

Chapter 21

By the time McCain regained cell service and received the voicemail messages from Sinclair, he was down the hill and running out of daylight. He decided he would head back up to the coordinates she had given him in the morning. His search for the tiger tracks could wait until he'd slept.

After Sinclair sent Spearman with the Seattle police officers to be placed in the city jail, she called the Kittitas County Sheriff's Office and chatted with Deputy McDonald. She told him that she had taken one of the suspects in the stolen cat trailer case into custody. Sinclair confirmed that there was, in fact, a tiger loose up in the Cascades west of Roslyn. She told him they knew where it had been released.

It only took McDonald ten minutes to put together a press release which he sent out immediately to the long list of news media and reporters he had accrued. Twenty seconds after he hit send on his press-release email, his phone started ringing.

Yes, he would be happy to do an interview immediately. Yes,

he could go live at five. Yes, he would do a satellite hookup with London. Yes, yes, yes. Ronald McDonald was loving it.

Unfortunately, Public Information Officer McDonald would not be loving it for long. A short time after his Live-at-Five interview, the call came into the sheriff's office about a dirt biker who had been mauled by a large cat near where the tiger had been released. According to the caller, the motorcyclist was dead, and the people who had found him said it was a horrifying scene.

McCain and Sinclair had just finished with the dinner dishes and were discussing how Sinclair had found Spearman when calls about the dead motorcyclist started coming in. Sinclair was speaking with one of the Kittitas County deputies when McCain's phone rang. It was KCS Deputy Hernandez.

"I don't know if you heard," Hernandez said, "but we have a real mess up here. A guy riding a dirt bike on one of the ATV trails got jumped and mauled. I haven't seen the body or the scene, but the people who found him say it is definitely a cat attack. And they're thinking it's the tiger."

"I just heard a couple of minutes ago. Agent Sinclair just took a call from one of your other deputies."

"I heard she found one of the people who let the tiger loose."

"Yeah, she followed up on the photo of the truck that you got from North Bend and found the owner, who evidently loaned his truck to a couple of co-workers. They planned the whole thing and staked out the truck and trailer as it arrived in Washington."

"We called the owner of the tiger," Hernandez said. "He's on his way over here now, and he is pretty confident his tiger did not maul anyone."

"Well, it will be interesting to see. Have your people gotten up there and secured the scene?"

"Yes, but there were a bunch of riders there, and the sergeant said everything is pretty well trampled. Do you think that dog of yours can track the cat?"

"Yes, I do, if we can find some tracks that haven't been obliterated by people."

"Okay," said Hernandez. "I'll get the sergeant to keep everyone away. They need to bring the body down, but we'll take care of the area and keep a couple deputies up there."

"Tell them to keep their eyes open. If there is a killer cat up there, they don't want to be sleeping on the job."

"I don't think that will be a problem. They said the dead guy is a mess. They'll be too afraid to sleep."

After he hung up the phone, McCain turned to Sinclair.

"Well, this is one for the books," she said. "We confirm a tiger has been turned loose, and the next thing you know, a trail rider gets attacked. Can't be a coincidence, can it?"

"It's hard to believe that it is," McCain said. "But Hernandez said Sam Banister doesn't believe it's his tiger."

"Should you talk to him?" she asked.

"Yeah, I'm going to. But it can wait until the morning. They're asking if Jack and I can track the cat that did the killing, so I'm pretty sure I'll see Mr. Banister first thing tomorrow."

It didn't take long for news of the possible tiger mauling to leak. It was the main story on every TV channel at eleven o'clock, each of the stations running teasers every twenty minutes during the earlier shows to promote their breaking story.

"This just in," a very serious reporter would say while staring into the camera. "A man riding a motorcycle has been killed by an animal in the Cascades. Officials fear it is the work of the tiger that has been running free for the past several days. Stay tuned. Full story at eleven."

"It looks like it'll be a media circus up there, too," Sinclair said as she and McCain were getting ready for bed.

"Ronald McDonald will get to handle that part of it," McCain said.

Sinclair grimaced and said, "Why doesn't he go by Mac or something?"

The couple went to bed, but they couldn't sleep. Sinclair retold the story of spotting Cassidy Sutcliff and Cory Spearman at the restaurant and how she'd caught Spearman trying to leave out the back door.

"That was some good bit of police work there, Agent Sinclair," McCain said. "And it wasn't even your case."

"If I'd been quicker, I would have caught both of them."

"Don't worry. She'll pop up again," McCain said of Sutcliff. "She sounds like she might be a little radical."

"Spearman said she's crazier than a loony bird and will do just about anything to free any caged animal."

"Like I said, she'll pop up again."

*

McCain had trouble sleeping, thinking about the attack on the rider. Finally, at four o'clock he rolled out of bed, grabbed a quick shower, and got dressed to head out.

"Couldn't sleep, huh?" Sinclair said from bed.

"Sorry if I woke you, but I really want to get up there and see what happened."

"I understand. You guys be careful. Let me know what's happening when you can."

"Will do," McCain said as he leaned down and kissed his wife. "Love you."

"Love you, too. I'm glad Jack will be with you. Be safe."

When Jack heard his name, he padded into the bedroom to see what was going on.

"We're off to work early, boy. Come on."

McCain headed to the door with the big yellow Lab right on his heels. As he walked by the closet, McCain reached in and grabbed his to-go bag, a backpack filled with everything he might need to spend a night or two in the woods. Its contents included a one-man tent, sleeping bag, and rations for him and Jack. There was extra water in the pack, snack bars, batteries, two headlamps, and a few other items, none more important than toilet paper.

He threw the backpack into the back seat after Jack and headed out to the highway leading to the Kittitas Valley. Hernandez had given him directions to the location the night before. At the site, there were three Kittitas County Sheriff's SUVs and two big satellite

TV trucks – one from the NBC affiliate in Seattle and another from CNN – parked off the road.

As McCain drove by, he wondered how they had made it up this far. A couple places on the road were very narrow because of trees. Evidently, the truck drivers had just taken on the low branches and would worry about scratches and gouges later.

McCain parked his truck, grabbed his pack, and walked over to talk to a KCS deputy standing near the spot where the motorcycle trail crossed the Forest Service road.

"How's it going?" McCain asked as he walked up to the deputy, Jack at heel by his side.

"I've been better," the deputy said. "I've been standing here for the last six hours, trying to keep the lookie-loos at bay."

"Well, it looks like you are doing a good job," McCain said. "I'm Luke McCain, and this is Jack. Deputy Hernandez asked me to come in and have a look around."

"Yes sir, Officer McCain. I'm Tate Buckley. I know all about you and Jack from when you helped find that serial killer a couple years ago. Pleasure to meet you, for sure."

"Nice to meet you, too, Deputy Buckley. So, where are the news people who are with these trucks?"

"They left after their live reports last night around eleven thirty. They all piled into a big SUV and headed down the hill. I'm guessing they're staying at a motel in Ellensburg. I expect they'll be back here before too long."

"Most likely," McCain said. "Were they trying to interview anyone?"

"Yeah, they cornered a couple of motorcycle riders who knew the dead guy. They tried to talk to me, but I'm under strict orders not to comment to anyone. PIO McDonald is handling all of that."

"Probably best," McCain said. "Do you expect PIO McDonald up here today?"

"Not that I know of. He likes working from his computer, doing the interviews on Zoom. That way he can keep his hair combed just right."

"Well, that is important. If he does show up, I'd like to meet him."

"My shift's almost up. But if I see him, I'll let him know."

"That'd be great," McCain said. "C'mon, Jack. We have a killer cat to track."

When McCain got up the hill to where the attack had taken place, there were two more KCS deputies. A large circle around the trail and surrounding area had been taped off with yellow crime tape, and the two deputies stood chatting on the outside of the taped circle. A black motorcycle was tipped over in the grass just off the trail.

McCain had heard Buckley radio up to the two deputies that he was coming, so they were expecting him. As McCain approached, one of the officers, a tall, lanky African American man of about forty said, "Officer McCain, I'm Sergeant Harper, and this is Deputy Hall."

The second deputy was a woman in her late forties of medium height and build. She had what looked to be sandy brown hair piled up under a KCSO ball cap.

"Nice to meet you," McCain said as he shook their hands. "So, can you tell me what you know about what happened, and without getting too close, show me where?"

Sergeant Harper took McCain through everything they had learned and pointed out where the attack had taken place, right below a big rock at a tight turn on the trail. From where he was, McCain could see blood in the grass and on some of the nearby brush.

"Did the coroner indicate how the man died?"

"No, he didn't," Harper said. "But I've seen plenty of car wrecks, a couple suicides, and a homicide where the people died from exsanguination. The amount of blood spilled here tells me the guy most likely died from loss of blood."

"I'd have to agree," McCain said as he looked around at the massive blood stains on the grass.

"What about the motorcycle over there? Was the engine still turned on?"

"I don't know," Harper said. "Not sure anyone looked. It wasn't running when we got here, so I guess it could have run out of gas."

McCain walked over and saw that the key was still in the on position.

"That would coincide with an animal attack," McCain said.

"Oh, it was an animal," Harper said. "You should have seen the slash marks on the victim's body. I've seen some knife wounds in my day, and those cuts were not made by any knife."

"And there are plenty of animal tracks around the area where the man was," said Hall. "I don't know much about tracks, but I would venture to say the prints were from a cat of some kind."

McCain told Jack to sit and stay, and then he walked under the crime tape and started to look around. The deputy was correct. The tracks McCain saw were definitely made by a cat: four fairly round toes off of the main oval pad. But he instantly knew the tracks were not that of a Bengal tiger. They were too small.

Before he said anything to the deputies, he looked around some more. All he found were the same sized tracks. McCain was positive the tracks were made by a cougar, but at first glance the tracks seemed off in some way.

"Well, it wasn't a tiger that attacked the man," McCain said.

"I thought the same thing," Harper said. "I'd say they're cougar tracks. I've never seen tiger tracks, but from what I've seen of the animals at the zoo, they have much bigger paws than this cat."

"Exactly what I was thinking," McCain said. "I've seen lots of cougar tracks over the years, and those are definitely some. And they're not from a really big cougar."

"Strange that a cougar would jump a man on a motorcycle," Harper said. "They always shy away from man-made noises from what I've seen."

"That's true," McCain said. "But sometimes a younger cat that is really hungry will be driven to get food any way it can. Attacking a man is very rare, and one on a motorcycle, well, I've never heard of such a thing."

"There was that attack by a cougar a few years ago over near

Snoqualmie when a mountain biker was killed," Harper said. "But that was a pedal bike, and if I remember right, the man and woman who were attacked stopped and tried to scare the cougar away."

"I guess that could have happened here," McCain said. "The rider could have stopped his bike to take a drink. Or if he saw the cat run across the road, he could have stopped to take a look."

Both Harper and Hall were now searching the surrounding woods to make sure the cougar wasn't back, watching them.

"It'll be interesting to see what the coroner has to say," McCain said.

McCain had once watched a cougar kill a mule deer buck, and while the cat used its front claws to catch and hold the deer, it raked the underside of the deer with its hind feet and killed the buck with its teeth by biting into its throat.

"Yes, it will," Harper said. "What a terrible way to die."

McCain looked around a bit more and chatted with the deputies, but he learned nothing more that might help him. It was time to get tracking.

Jack had done some amazing tracking work in the past. He'd even found the body of a dead woman killed by the serial killer that came to be known as the Cascade Killer. And, in fact, Jack had helped track down the killer. He had also tracked wounded animals several times, so tracking was not new to the yellow Lab.

As McCain prepared to set Jack on the tracks, he looked again at the different cougar prints in the dirt. He saw that several prints went one way over to a group of trees, while more prints went up a side hill in the opposite direction.

McCain followed the ones to the trees where he found some wet dirt, as if something, or someone, had urinated there.

"Excuse me, sergeant. Could you come look at this?" McCain asked.

Harper came over, and McCain asked, "What's that look like to you?"

"Looks to me like someone stood here and took a piss."

"That's what I thought. But the tracks leading this way are the cougar's. I guess it could have been the cat, but any cat I've ever seen tries to cover their urine and scat with dirt."

"You want me to get a sample of it?" Harper asked.

"If you wouldn't mind. It can't hurt. You got any evidence bags?"

Harper did in his patrol rig, and he went to get them.

"Have Deputy Hall take some photos of the spot, and of you putting some of the wet dirt in the bag. Get a wide view shot or two as well."

"Good idea," Harper said. "Will do. Now you go find that cat. And be careful. It might be a killer."

Chapter 22

Cassidy Sutcliff felt very lucky to not be in jail. She hadn't heard from Spearman since she saw the cop talking to that idiot Scott Cramer. She figured Spearman had been caught and put under a little pressure. He had probably told the pretty police officer everything he and Sutcliff had done.

She would miss Spearman. He was easy to manipulate and would do most anything she wanted him to do. And she'd miss the sex. He was one of the few men she'd been with who could keep up with her.

Now, on her own, Sutcliff wondered if she would be able to do what she knew she must. She had to get into those fairgrounds after hours and figure out a way to free that lion and those other poor cats.

Their apartment most certainly was under surveillance, so she couldn't risk going back there. She jumped on the light rail and rode it all the way to SeaTac, where she exited and walked to one of the less expensive motels nearby. She needed a good night's sleep, and then she would figure out what her next step would be.

When Sutcliff finally got settled into the room, she stripped and took a shower, standing in the spray of hot water for a long time. In the shower, she thought again about how close she had come to getting a free night's stay in jail.

After showering, she wound her wet hair up in a towel, wrapped her body in a second one, and clicked on the TV. The eleven o'clock news was just coming on. The top story was about a motorcycle rider who had been attacked and killed by a large cat in the Cascades. The speculation was the cat that had done the killing was the tiger that she and Spearman had released a week ago.

As soon as the reporter started talking, Sutcliff perked up and listened to every word. She scrutinized the trees and hills on TV. Could they have been that lucky? Not only was the tiger still running free, but it was exacting revenge on people for keeping it captive. She couldn't have scripted it better. She was so happy, she wanted to celebrate. She needed Spearman. Now.

*

After sniffing around the bloody clothes she had found on the trail, the tiger kept wandering. She had excellent night vision, and her nose picked up many interesting smells. She would follow one scent or another, hoping to find something else to eat.

The elk meat from the day before was enough to keep her going for a while, and there was plenty of water in the creeks and springs to keep her hydrated.

At one point, she smelled a deer ahead and instinctively dropped down, her belly barely off the ground, slowly stalking toward the deer. As she got closer, she saw two deer feeding on some brush. There was an urge to spring and run at them, but she stayed frozen in the grass, observing.

A second later, a slight breeze blew at the back of the tiger's head. Both deer threw their heads up, and in an instant, they were sprinting away. Timba just watched.

With the deer and their enticing aroma now nothing more than a lingering scent, Timba continued walking, knowing not where she was going or why.

*

If Dobbs had been a little more observant, he would have noticed the big cat prints in the dirt not far from where he had piled the bloody clothes and cougar hide. Frankly, he was a little groggy. The physical exertion and the adrenalin rush he had experienced ten hours before had really affected him. Plus, there had been the laborious hike back up the hill.

He should have slept, he knew, but there was plenty to keep him awake through the night. Mostly it was the noise of vehicles coming and going three miles down the hill. The noise wasn't deafening by any means, but it was loud enough that he could hear it all night long.

Dobbs had gone over his attack several times. It happened nothing like he had envisioned and after analyzing it again and again, he believed he'd been quite lucky. Still, he had accomplished his goal. He was confident that when the officials determined there was a killer cougar on the loose, they would warn everyone off, and he'd have the serenity he so desired.

He thought about throwing the cougar paws in with the bundle of stuff he was going to burn but decided there might have to be a second attack at some point. If that was necessary, the paw prints should match. Plus, the work he had done to create the cougar paw weapons and the printmakers was extremely time-consuming. He really didn't want to have to do it again.

So, with all the bloody clothes and the hide in his arms, Dobbs started down the hill, in the opposite direction of the attack, to find a place where he could burn everything.

*

Jack started out slowly, sniffing the tracks. McCain noticed that as he tracked, Jack would sometimes stay to the side of the cougar tracks, as if there was an unseen source of scent there. He'd never seen the dog do that before.

They were only about seventy yards up the trail when McCain heard a vehicle approaching from below. He turned and saw another Kittitas County Sheriff's SUV driving up. It parked on the road below him. It was Deputy Hernandez, and with her was Sam Banister.

McCain really wanted to stay on the tracks but decided he'd go down and chat with Hernandez and Banister before continuing. He told Jack to sit and stay and headed down to the SUV.

"Have you found anything, Officer McCain?" Banister asked.

"Well, as a matter of fact, we have. You can rest assured your tiger wasn't involved in this. The cat tracks that we found are all too small for a tiger. We believe it is a cougar."

"Would it be possible for me to see the tracks?"

"Sure," McCain said, leading Banister up the hill to the area circled with yellow tape.

When they got to the motorcycle trail, McCain pointed out some of the tracks. Banister studied them closely.

"No, those aren't Timba's tracks," Banister said. "You're right. They're too small. And Timba has a scar on the pad on her right front foot. It leaves a distinctive mark in her track. What a relief! I just didn't think she could do something like this."

"Officer Hernandez and Sergeant Harper will let their public information officer know immediately that we have ruled out your tiger as the cat who killed the rider," McCain said.

"So, nobody has reported any sightings of Timba?"

"No, nothing so far. As you know, one of the people who stole your truck and trailer was caught, and he pointed us to where Timba was released. I was all set to go locate the spot and try to track her from there when all of this happened."

"She's been up here for a week. She could be fifty miles from here by now."

"Sooner or later, someone will see her, or find a track, and we'll locate her."

"I hope so. I worry so much about how she is going to survive without any hunting knowledge."

"Mother Nature has a way," McCain said. "I'm sure she's doing fine. Now, if you'll excuse me, I have a killer cougar to run down."

Jack was still sitting patiently when McCain returned to the dog. "Okay, boy," McCain said. "Let's go find that cat."

McCain pointed to the last track he could see. Jack put his nose to it and started working up the hill again. As McCain watched the yellow dog work the trail, he was intrigued by how Jack continued sniffing to one side of the cougar tracks. They worked into a large patch of grass, and Jack kept his nose to the ground even though McCain could no longer see any cougar tracks.

Then, in an area where the grass thinned, McCain saw an imprint in the dirt. It was a human-sized print, but it was totally smooth, like it had been made with a shoe without tread. The human prints were right in line with the track Jack was following.

So that he could find it again, McCain stopped, removed a piece of bright orange surveyor's tape from his backpack, and tied it to a nearby bush. That way, if he needed to come back and find the print again, it would be marked.

As he continued to follow Jack, McCain thought about the human track. Of course, hikers and hunters had most likely walked this same hillside over the years, but their tracks would have been obliterated by the weather. Almost all hunters wear boots with a sole or tread to give them traction as they hunt, although McCain had read that some archery hunters actually did wear moccasins, or they would take off their boots and just wear an extra pair of socks when they stalked an animal. Maybe that is what the tracks were, McCain thought. But then why would they be in the exact line of the tracks Jack was following? Maybe Jack got sidetracked and was now following the wrong scent.

"Whoa, Jack," McCain yelled. The yellow dog stopped where he was and waited for McCain to catch up.

The dog was now just beyond the grassy slope, back into some trees where the ground was mainly dirt. When McCain arrived, he looked down and there were the cougar tracks. Jack hadn't gotten sidetracked.

Now, because the tracks were so obvious, McCain took a closer look at them. He'd followed cougar tracks before, and while these followed a similar pattern – with the back tracks almost touching the front tracks in a fairly straight line – something seemed out of place. Could the cougar have some kind of a birth defect, or more likely, had it been injured? Either way, something could be affecting the cat's stride. It certainly was possible. Maybe that is why it turned to killing a human.

As McCain hiked behind Jack, he would check regularly to see if the dog was on the cougar tracks. But, after about a mile of crisscrossing the hillside, moving through one draw, up the next side hill, over the hogback and down into the next draw, the cougar tracks disappeared in a large shale rockslide.

Jack followed a scent trail into the rocks but soon seemed lost. He started circling, trying to relocate the scent. Rocks were the worst at holding scent, especially when it was so dry. It quickly became obvious that Jack had totally lost the scent.

McCain watched as Jack kept searching. The dog would often come back to a spot about ten yards into the rocks, but from that spot, he just couldn't find anything.

Looking for the tracks did no good. McCain tried to find anything that might help his tracking partner get back on the trail, but it was fruitless. Finally, with no other good ideas, McCain decided that they should make a big circle around the rockslide to see if they could again pick up the cougar tracks.

At the northeast corner of the slide, they found some prints. But they weren't cougar prints. They were boot prints. If McCain didn't know better, it was like the cougar magically transformed into a man.

The boot prints were fairly fresh and headed up the hill. Jack was following the tracks, but it wasn't boot prints they needed to find, so McCain called Jack back, and they continued their search around the perimeter of the shale slide.

When they made it all the way around the rockslide and were back at the spot where the cougar tracks entered the scree, McCain decided to sit down, take a breather, and think about it for a few minutes. He called Jack back to him, pulled out a bottle of water, and they both drank from it.

"How could the cougar tracks just disappear?" McCain asked Jack. The Lab just gave him an inquisitive look, trying to understand what McCain was saying to him. "It's like the thing grew wings and flew right out of here."

Again, Jack just cocked his head and stared back.

"I don't understand it either, boy. But we'll figure it out."

Chapter 23

After a restless night, sleeping by herself for the first time in years, Sutcliff had a plan. Or at least she had the start of a plan. She would head to the fair in Puyallup and do a little reconnaissance on the Wild Cats of the World show.

When she got to the fair, she was amazed that it cost her fifteen dollars to get in. But she paid it, figuring it was going to be money well spent when she had her plan finalized.

As she wandered around the fair, she took in some of the other sites, and when she saw the big trailer for the Fisher Scones, she realized she was hungry, so she waited in a surprisingly long line and bought two.

Finally, in one of the smaller buildings toward the back of the fairgrounds, she found the Wild Cats of the World exhibit. The female lion was at the center of the exhibit, with the smaller exotic cats in enclosures around the lion. All the cats were snoozing on soft beds or carpet as the hundreds of fairgoers strolled by.

Sutcliff watched the cats lying there for a long time, and then she spent some time looking at the building. There was a man door next to a big roller door in the back of the building. She acted like she wanted some privacy to talk on her cell phone and wandered back by the doors with the phone to her ear. No one paid any attention to her.

The man door opened from the inside easily as she tried the knob. But after she opened it and reached around to try the outside knob, it would not turn. That told her it was locked at all times and would take a key to open. She guessed there would be security in the buildings, but most of the security at these places were not overly trained.

Sutcliff's plan was coming together. She would spend the day at the fair and then stow away somewhere in the fairgrounds, hopefully close to the cat enclosures. Then, in the middle of the night, she would get into the building and release the lion and the other cats.

During her reconnaissance, she had noticed that the locks on the doors of the different cats' cages were not the same as the ones in the trailer. They were smaller locks, which would be much easier to cut. Sometime in the next several hours, she planned to get a security company's blue shirt and a bolt cutter. Getting one of the blue shirts would make the second task that much easier.

*

When he needed to get supplies, Dobbs would walk four miles to one of the main Forest Service roads. From there, he usually caught a ride with someone going down the hill to Roslyn or Cle Elum, where he'd purchase what he needed. Then he would start walking home, trying to hitch a ride along the way. On these rare excursions, he might end up walking eight miles or more in a day.

The hike he was on today might rival those trips; he wanted to get a good distance away from his cabin. There were undoubtedly law enforcement officers down where the attack had occurred, and Dobbs didn't want any smoke from a fire to catch their attention. So, he walked. He was tired, but most of the hike would be downhill. It was the hike back up the hill that he dreaded.

As Dobbs walked, he again thought about what he had done to the motorcycle rider. It had happened very quickly, but as he thought about it, he remembered every single swing of the cougar paws, every slash the claws made. He thought about how he punctured the man's wrist, and about how the blood pumped from the wound when he pulled out the claws.

And, he remembered the final slash, across the man's throat, which ultimately killed him. He'd remember that for the rest of his life.

When Dobbs had walked about five miles, he started looking for a good place to burn his stuff. It had been the typical hot, dry summer in Central Washington, and setting the forest on fire was definitely possible if he wasn't careful. There had already been a terribly destructive fire that summer up near Blewett Pass. No way did he want a fire in his neck of the woods. His cabin could burn, and even if it didn't, there was a good chance it would be discovered.

Ultimately, the place he chose for the fire was in a slash pile that had been burned earlier in the spring. The logging company that had cut the trees in the area had picked a good spot for it, away from anything that might burn. It was perfect.

Dobbs had packed a small Mason jar filled with lantern fluid, and now he opened it and sprinkled the gas on the articles of clothing. As he was doing so, he noticed his pair of homemade moccasins was not there.

He looked all around, and then again in his pack. He started to panic. He really liked the moccasins, but he knew they too must burn. They were another piece of evidence that could connect him to the murder. The dead man had bled on the moccasins. They needed to be gone.

Dobbs stewed about the leather slippers for a bit. Then, figuring there was nothing he could do right now, he struck the wooden match on the leg of his denim britches. Dobbs dropped the match onto the pile of clothing and watched as it erupted into flames.

After the fire got going, he placed a few dry branches and moss on top to keep it burning. Then he added some bigger pieces of wood he'd found nearby. Dobbs figured it would have to be good and hot to burn the tanned cougar hide.

A half hour later, when he was convinced every bit of clothing and hide was reduced to ash, Dobbs stepped over to the dying embers and urinated on them. The last of the fire sizzled under the stream of pee, sending ashes and black smoke into the air.

When he was done peeing on the fire, Dobbs broke a green branch off a nearby pine tree and stirred the ashes. Then he kicked dirt on what was left of the fire. Convinced the fire was no longer a threat to the forest, Dobbs pulled a bottle out of his pack, drank half of the water inside, threw the bottle back in his pack, and pulled the pack's straps onto his shoulders.

He'd been gone from the cabin a little over two hours. Hiking steadily, mostly uphill, Dobbs would be back to his cabin in another three. He put his head down and started walking.

*

After a good rest, McCain decided they should walk the outside edge of the shale rockslide one more time. The cougar had walked into the rocks, and it most certainly had walked back out. He figured he and Jack had just missed where the mountain lion exited the shale.

So, up the hill they went, working slower this time. McCain looked for anything that might indicate where the cougar left the rocks, while Jack, nose to the ground, searched for the scent. Once again, they hit the human footprints in the upper corner of the slide. And once again, Jack started following them.

"Wrong tracks," McCain said to Jack. "We're looking for a cat, not a man."

McCain whistled, Jack reluctantly came back, and they continued their slow search around the slide. As they searched, McCain was trying to figure out how the cougar could just magically disappear. There was a chance the thing had a den in the rockslide, but when he examined the slide, the rock quality was all wrong. There were no rocks bigger than a basketball and almost all the rocks were flat and slick. It was not a place where a cougar would den up.

It was starting to get warm. McCain considered giving up, but the thought of losing the cougar's fresh trail made him press on. This time, he decided to work Jack in a bigger circle around the rockslide. Maybe the cat had made some miraculous jump from the rocks into a nearby tree.

So up the hill they went, this time twenty yards outside the perimeter of the shale. Jack showed no interest in anything until he again hit the boot tracks and started trailing them.

McCain thought about letting the dog go and following him, but again, it wasn't a man they were trying to find. It was a mountain lion. So, once again he called Jack back and had him work wider into the grass and trees around the rockslide.

As they worked, McCain not only looked for the tracks in the dirt, but also kept his eyes in the trees. Nothing at all caught his attention. Nothing caught Jack's interest either. When they again made it back to the place where they had lost the cougar tracks in the shale, McCain decided to call it a day.

Walking back down to the truck, McCain thought about the boot tracks leaving the shale slide. It was archery elk season. The tracks were most certainly made by a hunter. Maybe it was the same hunter who had left the sole-less imprint in the grass, lower on the hill. Something wasn't computing in all of this, but he wasn't sure what was off.

McCain lost his train of thought quickly. When he looked down at the two big satellite TV trucks, he realized the area had become a beehive of activity. There were two or three more cars parked nearby and people walking around. Two guys were dragging cables up the hill toward the yellow tape where the cougar attack had happened, and other people were carrying cameras on tripods.

As McCain descended the hill, he saw that one of the new arrivals was none other than Simon Erickson, the energetic news reporter from the ABC affiliate in Yakima. While the other people hustling about hadn't noticed McCain and Jack approaching, Erickson had. He threw his camera up on his shoulder and started filming as the officer and his dog trudged toward him.

"Officer McCain," Erickson said. "Can you do a short interview wid me?"

McCain should have told him no, that he needed to talk to Deputy McDonald with the Kittitas County Sheriff's Office, but he liked the kid and told him he would do a short one.

After attaching the microphone to McCain's shirt and getting his camera on a tripod, Erickson went to work.

"So, we heard dat da cat dat killed da rider up here on da hill was not da tiger dat was turned loose up diss way. Is dat correct?"

"Yes, it is," McCain said. "We are of the opinion that it was a cougar that attacked the motorcyclist. The tracks at the scene of the attack are too small for a tiger. They are those of a cougar."

"Do you tink you can find diss particular cougar?"

"We hope so."

"Is it safe for udder people to be up here hunting or hiking?"

"I think until we find the cougar, it might be prudent to recreate in other parts of the Cascades," McCain said.

"Is it normal for cougars to attack people?"

"No, it is extremely rare. But until we determine what made this particular cougar attack, we're recommending people find other spots to hike or ride or hunt. At least for the time being."

"What about da tiger? Do you tink you'll be able to find it? And do you tink it is a danger to people?"

"I don't know what to think about the tiger. I'm sure we will find her. How soon is another question. Now that we have a little more information about where she was turned loose, we'll have a better chance of finding her."

"Can you tell us where da tiger was released?" Erickson asked.

"No, I really can't. Just know the Kittitas County Sheriff's Office and other law enforcement officers are giving it their best effort to find the tiger."

"I see you have your dog wid you," Erickson said, as he panned the camera over to show Jack, resting in the grass. "Did he help track da cougar?"

"Yes, he tracked it for over a mile and then lost the trail in a shale rockslide."

"Is dat normal?" Erickson asked.

"No, it is not normal for Jack to lose the trail, but it is extremely tough to track across sheer rock."

Erickson asked a few more questions and then thanked McCain for talking with him. He was just turning off the camera when they both looked up and saw April Scott marching toward them.

The young reporter was not wearing four-inch heels today, McCain noticed. But she still was done up more than anyone else in these woods.

"Excuse me, officer," she said. "Could I talk to you for a moment?"

McCain felt like asking if she really wanted to talk to a nobody but agreed to talk to her for a minute. She'd seen him talking to Erickson, and he really couldn't show any favoritism.

Erickson was still taking the camera off the tripod when Scott set hers down right beside his, almost knocking it over. McCain looked at Erickson, and Erickson looked back at him, shaking his head.

Erickson smiled and said, "Tanks, Officer McCain. See you later, Jack."

"Oh, is this your dog?" Scott asked as she walked over to Jack to pet him.

McCain could see Jack starting to cringe. One thing he'd learned from his life around dogs is that they are pretty good judges when it came to people. Most dogs can tell immediately if a person is genuinely nice and good. Jack lowered his head and avoided eye contact with the obnoxious reporter. That told McCain everything he needed to know. Although he'd already made his mind up about this woman.

"Yes, his name is Jack. Be careful. He will bite sometimes,"

McCain said with the slightest of grins.

At that, Scott pulled her hand away from Jack and turned back to McCain. Jack gave McCain a look of gratitude, then walked to McCain's truck to lie down in the shade.

"So, what can you tell me about your investigation?" Scott asked after she had the microphone on McCain and her camera set up. "We've been told it wasn't the tiger that attacked the motorcycle rider."

"We're now looking for a mountain lion," he said. "And we believe it is what attacked the rider."

"I thought you said you were looking for a cougar," she said.

"We are," McCain said.

"So why are you looking for a mountain lion, too?"

McCain knew he was going to regret this interview.

He explained to her that a mountain lion and a cougar are one in the same. In fact, they are even called a panther or a puma sometimes. He told her they were fairly plentiful in this area.

"Do they attack people often?" Scott asked.

"No, very rarely," McCain said. "Sometimes if they are injured or starving, they will go after domestic animals, but attacks on humans just don't occur very often."

"Like horses and cows?" she asked.

"No. Smaller animals, like goats or sheep. They might even grab the occasional small dog or cat."

"Uhhhh!" Scott gasped. "Really. They will kill someone's pet?"

McCain took a deep breath, trying to stay patient.

"Yes, they will. They are predators and will take any small animal they can. And not just small animals. Cougars will kill one deer a week to eat."

"Uhhhh!" Scott gasped again. "They kill poor, innocent deer, too?"

McCain said nothing in reply. He thought Scott might break into tears.

"Well, this has been very informative and disturbing, officer…"

"McCain," McCain said.

"Yes, Officer McCain," she said and turned to the camera, flashing her blinding smile. She gave a recap of what McCain had just said and then finished off the interview with, "From somewhere deep in the Cascade Mountains, I'm April Scott reporting."

McCain already had his microphone off and was handing it to Scott when a yellow jacket appeared out of nowhere and started buzzing around her face. The reporter squealed, grabbed the microphone out of McCain's hand, and ran down the road, leaving her camera sitting on the tripod.

"You're welcome," McCain said, but the squealing reporter didn't hear him.

He walked down to his truck, looked at Jack snoozing in the shade and said, "Come on, boy. Let's go try to find a Bengal tiger."

Chapter 24

It hadn't been difficult to find a blue security shirt. Sutcliff had looked around the fairgrounds and soon found where the security office was located. She watched for a while and saw that there were two doors to the office, one for the public and a second for employees. After watching a few people, both men and women, coming and going out of the employee door, she decided to just walk in and see what she could find.

Sutcliff believed there must be a hundred or more members of the security team working for the fair, and nobody, except for the main supervisor, knew everyone. That meant if she walked in there like she was one of the team, nobody would really pay any attention. Unfortunately, Sutcliff couldn't walk into any room without drawing some attention. It had been a blessing and a curse for years. People, especially men, noticed her. Over time, she had learned just to ignore the stares. If she just went about her business, the long looks might not stop, but they'd be less intrusive.

There were only three people in the room when she opened the employee door and walked in. Two women looked at her and sneered. A young man in a blue security shirt and hat stared with his mouth open. Realizing he must look stupid, he gathered himself and said, "Can I help you?"

Sutcliff walked over to the man and said, "Yes, you can. I'm a new employee." She quickly checked out the name badge on the guy's shirt and said, "I'm supposed to ask for Noah."

"That's me," Noah beamed.

As he sized her up, she looked at the clipboard on his desk. There were a bunch of names listed on a clipboard.

"And who are you?" Noah asked.

"I'm Lacey Grant," she said, hoping that Noah hadn't met the real Lacey Grant.

He checked his list, found the name, and smiled. "Here you are Lacey. But you aren't supposed to be here until tomorrow."

"Yeah, but I wanted to come get my gear and be ready to go when my shift starts tomorrow. Is that okay with you, Noah?" she asked, giving him her best smile.

"Oh sure, that's great," he said, handing her a different clipboard. "Read this, fill out the back page, and while you're doing that, I'll get you your shirt. What size?"

Sutcliff told him her shirt size and filled out the back page with a bunch of false information. When the real Lacey Grant arrived tomorrow, Sutcliff would be long gone.

Noah came back into the room with a shirt and said, "You'll still need to check in tomorrow to fill out a timecard and punch in. We'll give you a radio and show you what zone you'll be covering."

Again, Sutcliff gave him her nicest smile and said, "Thank you. You've been very helpful, Noah. I'm looking forward to working with you."

Next on her agenda was to locate some bolt cutters. Sutcliff went into the nearest women's restroom and came out a couple minutes later wearing her nice, new, blue polo shirt. It had SECURITY printed in big, bold white on the back of the shirt and on the upper right chest on the front. Now, she figured she could go just about anywhere without being questioned.

Knowing there must be a maintenance shop on the grounds, she headed toward the back of the property. That was the most likely place to find it, out of sight from the fair's many visitors.

She found the building quickly. Three men, wearing Washington State Fair shirts, were in the shop tinkering with stuff. When Sutcliff walked in, they all stopped what they were doing and stared.

"Can one of you guys help me?" she asked. "My boss sent me over here to get a bolt cutter. Seems one of the exhibitors has lost the key to his trailer and needs help getting in."

The three guys looked at each other.

"I thought you had bolt cutters at your office," the oldest of the three men said.

"We do, but one of the other security guys has them, and my boss wanted me to check with you. I'll bring them right back."

"I guess it would be alright," the oldest shop guy said. "Dean, go grab that cutter with the red handles."

The youngest of the three guys finally took his eyes off Sutcliff and wandered to the back of the shop. A minute later, he reappeared with the bolt cutters and handed them to Sutcliff.

Again, with a heart-melting smile, she looked each of the men in the eyes. When she got to the oldest man, she said, "Thanks a bunch, guys. I'll bring them back soon."

She could feel all three of them staring at her ass as she walked back out the door. She glanced over her shoulder just to embarrass them as she left.

*

When Dobbs was still three miles from his cabin, he took a breather. He was still wondering where he had put those moccasins. At the same time, the chances were slim that anyone would be up near his little abode. He had lived there for four years, and so far, he'd had no visitors. It was just the way he liked it.

As he sat, he again replayed the events of the evening before. He wondered if he would ever get used to seeing it in his memory, especially the final fatal blow. He was thinking about that when he got another weird feeling. The hair on the back of his neck literally stood straight up.

Something was looking at him. He knew it. In the time he had lived in the mountains, he had seen plenty of bears and a few cougars. He figured it might be one of them now.

Dobbs slowly turned and looked around, but he saw nothing. He looked up the hill. Nothing. He looked down the hill. Nothing. He even looked up into the nearby trees. Still, he saw nothing. But the feeling of being watched did not disappear.

It was so pronounced and chilling, he decided to hustle up the hill. He wanted to get to the safety of his cabin, where his rifle sat in the corner, ready to fire.

*

Timba had spotted the man walking up the hill and watched with interest. She'd seen thousands of people before but hadn't seen a one since she'd landed in this strange place, outside of her normal enclosures.

The man smelled funny. He smelled of smoke and blood and perspiration. He moved slowly. She stalked him for almost a mile before he sat down. At one point, the man looked right at her, but being pressed down in the grass near some brush, she was virtually invisible.

Now, as he walked faster up the hill, she had an urge to chase him. Instead, she just lay in the grass and watched. Soon the man was up over a little rise in the hill and out of her sight. Timba decided she would follow him.

*

When he arrived at the place Cory Spearman had pointed out on the map, McCain was confused. There were no side roads or jeep trails off the main road. He guessed the man could have been telling Sara a lie, but he didn't think so. He was probably just confused.

For the next forty-five minutes, McCain drove the road. Every time he came to a side road, jeep trail, or two-track that ventured off the main road, he would stop, let Jack out, and they would walk it.

On the sixth side road, they finally found what they had been looking for. For over a week they had searched high and low. And now, finally, here were some tiger tracks. McCain was surprised when he realized that during one of his previous days of searching, he had been only a mile or two from this very spot.

McCain and Jack followed the tracks for a couple hundred yards, up over a small hill and down into a draw where there was a small, spring-fed creek. There was a particularly good print in some wet dirt near the creek and, looking closely, McCain could see the line in the pad of the front paw. It was just as Banister had described.

Jack had a great nose, but even with this incredible ability, there just wasn't much of a trail left. Scent particles can stay around for up to seventy-two hours, but it had been eight days since the tiger walked through this area. There was nothing for the dog to smell, meaning that McCain would have to do the tracking through the dirt, grass, rocks, and trees. It was not going to be easy. In fact, it was going to be nearly impossible. As Banister had said earlier that morning, the tiger could be fifty miles away by now, which would make the task even more difficult.

McCain checked the time on his phone. It was 3:30 in the afternoon. There were still about four hours of daylight left. Heading out now, following tracks that were over a week old, didn't make sense. He decided to mark the spot on his GPS, hike back to the truck, and head for home. He'd talk it over with the Kittitas County sheriff and see what he thought about what should be done next.

It seemed to McCain that trying to find the killer cougar might be a better use of his time, but even that really wasn't his first priority. It was still archery elk season, and he felt he needed be out there doing what the people of Washington State paid him to do.

Once he'd come out of the mountains and hit I-90 eastbound, McCain called Mark Anderson, the Kittitas County sheriff.

"Hey, Officer McCain. Thanks for all your help on that mauled dirt bike rider," Anderson said after he answered the phone. "I think our deputies would have figured out it was cougar tracks fairly quickly, but that whole deal with the tiger running loose up there kinda got people thinking one way."

"I understand, sheriff," McCain said. "And I wish Jack and I could have found the cougar. We lost its tracks up in a big shale rockslide about a mile from the incident."

"We have a guy with hounds who is just chomping at the bit to try and find the cougar. You think his hounds can do better than that famous dog of yours?"

"It might be worth a try. I'm guessing the dogs will hit the same dead end that we did, though."

"Okay, well, I think I'll give him the go-ahead. The sooner he and his dogs hit the trail, the fresher the scent will be."

"Roger. If he wants to talk to me before he goes, let me know. I might be able to help him some."

"I'll let him know," said Anderson. "Thanks."

McCain told the sheriff about finding the tiger tracks and what he was thinking about them.

"You think the hounds can track it from there?" Anderson asked.

"I doubt it, but I guess they could give it a go. Jack couldn't pick up any scent. Maybe the hounds can."

"I'll tell them about that too," Anderson said.

McCain gave him the GPS coordinates of the last best track he had seen at the spring, and then he asked about the man who was killed.

"His name is Mike Hodges," the sheriff said. "Thirty-seven years old. Rode dirt bikes for many years and was very familiar with those trails. His buddies said they rode all summer long and never had one incident with cougars. In fact, they said they've never even seen one in all the years they've been riding up there."

"I'm not surprised," McCain said. "They usually stay far away from man-made noises. That's why this thing is so perplexing."

"I know," Anderson said. "We did get a preliminary from the coroner. Said Hodges definitely died of blood loss. Looks like there were at least two wounds that could have killed him. One in the wrist, where the main artery was punctured, and another in the neck, where the carotid artery was slashed."

"Doesn't surprise me either," McCain said. "There was plenty of blood in the dirt and on the grass at the site. Were there any bite wounds on the man, in the head or neck?"

"The coroner didn't say anything about bite marks. Just said his arms and face were slashed up real bad. Hodges was wearing a helmet. It must have protected his head."

"Hmmm," McCain hummed. "Cougars kill by biting their prey. Either in the back of the neck, paralyzing them, or grabbing them by the throat to cut off their windpipes."

"Well, it looks like this one got the job done with its paws," Anderson said. "Anyway, the poor guy is dead, and it looks like it was a pretty horrifying few seconds."

McCain didn't answer. He was still thinking about there being no bite wounds on the victim.

"I'll let you know what the hound guy says, and either he or I will get back to you. Thanks again, Luke," Anderson said before hanging up.

The rest of the way back to Yakima, McCain thought about the victim, the cougar tracks, the possible urine in the trees near the sight of the kill, and the moccasin tracks. Something just wasn't adding up.

Chapter 25

With bolt cutters in hand, Cassidy Sutcliff walked briskly over to the building where the Wild Cats of the World exhibit was housed. She went behind the building and stashed the cutters in a large garbage dumpster. She assumed they wouldn't let any garbage trucks on the grounds during open fair hours, so the cutters would be safe there until she needed them.

With several hours to kill, she went into a nearby restroom, changed back into the shirt she had worn earlier, and went out to see more of the fair. Some big country music star was set to play that night, and already there were people streaming through the gates, most dressed in their wannabe cowboy boots, shirts, and hats.

Sutcliff hadn't eaten since she'd had the scones earlier that morning, so now she looked for something more substantial. People were walking by eating corn dogs and hamburgers, and it made her want to puke. She wanted to remind the passerby of the poor animals that were mercilessly slaughtered, just so they could eat a gross concoction of meat and innards, slathered in mustard and ketchup. But she refrained from lecturing anyone. People were basically stupid, and the more red meat they ate, the quicker they'd get some kind of heart disease and die.

She had all but lost her appetite from watching the people eat until she came upon a trailer that was selling Chicago-style pizza. She asked the lady at the window if she could have a slice with just veggies, and the lady said, "Comin' right up."

Sutcliff was digging into the slice when someone tapped her on the shoulder and said, "Hey, Lacey."

Shit, it was that idiot from the security office.

"Oh, hey, Noah. What's up?"

"Just wanted to say hi. How's the pizza?"

"Pretty good actually. First time I've eaten here."

"Well, get used to it. This is a long fair, and if you are going to eat, you'll probably eat here. Although, I do bring my own lunch now and again. We have a lunchroom over in the office."

"Good to know, thanks. Well, I'm heading out. See you tomorrow."

"Okay, see you tomorrow," Noah said.

Sutcliff tossed the crust of her pizza and napkin in the garbage barrel and walked toward the closest entrance. Before she walked out, she acted like there was something she wanted to see in the building closest to the exit. Sutcliff turned and walked that way, looking over to where she had left Noah. He was still standing there, watching her, with a stupid grin on his face.

She went into the building and stood just far enough from the door to see if Noah was following her. She waited a good five minutes, and when he didn't come through the doors, she went looking for another exit at the rear of the building. She wanted to get back to the cat building and start reconnoitering.

*

Noah Blakely knew the woman who claimed to be Lacey Grant was not Lacey Grant. He had met the real Lacey Grant in a pre-fair job orientation. But this new woman intrigued him. Not only was she drop-dead gorgeous, she had the guts to enter a security office and say she was somebody she wasn't, just to get a security shirt.

Blakely was bucking for a promotion, and he figured if he could catch this new woman stealing from some vendor, he might just get that promotion, and a raise to boot. So, when he saw her walking through the food court, he decided to keep an eye on her.

After he had chatted with her at the pizza vendor trailer, she'd gone into the arts and crafts building and hadn't come out. That meant she wasn't actually leaving the fairgrounds. He decided to go into one of the adjoining buildings and head upstairs where he could watch for her from above through the windows.

He'd been waiting for a few minutes when he spotted fake Lacey coming back outside. Blakely quickly lost track of her in the crowds of people. At least he knew she was still on the fairgrounds, and that she was up to something.

Blakely walked back down to ground level and went the direction he had last seen the woman go. It was prime time on a Saturday, and there were literally tens of thousands of people on the grounds. Locating her again would be a challenge. But he was going to do his best. He could really use that raise.

*

It had taken Dobbs a little over two and a half hours to get back to his cabin. Throughout the entirety of his hike home, he had the eerie feeling something was following him. He turned around two or three different times, thinking he heard something, only to find nothing there. Or nothing that he could see.

When he finally reached his little shack, he got inside, grabbed his rifle, made sure it was still loaded, and sat watching the door.

Dobbs awoke a few hours later, feeling totally disoriented. He flailed around for his flashlight and clicked it on, moving the beam of light around the inside of his hovel. Nothing was out of place that he could see. It scared him that he had been so sound asleep that he'd lost all sense of place and time.

Later, after firing up the gas light, Dobbs wrote about the experience in his journal. Then, after heating up a can of soup and eating it, he went to his manifesto and started scribbling in it. He wrote of the need to silence the incessant noise and what he had done to make it stop. He described tanning the cougar hide and creating weapons out of two cougar paws.

Then, in an effort to stop the reoccurring visions of the motorcycle-rider attack, he wrote it all down. He explained why he did it and described every single blow as he remembered. There was no emotion in his description – just cold, detached observations. Dobbs wrote for another hour before the exhaustion again took over, sending him to bed. Just as he was fading off to sleep, somewhere out in the darkness, he heard the roar of an animal. It made him shiver, even though it was still over seventy degrees inside his shack.

*

Sutcliff sat in an area not far from the concert venue. She could hear the country music star singing as his band played along. The music was a little too twangy for her liking, but it wasn't terrible. It definitely helped pass the time until she could get into the cat building and do what she had to do.

As she sat listening to what she guessed was a steel guitar, she thought of Spearman. She wondered what he was doing. He was probably still in jail, although Seattle was going through one of those times where you just about had to murder someone before they would prosecute you.

If she could somehow reach him tonight, he might be up for helping to free the cats, and then they could go find a motel room and have a little fun. Sutcliff pulled the phone from her bag. No missed calls. Well, maybe Spearman wasn't out of jail yet. Or maybe he was done with her. She wouldn't blame him. But good luck finding someone as good as she was in bed. She knew he would miss that.

The concert was over a little after ten o'clock, and soon people were out of the stadium and looking for the beer garden and places to buy food. Sutcliff wondered when they would start sweeping people off the grounds. Maybe midnight, she thought.

While there were still some people who gave her cover, she followed a crowd out of the concert as they headed in the direction of the cat building. The last thing she needed was Noah spotting her again.

Once she got to the cat building, she went around back, changed back into her blue security shirt, and then went into the building. There were a few people milling around, looking at the cats, but none paid any attention to the tall, slender, pretty security officer.

Sutcliff had seen the guy who owned the cats on TV the night after she and Spearman had let the tiger loose. She looked all around but didn't see the man. That was just fine with her. She didn't know that he had traveled back to the other side of the mountains because of the investigation involving the mauled dirt biker.

When there was a break in the people, Sutcliff went to the back door and opened it, putting a tiny piece of wood into the jamb so the door wouldn't close all the way. Then, she worked her way back out the front door and around back to wait for the fairgrounds to close down.

*

He spotted her just as she was leaving the building where the Wild Cats of the World were housed. She was wearing her security shirt and heading around to the back of the building. Blakely wondered what she might be able to steal in that building. Certainly not one of the wild cats. There were T-shirts and other knick-knacks for sale at a table near the cat exhibit. Maybe she wanted some of those? It made sense, given how popular the show's tiger merchandise had become.

Blakely cut back behind an adjacent building just in time to see fake Lacey jump into the dumpster. That was okay with him. He'd just sit and watch until she made her next move.

The gorgeous faux Lacey poked her head out of the dumpster at two o'clock in the morning. He saw her look around, then hop down. Next, she reached back in and grabbed some kind of a big tool – he couldn't tell what – and entered the locked back door.

Blakely wondered how she got a key to the door, but then realized he hadn't seen her use one. Was someone on the inside to let her in? Maybe he could catch two thieves in one. All the better for his promotion and his raise.

After the door closed behind her, Blakely moved quickly to the back door. Fake Lacey hadn't had a key, but he did. It was a master key that worked on virtually every door throughout the fairgrounds. He slowly put the key in the lock and turned it.

*

When she saw it was two o'clock, Sutcliff jumped out of the dumpster and reached back in for the bolt cutters. Then she opened the jammed back door and went inside.

It was dark, but not so dark that she couldn't see. A few security lights illuminated the walls along the inside of the building. After entering the building, she stopped and listened. There might be a security guard inside, or the guy who owned the show might sleep with the cats. She didn't know, so she stopped and listened for any sounds that might tell her she wasn't alone.

After what seemed like ten minutes but was probably only two, she took a few steps. She heard nothing except the cats rustling around in their pens. Soon they'd be prowling the fairgrounds, finally free, as their creator meant them to be.

Sutcliff got inside the roped-off area and approached the first pen. Inside was the caracal. The smaller cat was nervous and made a high-pitched squeal, similar to a house cat's meow.

"Don't worry little cat," Sutcliff said in a soothing voice. "You'll be out soon."

The smaller cat with tufted ears squealed again. Sutcliff got the bolt cutters on the small lock's shackle and squeezed. The cutters worked like a charm. As soon as she made the cut, the lock fell to the floor. At the same time, she thought she heard something near the back door. Sutcliff turned but saw nothing. Had she really heard the door?

She opened the small cat's cage and stepped back. As soon as the door was open, the caracal jumped out and ran to the front of the building. Sutcliff smiled.

The next cage was the female lion's enclosure. The lion also looked nervous, pacing back and forth at the back of the cage. Again, Sutcliff talked to the cat in a soothing voice. It did no good.

She moved the bolt cutters toward the lock on the door, and the lion jumped, bouncing off the side of the enclosure. Sutcliff worked the cutters on the lock's shackle, and just like the last lock, it fell to the ground after she cut it. Sutcliff looked in, and the lion stared back at her. Her ears were back and she was snarling.

Sutcliff was just reaching up to open the door when a voice behind her said, "I wouldn't do that." She just about peed herself.

"Holy shit, Noah," she said after she turned around. "You scared me half to death."

"I'm serious. Don't do that. I've radioed for security, and they'll be here in a minute. Step back, and let's walk out of here."

Just then, the lion rushed the door of the enclosure, hitting it hard enough to knock Sutcliff backward. The cat flew out of the cage and pounced on Blakely. Luckily, he had thrown an arm up just in time, and the lion grabbed it instead of his throat. The predator shook him like a rag doll.

Blakely began screaming. "Get it off me!" he managed.

Three blue-shirted security guards came running through the front door shouting "freeze!" The number of people rushing in, and the yelling, made the lion drop Blakely's arm and run for the back corner of the building.

"She's right there," Blakely said.

"Yeah, we saw her. She ran over there. Where'd she get you?"

"Not the lion – the woman who let the lion out! She was right there."

The security guards pointed flashlights in every direction, but no one was there.

"Shit," he said. "She was there fifteen seconds ago. Tell the rest of the grounds security to look for a tall, thin, thirty-year-old woman with brown hair. She is probably wearing a blue security shirt and blue jeans. If she looks like a model, that's her. And get me an ambulance, please."

Chapter 26

After grabbing breakfast sandwiches at the mini-mart for him and Jack, McCain headed back up to Kittitas County. The man who had a small pack of hounds had called and talked to him the previous evening, and McCain had filled him in, both about tracking the cougar and the tiger.

The tracker, Chet Henderson, knew all about Jack from his past tracking exploits. Still, he didn't seem to be overly impressed.

"My dogs have tracked cats over rocks, up creeks, even down concrete roads," Henderson said in a bragging tone. "We'll have that cougar before the day is over."

"Okay, Mr. Henderson," McCain said. "Good luck to you."

"No luck involved," Henderson said. "Just good dogs."

Afterward, McCain reflected on the call. He wished he could be up there to watch the dogs work. Maybe they really could unwind the puzzle of the disappearing cougar. He'd thought about it a lot in the hours after he and Jack had left the hills, and a couple things kept nagging at him. Where had the man in the boots entered the rockslide? He had only found boot prints leaving the area. And McCain was regretting not following Jack when he wanted to follow those boot tracks.

He'd learned a long time ago, as a young boy following the family Lab on pheasant hunts, to trust the dog's nose. Several times, McCain would have sworn there wasn't enough cover to hide a sparrow, but their Lab insisted there was a pheasant there, and the dog was always right.

He'd been stewing about the cougar all the way up the hill, but it was out of his hands now. At least, it was for the time being. Right now, he needed to go check on the elk hunters still in the area.

*

Two bloodhounds and a bluetick coonhound made up Chet Henderson's string of tracking dogs. He and his dogs had worked for the Kittitas Search and Rescue, helping to find lost hikers and hunters. On occasion, the Fish and Wildlife Department had hired him to track down a cougar or a bear that was creating problems in the more populated areas of Central Washington.

The people of Washington had voted to eliminate hunting mountain lions and bears with hounds several years prior, but there were still occasions when hounds were used to hunt them when called in by authorities. Otherwise, hound hunters like Henderson had to hunt raccoons with their dogs.

The chance to run down a cat was like Christmas to a hound hunter. When Henderson got to the spot of the attack, his dogs were ready. And he was prepared to show McCain and everyone else that nothing beats a well-bred, well-trained hound.

One of the TV satellite trucks was still there when Anderson showed up with his three hounds. Before he let the anxious dogs loose, he did a quick interview.

"This is Chet Henderson," the reporter said. "He and his three dogs have been hired to try to track down the cougar that killed a motorcyclist here a little over twenty-four hours ago. Do you think your dogs can find the cougar?"

"I don't think they can find the cat," Henderson said, puffing out his chest. "I know they can."

"We understand another dog was up here with a game warden yesterday morning, and they didn't have any luck."

Henderson just smiled. "Well, I don't think that dog has had much experience tracking mountain lions. It's a whole different deal. Me and my dogs, we'll find it, and then everyone can stop worrying."

With that, he turned and went to his truck. The bed had been rebuilt to hold several dog kennels, and the noses of three dogs were sticking out of the holes on their individual kennels.

The reporter turned the camera and filmed as Henderson opened a kennel door, clipped a lead on a dog, and did that two more times before letting all three out of the kennels. He then followed the dogs on long leads up the hill to the yellow tape on the hillside.

Henderson took the dogs and had them smell the tracks, but they seemed confused. The game warden had told him that his dog followed the tracks up the hill to the northwest, but his dogs showed no interest in going that way.

After looking around and seeing that the cougar tracks actually did go northwest, he started coaxing his hounds that way as well. Henderson couldn't figure out why the dogs couldn't smell the tracks when he could see them right there in the dirt. He kept working the dogs up the hill, watching the tracks and hoping they would hit the scent and be off.

What Henderson didn't know was that in the middle of the night a real, live cougar had cut across the hillside about three hundred yards above the sight of the attack. When Henderson's dogs finally did hit the scent of cougar, they lit up in an instant. It didn't matter that it was the wrong cat. As soon as his three hounds hit the fresh cougar scent, they were off and running, bawling and baying the whole way up the hill.

*

Carson Dobbs awoke the next morning feeling a little better. Writing had helped him fall back asleep. As he sat at his makeshift table, he listened to the morning woods waking up. There was the stuttering call of a pileated woodpecker followed by knocking on wood as the bird searched for its breakfast. Gray squirrels chattered. Stellar jays squawked. The sounds of nature brought him joy.

He also listened carefully for the unique roar from the night before, but he heard nothing. As he listened, he realized there was none of the motorized ear pollution he'd been hearing constantly for months. Maybe, just maybe, his attack had worked, and now the riders were staying well away from the area where a man-killing cougar lurked.

He began planning his day. First on the agenda was to procure some meat. Dobbs had run out of meat nearly three weeks ago. His obsession with getting everything ready for the attack had taken up almost every waking moment. Now, with that deed accomplished, he needed to restock his larder. Canned soup was okay, but he needed protein.

A deer would do, but what he really wanted was an elk calf. The meat was so tender and mild, to him it was better than any restaurant steak he'd ever eaten. People had no idea what they were missing. Not that he really cared about them.

As he put a couple days' worth of supplies in his pack for an elk hunt, he heard the sound of baying hound dogs. The hounds sounded like they were near where he had killed the motorcycle rider, and they were coming up the hill.

Could they really track a person like they did in the movies, Dobbs wondered. Or were the dogs tracking the scent of his cougar paws? Either way, they seemed to be coming his way.

Dobbs didn't know what to do. He thought about running, but he didn't think he could outrun a pack of hound dogs. He decided he'd sit and listen.

The baying of the dogs drew closer, and then they headed east. Dobbs had no knowledge of how hounds worked, but he hadn't gone east at all on his way back from killing the biker. Why would they go that way, he wondered, unless they were on some other track? Maybe they were trailing a bear, or even a real cougar.

As Dobbs sat and listened, the bawling of the hounds got farther and farther away, and soon, he couldn't hear them at all. When he was finally convinced the dogs weren't coming his way, he went back to work, preparing for his hunt.

*

When Henderson's hounds hit the fresh cougar scent, they took off running. They headed north up the hill and then turned to the east. Each of his hounds had GPS tracking collars, so Henderson was in no big hurry to keep pace with them. Besides, he could hear their bawling as they trailed the fresh scent of the cougar.

Once the dogs caught up with the cougar, in an hour, or ten, or twenty, they would start baying differently. Hound hunters knew the difference in the dogs' bays when they finally had a lion treed.

Now, thanks to technology, hound hunters could follow their dogs via satellite. When the hounds finally caught up to whatever they were chasing, the hunter could simply find that spot on a map and drive as close to the dogs as possible. It saved him from doing a lot of long hikes, often through treacherous terrain.

As Henderson listened to his hounds get farther away, he thought about his conversation with McCain the night before. McCain had told Henderson that his dog followed the tracks up to the northwest until they lost it at a big shale rockslide.

The warden's dog, Henderson thought, must have been tracking a coyote or a raccoon, because that cougar most definitely went to the northeast. He chuckled and shook his head. He figured he'd be delivering a dead, man-killing cougar to the sheriff's office by supper time.

Chapter 27

Once again, Cassidy Sutcliff felt lucky not to be incarcerated. And this time, she felt lucky to be alive. While the lion had Noah pinned, she was able to slip away and head out the back door just as she heard people coming in through the front. She had no idea if Noah was alive or dead. If Noah had been killed, she wondered, would she be up for some kind of murder charges since she was the one who let the lion out?

There was no time to think about that. She still needed to get the hell off the fairgrounds and maybe even out of the Seattle area altogether.

Sutcliff quickly changed shirts behind a couple other buildings and then headed to the back of the fairgrounds where she spotted a gate that had been left open. As she stood in the shadows of one of the buildings, she watched as a bread truck and then a Pepsi truck drove through the gates. This, she surmised, was when the vendors restocked for the upcoming day. There was security at the gate, but the lady in the blue shirt was just waving the trucks through without checking their credentials.

Sutcliff decided she needed to use one of the trucks leaving the grounds. She only had to wait about three minutes for a truck to come along. As soon as the Charlie's Meat delivery van passed by where she was hiding, she ran across the road and jogged alongside it as it went out the gate. The van screened the security guard perfectly, and Sutcliff made it past undetected. As soon as Sutcliff was off the grounds, she turned and headed toward town.

Once back into the commercial part of Puyallup, she could request an Uber and get to the airport or the train station. As she waited for the Uber driver to show up, she thought about the cats she had set free. She hoped they were out of the building and finally feeling the joy of freedom.

*

McCain decided to head to the Colockum Wildlife Area to check on the archery elk hunters up that way. In all this tiger hubbub, and the attack on the motorcycle rider, he had not had a chance to talk to any of the hunters north of I-90. He drove through Ellensburg, out Cooke Canyon, and up toward the Colockum.

Throughout the morning, he ran into several archery hunters and chatted with them. Most reported seeing some elk, but none had any luck filling their tags. A couple of the hunters asked McCain about the tiger, and he reassured them that it was on the other side of the freeway, most likely up in the Taneum.

In reality, he had no clue where the tiger was, but he believed the big cat wouldn't come back down, cross the freeway, and skirt the town of Ellensburg to get up into these mountains.

Everything seemed to be pretty quiet in the area, so McCain headed back into Ellensburg for some lunch. He stopped at the Red Horse Diner, his favorite hamburger place in Ellensburg. They had excellent milkshakes too. Not that he needed a milkshake to go with his burger and fries, but today he decided to splurge. He'd share the burger and a few fries with Jack, which he used as justification for the shake.

Jack was waiting patiently in the truck when McCain got back with the food. The dog watched every move McCain made with the burger.

"Okay, jeez, here you go," McCain said as he tore off a piece of burger for Jack. The dog gobbled it up without chewing. "I could have just given you a piece of wood, and you wouldn't have known the difference."

McCain was just finishing up his burger and fries when his phone rang. He looked at the screen and saw it was Sara.

"Hey, there. What's up?" he asked.

"I thought you'd like to know that Cassidy Sutcliff has struck again."

McCain had to think about it for a minute. Cassidy Sutcliff, oh yeah, the hot chick who helped steal the truck and trailer and released the tiger.

"No kidding. What'd she do?"

Sinclair went through the story of her breaking into the Wild Cats of the World show at the Washington State Fair and turning a couple of the cats loose, including the lion, which attacked a security guard.

"Oh, man," McCain said. "Is the guard okay?"

"I guess his arm is torn up pretty good," Sinclair said. "But he'll live. He's kind of the hero of the hour."

"What happened to the cats?"

"Sam Banister showed up not long after it happened, and he was able to coerce the cats back into their cages with some meat. They seem no worse for wear."

"And what about Miss Sutcliff? Anyone have any leads on her?"

"No, not really. Her boyfriend was released from jail and returned to the apartment he'd shared with Sutcliff. He said she hadn't been there. The police tried tracking her phone, but evidently it was turned off, so no luck there. How are things going up your way?" she asked.

"Pretty good. Nothing too exciting. Jack and I just stopped for lunch in Ellensburg."

"Let me guess. The Red Horse?"

"Aw, you know me so well. I asked Jack where he wanted to eat, and when he didn't come up with anything, I decided the Red Horse would work. He loves their burgers, and so do I."

"Uh-huh," Sinclair said. "And I suppose there was a milkshake involved?"

"You are the best investigator in the whole world, Agent Sinclair."

"Wish I was there enjoying one with you," she said. "Can you bring me one?"

"Sorry, we're about to go back up into the Taneum and snoop around there. We'll be home by dinner. Not sure I'm going to want to eat much though. That hamburger with fries and the milkshake were soooo good."

Click.

"She hung up on me," McCain said to Jack. "That wasn't very nice. Oh well, let's go see if we can scare us up a tiger."

*

The sound of the hounds baying off in the distance was still on his mind as Dobbs shouldered his pack. He had surmised that, when he heard the dogs, they had been brought in to track the cougar that had killed the motorcycle rider. This, in essence, meant they were there to track him. But they didn't follow his tracks, and they didn't find him.

Of course, he had no way of knowing what law enforcement believed had happened. But after replaying it over and over again in his mind, he believed he had left all the evidence necessary to make them conclude a cougar had killed the man.

Dobbs grabbed his rifle and headed north toward where he'd heard some bull elk bugling a few hours earlier. He liked hunting this time of year because the animals were very vocal in their mating rituals which made it easier to find them.

He'd learned that the biggest males would have harems of female elk, but there were often some younger males hovering nearby the big herd. He'd killed a couple of young bulls with only single-point spikes for horns after finding the bigger herds and watching the trails nearby. The young elk were always excellent eating.

As Dobbs hiked up the hill to the north of his shack, he stopped and listened often for the elk and the dogs. He also listened for the unusual growls and moans he'd heard over the past couple nights at his cabin.

At one point, as he was sitting and listening, he heard some footsteps in the distance. Not wanting to be seen, he hid in a stand of small fir trees. Dobbs watched as two men carrying bows and dressed in full camouflage walked by at about a hundred yards. Dobbs knew there were hunting seasons in the fall but hadn't realized the archery hunting season was open. He let the men walk on by and then waited for ten minutes to make sure they were well past him. Then he continued up the hill toward the area where he had last heard the elk.

Dobbs had not been raised as a hunter. In fact, his father had left his mother when he was just three, and his mother was always working to try to support her small family, so he had no one who could teach him anything about the outdoors. Not that he had any real interest in it as a kid.

Living in the woods, needing to kill something to eat, had been a huge educational process for Dobbs. He quickly learned that the animals in the woods were alert all the time. They were always checking the wind for danger and had incredible hearing.

He knew that sometimes deer and elk had trouble seeing him, especially if he didn't move, so Dobbs would often sit downwind of the game trails he had discovered.

Dobbs had figured out that deer had a fairly small and predictable home range, but elk would roam around – sometimes for miles – as they looked for food. Because of that, it was more difficult to determine where they would be. That is until September, when the males started bugling.

It took Dobbs almost an hour to get to where he thought he had heard the elk last. He slowly moved along near to a ridgeline, staying just below it so his profile couldn't be seen on the skyline. Ahead was a saddle that looked to Dobbs like a perfect place to watch for elk as the day wore on.

Making sure the wind was in his face, Dobbs sat down with his back to a big pine tree and waited. What he didn't know was he was being watched. Not by a four-legged creature, but by one of the bow hunters who had passed in front of him a while earlier.

Dobbs had been sitting against the tree for about twenty minutes when he heard animals moving on the other side of the ridge. He heard footsteps on the rocks, moving closer to him and the saddle. When he heard the faint mewl of a cow elk, he knew he was in business. Dobbs pulled his rifle up and, using his knees to help support his elbows and arms, waited for the elk to come over the rise.

The first elk to come through was on older cow. A small calf followed. Dobbs had killed an older cow once, and while the meat was flavorful, there was too much of it. He had to let some of it go to waste. He'd also killed a four-month-old calf before, too. The meat was tender and delicious, but there wasn't enough there to keep him fed for long. What Dobbs wanted was a yearling. Bull or cow, it didn't matter.

A few older cows and some younger calves followed the lead cow. The seventh elk in the line was the elk Dobbs was hoping for. It was a yearling bull with single-pointed horns about ten inches long.

The elk were about seventy-five yards away and offered an easy shot. Dobbs found the young bull in his scope, put the crosshairs on its neck, and squeezed the trigger.

Elk scattered everywhere at the sound of the high-powered rifle. The bullet had flown true, breaking the bull's neck and killing the animal almost instantly.

Dobbs picked up his pack and hustled over to begin the challenging chore of butchering the elk.

CHAPTER 28

The Washington Department of Fish and Wildlife has a bonus point system for its special hunt tag drawing. Hunters accrue points for every year they purchase a special hunt application, theoretically giving a person better odds with each passing year. Although there are flaws in the system, hunters keep applying for permits in the hopes that sooner or later they might get drawn for a coveted sheep, moose, or goat permit. Other special permits for branch-antlered bull elk, or restricted areas for deer, are also coveted.

The department also has a policy that gives ten bonus points to hunters who turn in poachers or hunters who break the laws. So, when Braydon Hill saw the weirdly dressed dude shoot the spike elk with a high-powered rifle out of season, he immediately dialed 911.

"Nine-one-one, what's your emergency?" the operator said.

"It's not really an emergency . . . well, I guess it is," Hill said. "I just saw a guy shoot an elk with a rifle out of season."

"What's your location?"

"Up in the Taneum, east of Roslyn."

"Okay, what's your name, sir?"

"My name is Braydon Hill. Can you get a game warden up here?"

"I'll reach out to one now. Can I have him call your cell phone?"

"Yeah, sure. It's five-o-nine, nine-five-two – "

"Mr. Hill," the operator interrupted. "I have your number here. Someone should be calling you soon."

"Okay, I'm going to stay here and keep an eye on this guy. It isn't right, him shooting an elk out of season."

"Yes, sir, Mr. Hill. I'm going to let you go. Someone will call soon."

McCain heard the call come over the radio in his truck.

"Wildlife one-four-eight, can you check out a potential elk poaching up in the Taneum?" the dispatcher said.

"Wildlife one-four-eight. Copy."

The dispatcher gave a quick rundown of the call that had come in and gave McCain the phone number for Braydon Hill.

"I'll call him now," McCain said.

Unfortunately, McCain couldn't. He was driving up a Forest Service road in a big canyon near where the tiger had been released and had no cell service. It took him thirty minutes of driving over washboard roads until he finally hit one of the highest points in the area. From there, he had three bars of service. Good enough. McCain stopped the rig and dialed the number dispatch had provided.

The phone barely rang once when a man answered and said, "Hello, this is Braydon."

"Yes, Mr. Hill. This is Officer McCain with the Department of Fish and Wildlife. I understand you'd like to report the poaching of an elk?"

"Yes, sir. I'm up here bowhunting, and as I was watching this area, a dude dressed funny-like wanders in, sits down next to a tree, and about a half hour later a herd of cows and calves comes over the ridge. The last elk in the bunch was a spike, and the dude drops it with one shot, deader than Elvis."

"Okay, Mr. Hill. Where are you?"

"To hell and gone up here in the Taneum. I walked in about five miles."

"Do you have a GPS, Mr. Hill?"

"Sure do. It's a Garmin. Best one money can buy. Last thing I need to do is get lost."

"Alright, can you give me the coordinates of where you are on the GPS?"

"Let's see. I'm not sure. I'll have to do some looking here."

It took a while for Hill to figure out how to get the coordinates McCain needed. It was getting late in the afternoon, and if Hill really was five miles from the road, McCain would be doing a lot of the hiking in the dark. But, if he wanted to catch the poacher, he would first have to try getting there.

"Okay Mr. Hill. I have the coordinates and your information. No need for you to stay there. You might as well hunt back to your camp or your rig. I'll take it from here. And if I can find the guy, you'll qualify for ten bonus points toward a special hunt tag."

"That's the main reason I called. You should be able to find the guy. I've been watching him with my binoculars, and he's still working on the elk."

McCain thanked Hill for calling and hung up. He then called Sara.

"Looks like Jack and I are getting a chance to work off that hamburger and shake. I just took a call about a poached elk in the Taneum. Sounds like a long walk to the downed elk. It'll be well past dark before we get out."

"Is that the same area where the tiger is running around?"

"Yes, or it was anyway. Chances of the thing still hanging around here are slim. I'm not too worried about it."

"Okay. Be safe. Keep an eye on Jack. Call when you can."

McCain told her he would and then clicked off.

*

Field dressing an animal the size of a small horse was always a chore. Doing it in a hurry as darkness fell made it even more difficult. When Dobbs shot his first animal – a doe mule deer – a few years back, he had no idea how to clean the animal or how to break it down for transport back to his cabin.

The next time he went to town, Dobbs stopped by a bookstore and purchased a book on how to field dress big game animals. The book had all kinds of photos and the step-by-step directions for removing the entrails, separating the hide, and then breaking an animal down into quarters.

He'd cleaned a few deer, and they weren't too bad once he had some experience doing it. But an elk was tougher, mostly due to its size. Even though the young bull Dobbs had killed wasn't as big as a mature bull, it was still a handful.

Shortly after he started breaking down the elk, Dobbs thought he heard a human's voice. He stopped what he was doing, looked around, and listened. But he didn't see or hear anything out of place.

Unlike most hunters, Dobbs didn't care about the head and the horns. You couldn't eat them, and they just added weight to his pack. No, he wanted the meat. So, after he had skinned the elk, he removed the back straps and cut huge chunks of meat off one of the hindquarters. When he had his pack full of meat, he took the remaining neck, front shoulder, and hindquarter away from the carcass and stashed them in some brush. The meat would cool overnight, and he would come retrieve it in the morning.

With that done, Dobbs shouldered his heavy pack, grabbed his rifle, and started back to his shack.

The meat in his pack would last for a while, but there were still many pounds of good meat stashed up the hill. His plan was to get up early and return to the elk for as much of the remaining meat as he could carry.

*

It had taken Chet Henderson's dogs a little over three hours to catch up with the cougar that had wandered by above the bike trail where Mike Hodges had been attacked. The dogs caught up to the cougar lying in some rocky bluffs and pushed it up the mountain. When it finally tired of being pursued, the cougar climbed a big pine tree and looked down at the dogs which were barking and baying around the base of the tree.

Henderson had followed the three dogs on his phone, picking up their movements via their GPS collars. When he saw that all three were stopped in one place, he knew they had treed the cougar. From what Henderson could see, the cougar was in a deep canyon between two roads. It looked like he could get closer to their location from the lower road on the map, so that is where he headed. When he got within a mile of where the dogs still appeared on the map, he grabbed his .243 caliber rifle, and started up the canyon. He could hear his dogs baying in the distance.

Henderson had considered the idea that his dogs might have crossed the path of a different cougar at some point in their pursuit, but he believed it was highly unlikely. In fact, he was convinced this was the cougar that had killed the motorcycle rider on the trail.

After a steep but short climb, Henderson reached his hounds and the trapped cougar. He had authority from the Kittitas County Sheriff's Office to shoot the cougar, removing a man-killer from the mountain and making it safer for people who were up there hunting, fishing, riding, and camping. The shot would be simple. The cougar was fairly high up in the limbs of the tree, but it was stationary and looked straight down at Henderson. One shot in the head would take care of the man-killer.

At the shot, the cougar went limp and fell through the tree branches to the ground, where the three dogs were immediately on it. Henderson clipped leads on the three dogs and pulled them away from the dead cat. He was positive it was the right cat, but he still needed to provide the body to the US Fish and Wildlife Forensics

Laboratory in Ashland, Oregon to test that it was the right cougar. The last thing the lab needed was a chewed-up carcass.

Henderson tied the three dogs to a tree and took his phone out to take a couple photos. Then he went to the dogs, untied them, and took them down the draw to the truck. He made sure the dogs had plenty of water and food and then put them into their kennels. Finally, he went back up to where the dead cougar lay, pulled it up to his shoulders, and wrapped it around his neck so he could carry it down to the truck.

On the way back down, the dead cougar on his shoulders, Henderson again thought about his conversation with the game warden whose dog couldn't find the track on the hill. Not much of dog, Anderson thought. At least not much of one compared to his three hounds.

*

McCain opened his GPS unit and put the coordinates into the map. Once he had figured out where Braydon Hill had called from, he then considered how to get as close as he could via driving before walking in the rest of the way.

He studied the roads and the map, which showed the contours and topography of the area. He saw that one road got him closer to the coordinates, but it would mean having to hike up through some seriously steep country. Another road would put McCain farther away, but the hiking would be much easier. He chose the latter.

McCain parked his pickup off the road a bit, marked the spot on the GPS so he knew where it was in the dark, and let Jack out. From what he could tell from the GPS, he would have about a three-and-a-half-mile hike in. Braydon Hill had told him five miles, but that must have been from where he had parked.

He debated whether or not to take his state-issued Springfield Armory .223 rifle with him, and then remembered there might be a tiger prowling about. Better to be safe than sorry, McCain thought. He grabbed the rifle and his pack filled with survival provisions, then headed out.

With the GPS unit pointing the way, McCain, with Jack running back and forth ahead of him, hurried through the woods. Even at a faster pace, McCain knew he would be returning to his pickup in the dark. Still, he wanted to reach the elk kill while the hunter was still there working on the meat.

The average walking speed of a human is three to four miles an hour. McCain was pushing hard to get there as quickly as he could, hoping to be at the elk kill in forty-five minutes. Of course, there were a few obstacles along the way: a brushy creek bottom, downed logs, and a couple of up-and-down draws he had to traverse. Jack was enjoying the walk immensely, running along with his tail wagging. He loved to run, and McCain was happy for the dog, realizing Jack had been forced to spend an unusual amount of time in the truck the past few days.

McCain periodically checked the GPS and, as he got within a half mile of the coordinates, he signaled for Jack to come. They slowed down their pace. The last thing McCain wanted to do was crash through the brush and trees, alerting the poacher that someone was coming. Nothing good could come from that.

With Jack at heel, McCain slowly worked through the trees, searching ahead of him as he walked. At one point, Jack's ears went up, and he looked through the trees to the right of them. McCain stopped and looked in the direction but saw nothing. He waited for a while longer, looking and listening intently. Still, he saw and heard nothing unusual.

Soon, Jack lost interest in whatever it was he had smelled or heard. McCain moved forward, looking for a man or signs of a downed elk. As he searched, he found the saddle that Hill had described. McCain looked closer and saw the yellowish-tan-colored hide of an elk. Next to it was the severed head of the young bull. He walked over to the animal and saw that most of the meat had been cut away from the carcass. All that was left were leg bones, the spine, and its rib cage.

One man couldn't pack all that meat out on his back. There would be two hundred pounds or more. McCain looked around and, sure enough, in the shade of some small fir trees was about a hundred pounds of meat, including roasts from the hindquarters and meat from the shoulders and neck. In the soft dirt nearby were boot tracks very similar to the prints Jack had followed out of the shale rockslide.

McCain looked at his phone. It would be dark in a half hour. He figured he could get Jack to help track the man who had shot the elk, but if the guy had a rig parked on the road, he'd most likely get there well ahead of them and drive away. Of course, if the man was walking back to a camp, McCain could find him there. But he was almost positive the man would be coming back for the rest of the elk venison. So, he could stay the night and wait to see if the guy came back in the dark, or he could come back in the morning and be waiting for him at daylight.

He decided he'd call Sara and check in with her. If she was okay with it, he'd just pitch his one-man tent, and he and Jack would have a little campout.

McCain looked at his phone and saw he had no service. He knew that Braydon Hill had called from up here someplace, so McCain looked around. On the other side of the saddle, the ridge rose about five hundred feet. He climbed the ridge and soon found he had service.

"So, did you catch the guy?" Sara asked when she answered.

"Nope, but we found the dead elk. I'm of the belief the poacher will be back for more meat, either tonight or tomorrow morning. I'm thinking about spending the night up here with Jack."

"I'm not real wild about that idea. Remember the tiger?"

"Yeah, I don't think the tiger is going to be an issue. Its owner says it's a big pussy cat."

"A big pussy cat that could be starving to death. A yellow dog might look like the perfect meal."

"We'll be fine, I promise."

"Okay. So, did anyone tell you that the hound guy ran down the killer cougar?"

"No, really?"

"Yep. KCSO called me when they couldn't raise you on your phone. The dogs found it, and the hound guy shot it out of a tree. KCSO has it, and last I heard they were preparing to send it off to the Ashland lab. They need them to confirm it was the one."

"You know what? I'm coming back down tonight. I want to see that cougar for myself. It'll be late, but we'll be home."

They said their goodbyes, and then McCain turned to Jack and said, "Come on, boy. We'll go get some dinner."

Hearing that, Jack got excited and started heading back to the truck.

"Slow down. I don't want you leaving me up here with a tiger on the loose."

Chapter 29

The bus ride from Tacoma to Portland was not pleasant. There were strange people on the bus and most of them had spent the five-hour drive staring at Sutcliff. It was like some of them had never seen a woman before. To help ignore the leers, she'd bought a *People* magazine at the bus station and buried her head in the pages.

The bus stopped about seventeen times at every small town along I-5. At every stop, she thought about getting off and leaving behind the weirdos. She wished she could talk to Cory. She wondered if he was still in jail. She had her cell phone but knew from watching police shows that cops had the technology to track a person by their phone. Turning her phone on and hoping for Spearman to call wasn't worth the risk. Not that he would. But it would be nice to know.

Her plan was to get to Portland, find a job, and then start figuring out how she might get into the zoo to do a little early release program for some of the animals living in captivity there.

Maybe, she thought, she'd even get a job at the zoo. That would be perfect. Although she wasn't sure she could be around all those poor animals stuck in cages and behind Plexiglas walls without immediately trying to free them.

The other thing she needed to do was see if her photo was being circulated to police departments, wildlife parks, and zoos in the area. She didn't need that.

No, she'd get another waitress job, lay low for a while, and slowly start to develop a plan.

The bus had stopped at another mini-mart somewhere between Tacoma and Portland when one of the leering men on the bus stopped by her seat.

"Can I get you anything inside the store?" he asked.

"No thank you," she said with a half-smile. "I'm fine."

"Do I know you?" the man asked.

"I don't think so," Sutcliff said.

"My name is Kenny. Can I sit down?" the man said as he started to sit.

In an instant, Sutcliff had a six-inch knife out of her boot and was holding it at the man's crotch.

"I'd rather you not, but I'll let you make that call," she said as she pushed the point of the knife against Kenny's scrotum.

The man stopped himself mid-sit and somehow reversed course in an instant, turning and walking back to his seat in the back.

An older lady who was sitting across the aisle from Sutcliff saw everything.

"Good for you, honey," the woman said. "I was hoping he'd keep pushing and you'd cut his balls off!"

Sutcliff said nothing. She just slipped the knife back into her boot and returned to the story in her magazine about the latest uproar with the royal family in England.

*

The trip back to his cabin had been challenging, for sure.

Dobbs had loaded the pack with more elk meat than he'd ever tried to carry before. But he made it, arriving just after dark. He spent the next hour putting the meat in cheesecloth bags and hanging the bags in the higher limbs of the trees around his place. The last thing he needed was to have a bear, cougar, or pesky coyote come and steal the meat he'd gotten.

Dobbs planned to be up before daylight and head back up the mountain to get as much of the remaining meat as he could. Then he'd leave the rest for the wild scavengers. Over the years he had seen golden eagles, bald eagles, turkey vultures, bobcats, coyotes, and bears on meat he'd left behind. He figured cougars would scavenge meat, too, if they had the chance.

Leaving the meat overnight on the mountain meant potentially losing it to one of the nocturnal scavengers. But he was just too tired to make another pack out tonight. He would cut a nice steak from the backstrap, enjoy some good protein, and hopefully be recharged for the morning.

*

As soon as McCain had cell service on his drive out of the mountains, he looked up the phone number for Chet Henderson and gave him a call.

"Hey there, Officer McCain. Did you hear the good news?" Henderson asked.

"I sure did," McCain said. "That was quick."

"Well, my dogs are pretty good at what they do."

"I'm sure they are. Can you tell me where you picked up the cougar tracks?"

"Right there at the spot where the motorcyclist was attacked."

"And did you get to the shale rockslide?"

"No, sir. My dogs started cutting up the hill to the north and east about three hundred yards above the trail."

McCain thought about that a minute. Jack had tracked the cougar for a mile north and west.

"Any chance that could've been a different cat that walked through there after the attack?"

"Naw, my dogs can tell the difference between cougars. That's how good they are. We found the cat that did the killing. Mark my words."

McCain thanked the hound man, hung up, and kept thinking about it as he drove to the coroner's in Ellensburg.

Before he got to town, McCain called Deputy Hernandez at the Kittitas County Sheriff's Office and asked if she could coerce the coroner to meet him at his office.

"I'd like you there, too, if you could be," McCain said to the deputy.

"I'll call him and will meet you there," Hernandez said. "I'd like to see this killer cat for myself."

When McCain got to the coroner's office, Hernandez was already there. As soon as she saw him pull into the parking lot, she jumped out of her KCSO vehicle and came over to McCain's truck.

"Hey there, Jack," she said through the passenger window as McCain rolled it down.

Jack, always quick to get some good petting, nuzzled up to the window to let the deputy scratch his ears.

"Sounds like you've had a busy day," she said. "Did you catch the elk poacher? I was in the office when that call came in."

"Nope. We found the elk. We'll be waiting for him to come back to get the rest of the meat in the morning."

"If he shows," Hernandez said. "With those types, I wouldn't count on it."

"Yeah, well, we're going to give it a try, aren't we Jack? Is the coroner here?"

"Not yet. He was at a meeting with the county commissioners, but said he'd get here as quickly as he could."

They talked a bit more about the killing of the motorcycle rider and the tiger still running loose up in the mountains.

Burt Jansen, the Kittitas County Coroner, pulled into the parking lot a few minutes later.

"Sorry," Jansen said. "But when my bosses say jump, I ask how high and come running."

McCain thought that statement was a bit humorous because he couldn't see Jansen jumping and running anywhere. The man was a good sixty pounds overweight and was possibly larger than when McCain had seen him last.

"No worries, Burt," Hernandez said. "We've been catching up on stuff."

McCain left Jack in the truck with the windows cracked. He'd barely closed the door and the dog was curled up, sound asleep in the back seat, exhausted from the long hike.

The two officers followed Jansen through the front door, down the hall, and into a big room with large lights set up to shoot down on stainless steel tables.

"You want to see the cougar first?" Jansen asked.

"That would be great," McCain said. "Have you done any checking on the cat? Was it thin or injured?"

"You mean, besides the bullet hole in his forehead?"

"Yes, besides that."

"I'm no cougar expert," Jansen said. "As a matter of fact, we are going to ship the body to Oregon where the experts can do a more thorough examination. But I found nothing that says this isn't a healthy cougar. It might be two or possibly three years old and looked completely healthy. The only odd thing I found is the cat has only three toes on its left front paw."

"How would that happen?" Hernandez asked.

"Could be a birth defect, or an injury suffered when it was younger. Could even have frozen off, but that's a rarity around here."

Jansen went into a large cooler and rolled out a table with the dead cougar lying on it. McCain walked over and gave it a quick once-over. It was obvious where Henderson had shot the cat. There was a perfect bullet hole in its forehead, right between its eyes.

"I presume you have Mr. Hodges' body here as well?" McCain asked.

"Yes, we do. Would you like to see it too?"

McCain and Hernandez watched as the coroner walked back to the cooler and rolled out another gurney, this one holding a human body covered in a white sheet.

"I understand from talking to some other deputies that Mr. Hodges was slashed fairly severely in the attack. Would there be any way to match this cougar's claws with the slashes on the victim's arms or face?"

Jansen thought about that for a second. Then he walked over to the cougar and pressed in on the toe pads of the dead cougar's front paws. Claws magically appeared from under the hair on top of the toes.

"I believe we can," Jansen said. "I haven't spent much time here since the cougar came in, so I hadn't thought of that."

Jansen rolled the table with the dead man over to the table with the cougar. He then pulled the cougar closer to the edge of the table, nearer to the man's arm.

"This is Mr. Hodges' right arm, so in theory he would have been attacked by the cougar's right paw if he came at the man from behind. Officer McCain, can you please hold the victim's arm up?"

McCain did as he was asked, and Jansen grabbed the cougar's right paw and pushed the toes so all the claws were extended. He then placed them near the slash marks on the man's arm. They didn't match perfectly, but they weren't far off.

"It's so hard to tell," Jansen said. "The cougar might open its toes more when it attacks. It's certainly not conclusive."

"But a paw with only three toes would be," McCain said. "Let's look at Mr. Hodges' left arm."

Jansen spun the table around and pulled the sheet back. They didn't even need to try to match the cougar's left paw to them. Every wound on the man's left arm and face showed four distinct slashes.

"Well, I'll be," Hernandez said. "This isn't the killer cat. It's still up there somewhere."

"I'll let you be the one to tell Chet Henderson," McCain said.

"Although I'd love to be the one to do it. He's quite proud of his dogs. My guess is he won't believe you when you tell him he tracked down and shot an innocent cougar."

"I guess you could write him up," Hernandez said with a chuckle. "Cougar hunting season isn't open yet, right?"

"No, it is not, and it's never open to hound hunting. I could get him for about five hundred bucks anyway."

"He'd just turn it into the sheriff. It was Sheriff Anderson's call to bring his hounds in on this thing. I always thought you and your dog would track it down, but I'm a little partial. I saw what Jack can do."

"Well, if it's all the same to Sheriff Anderson, I think we'd all be better off, including the cougar population in Kittitas County, if Mr. Henderson and his hounds sat out the rest of this one."

"I will strongly suggest that to the sheriff," Hernandez said.

"I guess there's no need to send the cougar carcass to WSU then," Jansen said.

"No sir, there isn't," McCain said. "Say, the other day Sergeant Harper was going to bring in some wet dirt that we found up at the site where Mr. Hodges was attacked. Did you do anything with that yet?"

"No, because you can't really get any DNA out of urine," Jansen said. "It would have been a waste of time."

"Did you smell it?" McCain asked.

"As a matter of fact, it was hard to avoid," Jansen said. "It was pretty ripe."

"Did it smell like cat urine?" McCain asked.

"Well, no, now that I think about it. At least not like the cat urine I've smelled."

"Interesting," McCain said, more to himself than to the other people in the room.

CHAPTER 30

Timba the tiger had been running loose in the wilds of the Cascade Mountains for ten days. In that time, she had survived by scavenging other animal kills, but she was always hungry.

Twice, while she was out looking for food, she chased snowshoe hares that had burst from the brush. But the rabbits were too elusive, changing directions in an instant and disappearing into thin air. Timba had also come upon a big bull elk with huge antlers. Instead of running, the bull turned and dropped his head so the antlers were guarding him from an attack. She wasn't planning on trying to take down the elk because something inside told her to stay clear of the white-tipped antlers.

Later, as she walked up a ridge, she caught the aroma of a freshly killed animal. Warm blood had an unbelievably enticing scent, and the smell was like a siren, calling her to the dead beast. She found the hide and carcass of the elk in short order. A couple of coyotes were eating there, but as soon as they saw her, they ran off. Timba moved in and fed on the remaining organs and entrails of the elk.

When she was finished, she caught the scent of more meat in the brush nearby and went over and ate some of that too. There was more meat left, and although she was no longer driven by hunger, something made her lie down near the meat to protect it from the scavengers.

Her hunger totally satisfied for the first time in a while, she fell into a deep sleep.

*

Sore and stiff from the long hike with his heavy, meat-laden pack only a few hours before, Dobbs struggled to get up and retrieve the rest of the elk meat. He thought about it as his calves, hamstrings, and shoulders barked at him.

Did he really want to make another hike up the hill to retrieve the rest of the meat?

No, he did not. But obtaining such a prime elk, like the yearling bull he had killed the day before, was never easy. In fact, it might take him a month or more to find another one. And, as winter approached and the elk moved lower to avoid heavy snow, it would be almost impossible.

He got up and started moving. He would go get as much of the remaining meat as he could carry, but he was in no big rush to get there.

Dobbs cooked another elk steak for breakfast and fiddled around, getting his pack and rifle ready. He didn't intend to shoot anything else, but he liked to have protection from whatever might be lurking out there. He had heard the strange growls and other unusual guttural sounds at least three more times during the previous week. He still had no idea what was making the eerie noises.

With a couple bottles of boiled creek water in his pack, Dobbs put on his bag, grabbed his rifle and headed up the hill. The elk meat was about four miles from his cabin, he figured. In no rush, he walked slowly and steadily.

As he got closer to where he'd left the meat and carcass, he could hear magpies chattering. They'd surely found the carcass, but hopefully they hadn't found the meat he'd stashed in the bushes and trees.

Dobbs slowly approached what remained of the dead elk. He held back in the trees and just watched. The last thing he wanted to do was spook a bear or a cougar that may have claimed the carcass. He didn't know what might happen in a case like that, so he just stood and watched from seventy-five yards to see what was happening.

As he looked closer, Dobbs was surprised to see that the elk hide was torn apart and spread around several feet from the carcass. And, looking at the white ribs and backbone, it was obvious that the scavengers had been busy during the night. The magpies were still chattering, and Dobbs could see there were a couple ravens pecking away at the bones. He was surprised he didn't see any coyotes working on the elk's remains.

Dobbs turned his gaze to where he had stashed the hindquarters and saw something moving through the trees. He couldn't make it out, but it was big and floated through the brush like a ghost. He'd never witnessed anything like that before. It scared him a little.

Finally, after watching for ten minutes without seeing the aberration again, Dobbs moved slowly toward the carcass. The ravens and the magpies all flew into the trees to wait for another chance to steal more scraps of meat or tallow.

Looking at the carcass, Dobbs found that there was very little left except for the proverbial skin, scattered around in pieces, and elk bones. When he reached the spot where he had placed the hindquarter and other meat, he couldn't believe his eyes. The neck meat was all gone, and most of the meat from the hindquarter had been eaten. And there, in the dirt, was the biggest mountain lion track he had ever seen.

Chapter 31

McCain woke up early again. His mind had been turning the whole drive home from Ellensburg the night before, and then he hadn't slept well. Things were just not adding up on this cougar attack.

From what he had seen at the coroner's office, the victim's body had most certainly been attacked by a cougar. The slashes in his arms and face confirmed that. But why had the cougar not killed the man by biting his throat? Yes, Mike Hodges had been wearing a helmet, but the coroner said that the slashes on the man's throat had most likely killed him. McCain had seen many cougar kills in his days in the woods, and none of the animals had died from claw slashes to the throat.

Then there was the whole deal where the cougar had walked away from the spot where it had attacked Hodges and urinated. McCain had twice watched from a distance as cougars had peed on some brush. They didn't pee in one spot – they marked their territory by lifting their tail and spraying.

Finally, there was the issue of the cougar tracks disappearing in the shale rockslide, while boot prints on the other side exited the shale and went uphill. If you thought about it too much, you would think the cougar magically transformed into a man.

McCain certainly didn't believe that. But what if a man had somehow made it look like a cougar had killed Mike Hodges? That was at least plausible. If that were the case, how would the person make cougar tracks and not leave any of his or her own? Then McCain remembered the moccasin print he found in the sparse grass on the trail Jack was following.

Running all of this through his mind a couple times made him start to believe he was onto something. His intention when he left the house was to reach the dead elk and wait for the poacher to arrive. Now, as he drove toward Ellensburg and thought about the anomalies in this cougar case, McCain changed his plans.

He called Deputy Hernandez and got her voicemail. McCain thought for a minute and dialed KCS Sergeant Harper.

"This is Harper," the sergeant said.

"Hi, sergeant. This is Luke McCain with the Department of Fish and Wildlife."

"Sure, Luke," Harper said. "What can I do for you?"

"I was going to bug Hernandez, but she wasn't answering. I need to talk to someone with the sheriff's department and give them some ideas I have on the cougar attack from a few days ago."

"Okay, I'm listening," Harper said.

McCain spent the next several minutes outlining all the things he knew about the attack. And then he started telling Harper about his theory as the sergeant listened intently without saying a word.

"So," McCain said. "Do you think I'm crazy?"

"On the contrary," Harper said. "I think you may be onto something."

"My plan is to go up on the hill and get Jack back on the boot tracks leaving the shale slide. Between his nose and my eyes, I think we can figure out where the person went."

"Still could be a hunter or hiker," Harper cautioned. "But it would be good to know for sure. In the meantime, I'll do some work from this end. Since everyone was convinced Mr. Hodges had been killed by a cougar, nobody really did any other checking into his background. I'm going to talk with his relatives and friends and see if there might be someone out there who wanted him dead bad enough to fake a cougar attack."

"You might start with the guys he rode with," McCain said. "They know this area and would have known the perfect place to stage something like this."

"They were going to be my first call," Harper said. "Good luck up there and let me know what you find."

"Will do," McCain said and clicked off.

When he arrived at the spot where the motorcyclist had been attacked, McCain was surprised that the TV trucks were gone. But, as he thought about it, he revised his initial reaction. The reporters now knew that the missing tiger hadn't been involved in the attack, and the man-killing cougar had been hunted down and killed by Henderson. Story over.

Frankly, he was happy there was nobody else around. He just hoped all the different tracks he had seen a couple of days ago hadn't been totally obliterated.

McCain let Jack out of the truck and removed his pack. He had filled it with water and other provisions before leaving the house, so it was ready to go. He threw the pack on his back, grabbed his .223 rifle, and headed up the hill.

"Come on, boy," he said to Jack. "Let's go try to figure this out once and for all."

After spending a few minutes looking around, McCain took some photos with his phone at the site where the man was attacked. Then, he turned and headed to the spot where he had marked the treadless shoe print. Luckily, Henderson's dogs hadn't ruined the track. In fact, McCain found only Jack's prints in that area.

McCain was careful not to disturb the print. There was a chance the sheriff's office would want to make a cast of it. He took a photo of the print with his phone and then headed up the hill. As soon as they got around the shale rockslide and McCain found the boot prints heading up the hill, he whistled Jack over and had the dog sniff the tracks. McCain took another photo of the best boot print, marked it with bright orange surveyor's tape, and told Jack to "find him."

The dog spent a couple minutes circling around the print, moving up the hill and back down. McCain didn't know if Jack was going to cypher it out. There were probably a million other scents in the air and on the ground, and the boot tracks were three days old. McCain couldn't blame the dog for having issues trying to figure out what was what.

As Jack worked, McCain slowly moved up the hill in the direction of the tracks. Occasionally, he would spot a track or a partial print and kept encouraging Jack to "find him" as they moved up the hill to the northwest.

Finally, Jack seemed to catch on to what scent McCain wanted him to follow, and he headed up the hill in a slow but steady direction. McCain made sure Jack was still on the right track by keeping an eye on the ground, looking out for the boot tracks.

They gained elevation gradually – side-hilling, crossing over small hogbacks, dropping into draws. In some places the dirt was soft, and McCain could see the man's tracks from twenty yards away. At other times they were crossing over rocks and grass, making it nearly impossible to find a track. Still, Jack worked steadily up the mountain.

McCain told Jack "whoa" about a mile above the shale. They took a breather there. McCain drank from a bottle of water and gave another to Jack. He fed the dog some jerky and ate a piece himself.

After the ten-minute breather, McCain stood and said, "Okay, boy. Find him." In an instant, Jack was back on the trail.

They'd walked another forty minutes when they came upon a flat. The tracks led into a heavily treed area that, from the outside, looked almost impenetrable. It was the thick black timber that elk loved to bed down in during the day.

McCain looked again as Jack started into the timber. Sure enough, there was a partial boot track in some dirt next to a flat rock. Just inside the timber, the tracks hit a well-used trail. McCain whistled Jack back and said, "Slowly now."

With Jack right next to him, McCain crept down the trail. He kept one eye ahead of them and another on the trail that they had been following from the rockslide. They had gone about three hundred yards down the trail when the trees began thinning, allowing some light to stream through. There appeared to be an opening ahead.

When they got to the opening in the trees, McCain could hardly believe his eyes. There, right up against the hillside, tucked into some large boulders, was some kind of an abode. McCain didn't know how he would describe it. It was more shack than cabin. Or it looked like a hovel, or maybe a hut. Judging by the tools, garbage, and other items scattered around the place, someone was obviously living there, and had been for some time.

Before he went any closer, McCain stopped and listened. He didn't want to surprise whoever might be living there and risk being fired upon. Finally, hearing nothing, he called out.

"Hello? Anyone home?"

There was no answer, so McCain moved forward, looking all around him as he did. Jack stayed right beside him.

The more McCain looked at the place, the more impressed he was. The little shack was constructed so that the back of the abode sat flush against the hill's severe slope. On the hill above the abode, several large fir trees grew, with their lowest limbs forming a canopy thirty feet overhead.

Several large gray boulders, not as big as Volkswagen Beetles, but larger than beach balls, sat to the left and to the right of the shack. The rocks were not too big to block the view, but still added some camouflage for the hut. The dense growth of huge fir trees out in front of the shack formed a seemingly impassable perimeter for almost a hundred and eighty degrees. Of course, it did allow passage as Luke and Jack discovered. But from a distance, someone would have to be looking for this place to see it.

Again, McCain called out as he approached the front door of the shack. After no answer, he opened the door and looked in.

The place was bigger than it looked from the outside. There was a single bed toward the back and a roughly made table with a camp chair closer to the front. The bed was covered with a couple dirty blankets, and a pillow with no case, stained yellow with sweat.

A plywood shelf ran the length of one side of the shack. On it was a Coleman camp stove. A well-used black skillet sat on one of the burners. A few plastic plates, blue in color, and two red plastic cups sat near the stove. Three pots of various sizes hung from nails on the wall. Four Coleman lanterns were placed about, one on a tiny shelf next to the bed, one on the rickety table, and two on the long shelf. Stacked near the bed were two old plastic milk crates with articles of clothing folded and placed inside. Most of the clothes looked to be well-worn Army surplus items.

As McCain looked around, he thought there were worse places a person could live.

McCain had smelled cooked meat when he entered the shack but saw nothing that would tell him when or if the person had been there recently. Wondering what the resident did for heat, he looked and saw two of the propane heaters that campers use to warm tents. They were a passable heat source for several months of the year, but definitely not for the dead of winter.

On the table there were stacks and stacks of used books, some with dust on the covers. McCain looked at the titles and authors. The library was eclectic and weird.

There was also a stack of binders on the floor next to the table. One binder was open, and McCain could see the person had been writing in it. The handwriting was so poor McCain could hardly make out any of the words. From what he could decipher, the writer was railing against something the president had done in the Middle East.

McCain had left Jack sitting just outside the shack, and when he went back out, the dog was gone. McCain looked around and saw Jack sniffing in the dirt below four dirty white bags hanging from a couple tree limbs. The bags were dripping blood onto the pine needles on the ground below.

"What do we have here?" McCain asked as he walked over to Jack.

McCain untied one of the bags and brought it down to take a look inside. Meat was meat, so it wasn't apparent what kind of animal it had come from until he looked closer. Some stiff yellow hair he noticed told him it was from an elk.

"That's interesting," McCain said to Jack.

The dog just looked into McCain's face as if to say, "I have no idea what that means."

"We may have just found our elk poacher."

Chapter 32

After collecting what was left of the elk meat, Dobbs loaded it into his pack, threw it over his shoulders, and quickly headed back down the hill. After seeing the size of the cat tracks, he wanted to be out of the area and back to the safety of his cabin. He kept his rifle at the ready, just in case whatever he had seen in the trees decided to come back.

Dobbs was mad that he'd walked all the way back up the hill and was only able to retrieve twenty pounds of meat. But he was also glad to have a much lighter load on his back after the strenuous pack out the previous evening.

As he walked back down the hill, Dobbs would stop occasionally and listen to make sure nothing was following him. And he would listen for any motorcycle or ATV riders too. The sound of silence made him happy.

*

The tiger had heard and smelled the man coming toward her well before she saw him. When the man stopped and looked her way, she had backed off the meat. But she didn't go far.

She followed the man's movements to the carcass and then over to her stash of meat. She had the urge to rush in and scare the intruder off, but she held her ground. She lay silently in the brush only thirty yards from the man as he packed up the remainder of the meat.

When the man was over the rise of the hill, she moved silently to where the meat had been. Then, following the scent trail of the man and the meat, she stalked silently after him.

*

McCain didn't have a search warrant, although, since this wasn't actually a permitted permanent residence and the person who lived there was basically squatting on public land, he figured he could take a closer look around.

From what he could tell, the person – he presumed it was a man – had been living here for a while. Just by the collection of soup, chili, and beef stew cans piled under a tree, it looked like someone had been here at least a couple of years.

The person who lived here was definitely handy. Not only had he made a table and a bed in the shack, there were handmade items around the outside of the house, including a broom. McCain wandered around and found a place where it appeared a bear had been skinned. Coarse black hair was spread all over the dirt.

He was walking back toward the shack when a track in the loose dirt made him stop and stare. There, as plain as could be, was the track of the missing tiger, Timba. It had the same line in the paw that McCain had seen where the big cat had been set free from the trailer.

"Keep your eyes open, Jack," McCain said. "There's been a tiger lurking around here."

Jack was sniffing around the bear hair and some other lighter-colored hair McCain hadn't noticed before. He walked over to the dog, squatted down, and picked up some of the hair. It was definitely from a cougar.

"This guy's been busy killing," McCain said to himself.

A moment later, Jack caught the sound of something coming down the path. He turned toward the noise, ears up, nose working the air.

McCain pulled out his service pistol and walked in the direction Jack was looking.

"State police!" McCain hollered. "Come on ahead."

McCain watched as a man with worn and tattered clothes came out of the trees. His dark, dirty beard was long and scraggly, and his hair looked like it was cut by weed whacker.

"Set your rifle on the ground and keep your hands where I can see them," McCain ordered.

The man did as he was told.

"Now take your pack off, come over here, and sit down."

Again, the man did as he was told.

"What's your name?" McCain asked as the man slowly walked closer.

"Dobbs."

"Do you live here, Mr. Dobbs?"

"Yes."

"For how long?"

"I don't know."

"Did you kill an elk up the ridge a ways with your rifle yesterday?"

"Yes."

"And you know elk hunting season with a rifle is not open yet?"

"Yes."

"It looks like maybe a bear and a cougar were skinned over there in those trees. Did you kill them recently?"

"Yes."

"Did you have a hunting license and tags to hunt the cougar and bear?"

"No."

Every time McCain asked a question, he would look directly into the man's eyes. So far, it seemed like Dobbs was being very forthcoming and truthful.

"Did you know a Bengal tiger has been prowling around your place?" McCain asked.

At the question, McCain could see the surprise in Dobbs' eyes. The man didn't answer, he just turned his head as if he were thinking about something.

"Mr. Dobbs, my dog and I followed your tracks from down the hill a few miles. We picked them up near where a man riding a motorbike was attacked and killed. You know anything about that?"

Again, McCain watched the man's eyes. This time he didn't answer immediately, like he was thinking about it. Dobbs glanced over at Jack and back at McCain.

"Why would I know anything about that?" Dobbs asked.

"Well, again, we know you were down there. Just wondering if you saw or heard anything."

Dobbs eyes shifted again. "No."

McCain could tell the man was lying – or at least he knew more than he was telling.

"So, we have a little bit of an issue here, Mr. Dobbs," McCain said. "There are some serious game violations that need to be addressed. And I'm sure you know this, but building a cabin on National Forest land is not allowed. Plus, the Kittitas County Sheriff is going to want to chat with you some more about the rider who was killed."

*

The tiger had followed the man that smelled like dead elk until he disappeared into the trees. Then she heard people talking and listened to their voices. None were the voice of the man who had fed her all her life. She didn't know what to do next, so she lay down in some grass and listened.

*

How had the game warden followed his tracks from the place where he killed the motorcycle rider? He didn't leave any tracks.

The cougar left tracks, not him. What was he going to do? This police officer was going to ruin everything. He had to think and do something fast.

If he could get to his cougar paws, he might be able to kill the warden while making it look like another cougar attack. That was all he could do. If he didn't, he'd be out of his cabin. He would have to start all over, or worse. If they could prove he was the killer of the motorcyclist, he would go to prison. He absolutely could not go to prison. He would rather die first.

He had to get to the cougar paws.

*

Dobbs stood up and started walking toward his cabin.

"Where are you going, Mr. Dobbs?" McCain asked.

"If you're taking me away, I want to get some items out of my cabin," Dobbs said as he kept walking.

McCain pulled his pistol again and said, "Wait right there."

Dobbs stopped just short of the door to the shack.

About that time, Jack started with a low, deep growl. When McCain turned and looked at Jack, he saw the dog was not growling at Dobbs. Jack was staring back up the trail into the dark timber.

As McCain turned to see what Jack was growling at, Dobbs used the distraction to run into the shack and close the door.

"Crap," McCain said. "Stay here, Jack."

McCain ran to the door, keeping low and to the side just in case Dobbs was retrieving a firearm. The door to the shack was nothing more than a piece of three-quarter-inch plywood on hinges. McCain knew he could easily break through it, but he really didn't want to run into the muzzle of a pistol.

"Mr. Dobbs, you have nowhere to go. Come out with your hands where I can see them."

There was no answer, and McCain could detect no movement inside. Had he overlooked a back door or some kind of escape hatch in the floor?

"Mr. Dobbs, come out now."

Again, no answer and no sounds of anyone moving inside.

McCain turned to look at Jack. The dog was sitting where McCain had told him to stay, and he was intently looking into the dark timber. McCain gave a quick whistle. Jack turned and looked at him, and McCain patted his hip. Jack immediately ran to McCain's side.

"Stay here, boy," McCain said.

With that, McCain turned and, with one quick move, hit the door with his left shoulder. The door broke open even easier than he had expected, and his momentum carried him farther into the shack than he planned. It may have saved his life.

Dobbs was waiting just inside of the door with one of the cougar-paw weapons raised. But McCain basically flew by him. Dobbs quickly moved toward McCain, raising the cougar-claw hatchet to make his first strike. But suddenly, he felt a burning pain in his right leg, just below his buttocks. The pain of the bite, and the force with which Jack hit him from behind, threw Dobbs at McCain.

As he fell forward, Dobbs brought the claws down toward McCain's throat, but Jack had hit the man with such force that it threw him off target. McCain brought his right arm up and caught the downward swing of the hatchet on his forearm. The cougar claws ripped into McCain's arm, then stuck there.

Jack continued to hold onto Dobbs' leg as the man fell to the ground. Dobbs let go of the claw weapon, turned, and started to take a swing at Jack with his fist. But the dog saw it coming, let go of the man's leg, and spun around to McCain.

McCain was trying to figure out what the man had hit him with, and why his shooting hand wasn't working, when Dobbs ran out of the cabin with surprising agility, slamming the door behind him. Jack ran to the closed door to chase the man, but there was nothing he could do.

Forgetting about the cougar claws stuck in his arm, McCain rushed to the door. He opened it just in time to see Dobbs sprinting to where he'd placed his rifle. Then, out of the corner of his eye,

McCain saw something big and orange come out of the brush next to the house. In two fast, powerful jumps, the tiger hit Dobbs. The animal struck with such force, it knocked him down on his head and shoulder, sending the man rolling.

Luckily, Jack was just as surprised to see the tiger fly out of the brush, so he stood and watched, just in front of McCain.

"Stay," McCain hissed at Jack, and the dog didn't move.

McCain didn't want to watch a tiger kill a man, but he couldn't risk intervening, so he waited to see what would happen. For some reason, the tiger didn't stay on top of Dobbs, nor did it use its claws or bite the man. It was almost like it was playing with him.

It seemed to McCain that the tiger didn't know what to do next. Dobbs was just lying there, either knocked out or unwilling to move. Finally, the big cat sauntered over to where Dobbs had dropped his backpack, picked it up and walked down the trail, into the thick stand of dark trees and out of sight.

McCain watched the tiger leave, carrying the backpack with elk meat inside, and then looked back at Dobbs. The man wasn't dead, but the force of the hit had done something to him. It most certainly separated his shoulder and maybe broke his clavicle; McCain didn't know. Dobbs was obviously in pain because as soon as the tiger was gone, he started writhing around and moaning loudly.

McCain told Jack it was okay to move, and the dog ran over to Dobbs and stood a couple feet away, emitting a low growl.

"Are you going to live?" McCain asked Dobbs as he walked over to him. He had his service pistol in his left hand, the cougar-claw hatchet still stuck to his right forearm.

Dobbs just grunted.

"Don't get any more thoughts of running. My dog, unlike that tiger, will bite, as you found out earlier."

McCain put his pistol in its holster and, with his left hand, dug the handcuffs out of the pouch on his service belt and put them on Dobbs. The man screamed when McCain pulled his right arm behind his back to be cuffed.

"Watch him, boy," McCain said to Jack after he sat the cuffed Dobbs upright. "And if he runs, bite him in the other leg."

Dobbs kept moaning and acting like he hadn't heard McCain. But he looked at Jack with contempt.

After walking over to where he had put his own backpack down, McCain dug out a small first aid kit. He carefully worked the claws out of his forearm, scrubbed the four wounds with antiseptic pads, and then wrapped his arm with gauze and tape. When he was finished, he grabbed his radio.

"Wildlife one-four-eight needing assistance," McCain said into the radio. "Have a suspect in custody for the possible murder of the motorcycle rider. We'll need a couple KCS deputies up here as soon as possible. Also need medical assistance."

"Copy," the dispatcher said. "What's your location?"

McCain told the dispatcher to hang on a minute as he pulled out his GPS unit and turned it on. A minute later, the GPS had acquired three satellites, and McCain gave the dispatcher his coordinates.

"Tell them to come to where the motorcycle rider was killed earlier this week and then follow the coordinates up the hill."

"Do you need airlift for the medical situation?" the dispatcher asked.

McCain heard Dobbs mumble, "Yes."

"No, the injuries are not life-threatening. We'll be fine. Just have them here when we get down the hill."

"Copy."

"And can you figure out how to contact Sam Banister, the owner of the tiger running loose? Tell him we've found his tiger and would like his assistance ASAP."

"Copy that. Are you in danger?"

"Unknown," McCain said. "But I would really like Mr. Banister here. You might get someone up here with a dart gun too. Maybe a WDFW biologist."

"Copy. Hang in there. Help is on the way."

Chapter 33

McCain figured it would be two hours minimum before anyone showed up. He debated whether to stay and wait or get Dobbs on his feet and headed downhill.

After he rounded up Dobbs' rifle and unloaded it, he put it in the shack. Then, thinking about the cougar-claw weapon that Dobbs had magically come up with, McCain wondered if a second one might be hidden in the room somewhere. After looking more closely, he found a very simple door cut into the wallboard. McCain reached in and sure enough, a second cougar claw weapon was hidden there.

McCain walked back out holding the cougar-paw hatchet. Dobbs looked up at him with a pained smile.

"I should have killed you," Dobbs said. Then he looked at Jack and said, "You were lucky that dog was here. He saved your life."

"Not the first time, Mr. Dobbs. So why did you decide to kill Mike Hodges?"

Dobbs had a blank look on his face until it dawned on him

that Hodges must have been the motorcycle rider. "He was just the unlucky one," Dobbs muttered. "How were you able to follow my tracks up here?"

"You made several mistakes," McCain said. "If you've ever seen a cougar kill a deer, they kill with their teeth, not their claws. The cougar prints you laid down were somewhat convincing, but I found a moccasin print in the grass as we followed the cougar prints up the hill, which made me start thinking that maybe a person was actually making the cougar tracks. But the biggest error was having your fake cougar walk into that shale slide and never walk out. Only your boot tracks exited the rockslide."

Dobbs dropped his head and moaned some more.

As McCain continued talking to Dobbs, he kept a watchful eye out for the tiger. He noticed Jack, too, was again watching up the trail into the dark timber.

After considering whether to stay or go, McCain decided they should head back down the hill. But first he grabbed two bags of elk meat hanging from the trees, cut them down, and carried them up the trail. Just as he cleared the dark timber, he dumped the meat out into a big pile.

Then he walked back, put his pack on, grabbed his rifle, and helped Dobbs to his feet. The man moaned loudly with pain.

"Come on," McCain said. "The sooner we can get you down the hill, the sooner someone can help you with that shoulder."

He noticed Dobbs was walking with a limp too. He'd forgotten that Jack had bitten him in the back of his upper leg.

They walked around the shack and down the path that Dobbs had used two days earlier to go burn his bloody clothes. Once they were a half mile down the trail, McCain cut back to the southeast. They began the slow process of walking cross-hill, through draws and over small ridges, down to where his truck was parked. He estimated they'd get there about the same time the deputies and medics would arrive.

On the way down the hill, McCain got a call from the KCSO dispatcher. He told McCain that Deputy Hernandez and Sergeant

Harper were on their way, as was an ambulance. They had reached Mr. Banister, but he would not be there for a couple more hours. WDFW was sending a biologist with a dart gun.

"Copy," McCain said. "Thank you."

They stopped a couple times for a rest. Dobbs was clearly in pain, but there wasn't much McCain could do about that. He was in pain too. His arm throbbed, and blood was starting to appear around the edges of the bandage. A new dressing needed to be applied. There was no time for that though, so after taking on some water, McCain got Dobbs up and moving down the hill.

Two or three times, McCain stopped to look and listen. He wasn't overly concerned about the tiger, but he really didn't need to be dealing with it right now. He hoped the elk meat would pacify her for a while. Maybe she would even stay there long enough for Banister to arrive and figure out how to get her back to his traveling cat show.

McCain was really glad to have Jack along. He knew the dog would hear the tiger well before he would, and that gave him a little encouragement as they walked down the hill. He certainly didn't want to have to shoot the tiger, especially after she had helped catch Dobbs. But if it meant saving someone's life, he would certainly do so.

When McCain, Dobbs, and Jack finally arrived at his truck, the deputy sheriffs and two medics were there getting their gear ready. The medics jumped right in and started to work on Dobbs and McCain. McCain told the whole story to Hernandez and Harper, who stood there, staring in disbelief, as McCain described Dobbs' attack, the cougar claws in his arm, Jack biting Dobbs in the leg, and finally the tiger pouncing on Dobbs as he ran for the rifle.

"That tiger might have saved your life," Hernandez said.

"I think it did," Harper said. "If Dobbs would have reached the rifle, who knows where you'd be right now!"

"You don't know," McCain said. "I'm a pretty good shot left-handed."

"As I understand it," Hernandez said. "You're not even a good shot right-handed."

They all laughed.

"But he is the Rifleman," Harper said. "I know you can shoot a rifle."

"Where'd you hear that?" McCain said.

"Deputy Williams of the YSO and I talked the other day. Now, the whole Kittitas County Sheriff's Office knows about your nickname, Rifleman."

McCain shook his head. He'd get Williams back the next time he saw him.

They talked a little more, and it was decided that Hernandez would follow the ambulance down to the hospital in Ellensburg. After Dobbs was all fixed up and released, she'd get him processed and into the lock-up.

Harper radioed for more assistance and was told two additional deputies were on the way.

"One will be escorting Mr. Banister and the wildlife biologist," the dispatcher said.

"We'll wait here for them," McCain said. "I think it's best, what with the tiger still wandering around up there."

"Wait, who is we?" Harper asked. "You need to get down to the hospital to have those wounds sutured. Didn't you hear the medic?"

They argued for a couple minutes about whether McCain should go or stay, until they heard the sound of vehicles rumbling their way. Up the road came not one, but three TV rigs. McCain recognized the car of Simon Erickson, and almost decided he'd rush to the hospital after all when he saw the big blonde hair of April Scott in a second vehicle. The third car was from the Yakima CBS TV station. McCain didn't recognize the reporter driving that vehicle.

The rigs zoomed up the bumpy dirt road and stopped in a cloud of dust behind McCain's pickup. The three reporters piled out of the cars, grabbed cameras and tripods, and ran over to where McCain and Harper were leaning against Harper's SUV. Scott, McCain saw, was only wearing two-inch heels, and only tripped once as she hurried along the rocky, rutty dirt road.

"Okay, everyone hold it right there," Harper said as the three rushed up to McCain. "This is how we're going to do this. Officer McCain will talk to all three of you at once. Set your stuff up over there and when you're ready, I'll bring him over."

McCain just stared at Harper.

"This is a KCSO investigation," McCain said. "I thought you were going to talk to them."

"Sheriff's orders," Harper said. "Only Public Information Officer McDonald from our office can talk to the media about tiger stuff. And this is definitely tiger stuff. McDonald isn't here, so you're up. You should be thanking me. Now, you only have to do it once, instead of answering the same questions three times."

McCain looked over at the trio of young reporters. April Scott didn't look happy. As McCain recalled, she liked one-on-one interviews where she could ask the tough questions like what are the colors of a tiger.

The reporters had their cameras set up quickly, and soon all three were clipping microphones to McCain's shirt lapel.

"Say and spell your name please," the CBS reporter said.

McCain did, and then they were off and running. He went play-by-play through the day: following the tracks up the hill, finding the shack, confronting the suspect on the poaching charge, and then getting attacked by the suspect. He left out the part about Jack biting the guy but told how the suspect left the shack and got caught by the tiger.

"Oh my gosh!" April Scott said with a gasp. "But the man was okay?"

"Yes, he was in the ambulance you saw heading down the road," McCain said. "He should be fine."

"How did you determine dat da man might be da person who killed da motorcycle rider up here in da mountains?" Erickson asked.

"I found some incriminating evidence at the cabin," McCain said.

"Such as?" Erickson asked.

"He attacked me with the same weapon he used to kill the rider," McCain said, raising his bandaged arm.

"Oh my gosh!" April Scott said with another gasp. "Does it hurt?"

"Yes," McCain said.

"So, what about the tiger?" Scott asked. "What did it look like?"

Erickson turned and looked at Scott. "Probably like every udder tiger in da world."

"Shut up," Scott said to Erickson. She turned back to McCain. "Can you answer that please, Detective McClure?"

"It's McCain. And I'm a wildlife police officer. It looked like every other tiger in the world."

Erickson chuckled. Scott just nodded her head, with a concerned look on her heavily made-up face.

"So, the tiger," Scott said, still looking very concerned. "It must have found enough to eat out there in the wilds?"

"Must have," McCain said. "She's still alive and chasing down bad guys."

When the three reporters could think of no more questions, good or bad, they let McCain go, then scattered like a covey of quail, each to a different part of the forest to set up their cameras and shoot more footage.

McCain knew that even though the reporters had talked to him for more than ten minutes, they would only use about twenty seconds of his answers on the news. That was certainly fine with him. He'd returned to Harper's KCSO rig when Erickson came over.

"Could you tell me where dat shack is, Officer McCain? I'd like to try to go live from dare at five and six tonight."

"You know Simon, I like your gumption. But until we get that tiger rounded up, I don't think that's a very good idea. And besides, the shack is a live crime scene. Maybe you should go over into those trees and do your live shots from there. Tell the viewers the shack is just on the other side of the trees. They'll never know the difference."

Erickson thought about it for a minute, said, "Tanks, dats a great idea," and headed toward the trees to look for the perfect setup.

"You really do gotta like his gumption," Harper said with a laugh.

Chapter 34

They waited another forty-five minutes before Hernandez showed up. Banister trailed behind her in his black GMC pickup pulling the cat trailer. McCain hadn't thought about that, but if they were able to get the tiger somehow sedated, it would need a place to ride back to the fairgrounds in Puyallup.

A few minutes after that, a WDFW pickup arrived with Officer Stan Hargraves and Wildlife Biologist John Stanton.

"Hey, McCain," Hargraves said. "I heard you may have caught the guy who killed the motorcycle rider."

"I believe it is him. He even cougar-clawed me with the weapon that we believe was used in the killing," McCain said holding up his bandaged arm.

"What?" both Hargraves and Stanton said in unison.

McCain introduced the two men to Sam Banister and Deputy Harper, who already knew Hargraves, then told everyone the story about getting attacked by Carson Dobbs. They all laughed when he got to the part about Jack biting Dobbs in the back of the leg.

"Good dog, Jack!" Hargraves said.

Jack glanced up from where he was napping in the shade of McCain's pickup, then dropped his head back down and quickly fell asleep again.

"All in a day's work, I guess," Stanton said.

Then they all oohed and ahhed when McCain told them about the tiger running Dobbs down and pouncing on him.

"Did he need to change his shorts after that?" Hargraves asked.

"I can't believe Timba would do that," Banister said. "But at least she didn't really maul the man. It sounds like it was a game for her."

"Whatever it was, she saved me from a probable gunfight," McCain said. "Dobbs was running for his rifle."

They talked for a few more minutes, and then Stanton said, "So, where is this famous tiger?"

McCain really didn't want to go back up the hill. His arm was throbbing and frankly, he was tired. But he knew Banister and Stanton would probably never find the shack or the elk meat on their own. So, after Stanton and Banister figured out the right tranquilizing dosage for Timba based on her weight, the men packed up everything they needed and told McCain to lead the way.

"C'mon, Jack," McCain said as he again shouldered his pack and grabbed his rifle.

"You're not going to use that are you?" Banister asked, looking at the rifle.

"I don't plan on it, but I'd rather have it and not need it than need it and not have it."

"Timba's a pussycat," Banister said. "You won't need it."

As the three men hiked up the hill, Jack ran ahead. The occasional squirrel would skitter across a log, or from one tree to another, and he'd give chase.

It took them about an hour and a half to walk the three miles up the hill. As they reached the flat, McCain whistled Jack over to heel and said, "I placed the elk meat up by those trees about two hundred yards ahead."

All three men looked and didn't see anything. No tiger, no meat, nothing. As they walked a little closer, they found the blood stains where the meat had been placed by McCain. It was all gone.

McCain checked around for tracks and found some going through the black timber toward Dobbs' cabin. And there were more tracks leading back up the ridge.

"Let's go check down the trail. She might be staying near the cabin where there's still some meat hanging in a tree," McCain said.

Stanton put the dart in the chamber of his rifle, ready to take a shot if needed.

"I'm hoping she'll come to me and we can just walk down to the truck," Banister said.

"How realistic is that?" McCain asked.

"Well, ten days ago I would have said very, but now that she's been out here on her own, I just don't know."

"Let's hope that's how it works. If you think Jack might scare her off, I can take him back to the truck."

"As long as you keep him by your side, we should be fine," Banister said.

The three men and Jack walked slowly down the trail and through the thick stand of big trees until they reached the spot where it opened up in front of Dobbs' cabin.

"Here, Timba," Banister called in a high-pitched voice, like he was calling a house cat to come for a bowl of milk. "It's me. Come on, girl."

From somewhere over near the cabin they heard a growl.

"She's here!" Banister exclaimed. "Come on, Timba!"

The men looked around, and there, lying under the last bag of elk meat in the dried pine duff, was Timba.

Banister started walking toward the big cat, and her tail flipped from one side to the other.

"He's braver than me," Stanton whispered to McCain. "You might have that rifle ready."

"I think he's fine. Let's just see what happens."

They watched as Banister slowly walked up to the tiger and started scratching her ears. Then he put his arms around her neck and gave her a big hug.

"I've missed you," he said.

He stayed with the tiger for several minutes, talking to her like she was a person. His voice was soothing, and his actions were slow and deliberate. He pulled a leash attached to a collar out of his small backpack and placed the collar around the tiger's neck.

"You don't suppose he's planning on walking that tiger down the hill like it's some kind of show dog, do you?" Stanton whispered again.

"Looks like he's going to try," McCain whispered back.

Once Banister had the tiger on the leash, he called back and asked one of the men to come help him get the bag of elk meat down out of the tree. McCain told Jack to sit and stay, and then he went over to help. As he walked over, he gazed at Timba. The big cat looked as happy as could be to have Banister standing there next to her.

"If one of you men can carry the meat down to the trucks, I believe I can get her to follow you with me holding the leash. At least it's worth a try. I don't really want to dart her. And if we do, then how do we get her to the trailer?"

McCain had been giving that some thought. He figured they would have to radio a helicopter to come in and carry the tiger down to the trucks, like they do when they are transporting bighorn sheep. It was doable, but it might take a couple hours to get a helicopter up here. He really didn't want to sit around waiting with a tiger.

"I'm not sure I want to be the meat carrier," Stanton said. "I think a decent-sized German shepherd could break that leash."

"Let's give it a try," McCain said. "I'll put the meat in my backpack."

He put the meat in his pack, threw it over his shoulders, and started walking to where Jack and Stanton were sitting near the trail in the trees. Timba stood up and started following him.

When they got through the dense trees and out into the opening, McCain turned around and looked. Banister was coming up the trail, Timba by his side. He could have been walking a poodle.

Stanton was a little uncomfortable with the whole situation, and by the time they were a mile or so down the hill, he was five hundred yards ahead of McCain and Jack, who were about twenty yards ahead of Banister and Timba.

As soon as it looked like walking the tiger down the mountain was going to work, McCain radioed ahead.

"Wildlife one-four-eight to Sergeant Harper."

"Copy. This is Harper."

"We have a tiger on a leash and we're walking her down to the trucks now. We'll be there in about an hour. If you can get in touch with Simon Erickson with the ABC TV station, he might want to be here to see this. He left not that long ago."

"Copy," Harper said. "I'll get him turned around."

Chapter 35

When they broke over the crest of the last hill, McCain looked down at the road. Harper was there, and McCain could see Simon Erickson all set up with his camera. As they walked down the hill, McCain watched Erickson jump in front of the camera and start talking.

"Dis is quite a sight," Erickson said into the lens, his tone serious. "After ten days in da wild, Timba da tiger is on her way out of da wilderness."

Then he jumped back behind the camera and zoomed in on the men, the yellow dog, and the tiger as they walked down the hill and to the back of the long, white trailer. When they reached it, McCain pulled a bloody sack out of his pack. Banister grabbed some meat from the sack and threw it into the enclosure in the back of the trailer. Timba dutifully jumped into the trailer and into the enclosure, and Banister unclasped the leash and closed the door.

McCain walked over to the Kittitas County officers and watched as Erickson interviewed Banister. The man was obviously overjoyed to have the tiger back safe and sound.

When the interview was done, Erickson, for the second time that day, thanked McCain, packed up his equipment and headed down the mountain. The live shot at five and six had been cancelled, so he had to get down to the station to get his story ready for airing.

Banister got Timba some water, and after she drank, he closed up the trailer, fired up the air conditioner at the front, and walked over to McCain and Harper.

"I can't thank y'all enough," Banister said. "I really thought I'd never see her alive again. You don't know how much this means to me."

"Actually, I think we do," McCain said, shaking Banister's hand. "You have a safe trip back to the fair, and then home to Florida."

They all said their good-byes, and Banister jumped into the GMC and backed the trailer down the road a short way to where he could turn around. He got the outfit straightened away, gave a honk, and the truck rumbled off.

"This sure has been an interesting few days," Harper said to McCain after the truck and trailer were gone.

"The life of a game warden," McCain said. "It's never boring."

"Well, I'll remember this one for a long time," Harper said. "Guess there's nothing more for us to do here, so I'll get out of here."

"Thanks for all your help," McCain said as Harper walked to his SUV.

McCain walked over to his truck, where Jack was again lying in the shade napping. He sat down next to the yellow dog and rubbed his ears. Jack didn't even open his eyes.

McCain hadn't realized he'd fallen asleep beside Jack until his phone started beeping. He woke with a start, looked around, saw Jack still asleep in the grass, and answered his phone.

"Did the tiger get you?" Sara asked.

"Funny you should ask," McCain said. "I'll tell you all about it when I get home. We're on our way now and should be there in a couple hours."

"So, everything is okay?"

"Yep, everything is just great."

When he hung up, he grabbed two bottles of water and jerky from his truck. He and Jack drank and ate, then watched white clouds drift across a beautifully clear sky.

"This'll be one to tell the grandkids," he said to Jack.

Thinking of that made him sad. By the time he had grandkids, Jack would just be a wonderful memory.

"Enough of that," McCain said, wiping a tear from his eye. "We've got many more adventures ahead of us, and a whole bunch more pheasants to hunt."

Before they loaded up, McCain looked up at the yellow tape still around the spot where Mike Hodges had been killed just three days before. Was it really just three days, McCain wondered. It seemed like three weeks.

"Come on, boy," McCain said to Jack. "Let's go get some dinner and some rest."

Chapter 36

They watched the eleven o'clock news together. McCain's capture of Carson Dobbs and the retrieval of the tiger were the lead stories. In fact, they took up the whole first five minutes of the half hour news. Simon Erickson even did a live shot from the forest that looked suspiciously like the pine trees planted next to the TV station. He didn't come out and say he was at the site of Dobbs' cabin, but he didn't tell the viewers he was in Yakima, either.

McCain watched himself talking to Erickson. He actually got about thirty-five seconds of airtime. Banister had a little more, talking as the TV viewers looked into the enclosure while Timba happily lay there, gnawing on some raw elk meat.

When they cut to the story of McCain finding Timba and how the men had walked her three miles back to the trailer, Sara spotted Jack in the shot walking down the hill.

"There's Jack!" she exclaimed.

Jack was sound asleep on the cool linoleum kitchen floor and didn't even raise his head when she squealed his name.

Then she looked over at McCain, and he was also fast asleep, laid back in the recliner.

*

Erickson's video of McCain and Jack walking with the tiger down the hill had gone viral and was now on every news broadcast in the country. McCain had seen it once on one of the morning news shows, and that was enough for him.

Two days after catching Dobbs and helping to locate the tiger, McCain was in the hardware store in Naches, buying some shotgun shells for an upcoming sharp-tail grouse hunt in Montana with some buddies and their dogs. Jim Kingsbury spotted him in one of the store's aisles.

"Hey, Luke! Man, I see you made the national news finding that tiger," Kingsbury said. Today, the gentleman was wearing a bright yellow T-shirt with I AM SILENTLY CORRECTING YOUR GRAMMAR in bold purple letters printed across the front. "That must have been something, huh, catching the killer and then finding the tiger?"

"Yeah, well, it all worked out," McCain said. "It was good to catch the real killer and get the tiger back to her owner."

"And that recluse came after you, too, I hear? But Jack saved you again."

"Jack and Timba the tiger," McCain said. "It's good to have four-legged friends."

After Kingsbury left, McCain paid for his shotgun shells and walked out to his Tundra, where Jack was asleep in the back seat.

"You're a national celebrity, Jack," McCain said. "Don't get a big head now."

Jack didn't move.

"I guess we don't have to worry about that," McCain said after seeing the dog still snoring away.

*

Cassidy Sutcliff was watching the local Portland news, and the two overly cheery news anchors discussed how a game warden from Yakima had found Timba the tiger in the Cascades and helped reunite it with its owner. It was the "feel good" story of the night.

Only it didn't make Sutcliff feel good. Actually, it pissed her off. She had worked so hard to set the tiger loose, and that game warden had ruined it. Although, he was kind of hot, she thought. Just her type, in fact – tall, muscular, and obviously an animal lover.

Sutcliff was holed up in a cheap motel on the outskirts of Portland, across the street from a Wal-Mart and several fast-food restaurants. She thought about the news story and the game warden for a while. Then she went across the street to the Wal-Mart and purchased a map of Washington State, a few items to eat and drink, and went back to her room to think some more.

Yakima, she saw on the map, was about two hundred miles from Portland. Driving it would take three and a half hours, while riding the bus might take six. She had three hundred and seventy-nine dollars in her bag, but that, unfortunately, wouldn't buy a car. Riding the bus, as unappealing as it was, was her best option.

That night, as Sutcliff lay in bed, she thought about Spearman. She really missed him. She needed him. Then her thoughts turned to the good-looking game warden she'd seen briefly on TV. She smiled. Getting to know him was going to be fun.

*

McCain was just feeding Jack when Sara got home from work the following day.

"How was your day?" he asked. He put Jack's dish down and the dog tore into his food like he hadn't eaten in a week.

"Pretty good," she said. "Wanna go to Miner's tonight? I've been craving one of their burgers."

McCain was always up for Miner's. The longtime hamburger-stand-turned-restaurant was an iconic fixture in the Yakima Valley. He was always amazed by the times when he traveled somewhere in the country and mentioned he was from Yakima, Washington.

A person would often say, "Oh, I've been there. Love those Miner's hamburgers."

"Miner's sounds good to me," McCain said. "Anyone have a photo of the gal who stole the truck?"

"Actually, I do. I looked up her driver's license information after she left the restaurant in Seattle. Her name is Cassidy Sutcliff. The photo on the license is not great, but even with the crappy picture, you can tell she is very pretty."

"Tall, short, heavy, skinny?" McCain asked.

"Fairly tall, five-foot-eleven. And slender, one-hundred-and-twenty pounds."

"I guess that could qualify as swimsuit model material. E-mail me a copy of the license when you think about it."

"Will do. Now, let's go. I'm famished."

*

As Luke and Sara pulled into their driveway after dinner, Austin Meyers came running over from across the street.

"Hi Sara," Austin said before turning to McCain. "Can you help me for a second, Luke?"

"Sure, what's up?"

"I think I found a rig to buy, but I'd really like your opinion."

As he was telling McCain about the vehicle, Austin pulled out his phone and showed him the Craigslist post for a 2006 Toyota 4Runner. The rig had a lot of miles on it, over 158,000, but it looked to be in good shape otherwise.

After letting McCain look at the description and photos, Austin asked, "Well, what do you think?"

The SUV was listed for $4,500.

"It looks pretty nice. Do you have the money to buy it?"

"Not quite. I'm about a thousand short, but Charlie said he'd give me the rest. All I would need to do is work it off some time in the future."

Sara, who had been standing nearby, stepped in.

"Let me see this car you're all excited about."

She took the phone from Luke and started swiping through the photos.

"Boy, it does look like it is in nice shape. And that is awfully nice of Charlie to front you the rest of the cash."

"Yeah, he's pretty cool when it comes to money."

"What is it he does for work again?" Sara asked.

"Mom said he imports some stuff from South America. He said I could maybe help him with some deliveries when I get my driver's license and a rig to drive."

Sinclair gave McCain a look that said *I don't like this.*

"Well, that is very nice of him," Sara said. "Do you know the name of his business?"

"No. But I can find out if you want."

"No, that's okay," McCain said. "When can we go test drive this Toyota?"

"I can call and see if we can go look at it now," Austin said excitedly.

"Let's do it," McCain said. "Go tell your mom – maybe she wants to go too. And you'll need the money just in case you want to buy it."

"Okay," Austin said. "I have the money in my room. I'll ask Mom if she wants to go."

A few minutes later, Austin came running out of the front door, followed by his mom, Jessie Meyers.

"This is awfully nice of you to do this Luke," Jessie said. "About the only thing I know about cars is how to turn them on."

"Glad to help," McCain said. "I remember buying my first car. It's a big day in a kid's life."

As they drove out to Selah where the 4Runner was, McCain asked about how everything was going in Jessie's life.

"It's great!" she said. "Charlie has been really good to me and Austin. He's a really nice guy."

"He must be," McCain said. "It's very nice of him to loan Austin some money to help buy a car. Austin says he's in the importing business?"

"Yes, he has people who travel to South America and bring in items made by some of the indigenous people in Peru and Bolivia. It sells really well here in the States."

"Interesting," McCain said. "Does he have a catalog showing his products? Or a website?"

"Yes, his business is called SO-AM Tradex. Google it and you'll see everything he sells."

"I'll do that," McCain said. Then he turned to Austin. "Now, depending on if you like the 4Runner or not, how much are you going to offer for it?"

After taking the Toyota for a test drive, McCain told Austin that he had concerns about a noise the transmission made.

"I'd recommend not making an offer right now," McCain said. "Tell the guy you'd like to take it to a shop to have it checked out before you'd be ready to make an offer."

McCain could see that Austin was disappointed, but after his mother encouraged him to listen to Luke, he told the man that he liked the SUV very much but wanted to have it checked out at a shop first.

The man wasn't too keen on the idea, so McCain told him thanks, that they'd check back with him later to see if he would change his mind.

"I know you are disappointed," Jessie said to Austin. "But Luke knows what he is doing. There are lots of good used trucks out there. We'll find the right one for you."

Later, talking to Sara, Luke said, "I got the name of Charlie's company. Maybe you can do a little checking on it. It sounds legit, but anytime anyone is importing items from South America, who knows what is really going on."

"I'll check it out now. I just want to know Austin is working for a legit business and Jessie isn't going to be hurt again."

After looking into SO-AM Tradex, Sinclair could find nothing out of line. Everything she could find online made it look like the company was doing exactly as Jessie Meyers had described. Still, Sinclair had a weird feeling about the company and about the boyfriend, Charlie.

"It all looks like a legitimate business," Sara said to McCain from behind her laptop. "But I'd still like to check it out some more."

"Go with your gut," McCain said. "It is usually right."

*

Sutcliff wrote the address down on a piece of paper and headed for the bus. She didn't actually know what she was going to do if or when she met the officer, but she had her knife in her boot just in case. She hoped she wouldn't have to use it, either on the man or any other pushy bus passengers.

While she waited for the bus in Portland, Sutcliff risked turning on her phone and spent a couple minutes researching the Department of Fish and Wildlife in Yakima. She didn't know if the game warden she'd seen on TV spent time at that office, but she figured it would be a starting point.

The bus trip from Portland to Yakima was uneventful. Or it was as uneventful as a bus trip can be. A young woman had a baby with her that cried for the first two hours, and a man, who sat across the aisle from Sutcliff, had some form of illness that kept him coughing nonstop. She hoped she didn't contract whatever the man had.

The bus didn't arrive at a bus station. Sutcliff wasn't sure why, but it just pulled into an AM-PM mini-mart, and that is where the Yakima passengers disembarked. That was fine with her.

In some towns, there were taxi cabs waiting for Greyhound passengers when the buses arrived. Sutcliff looked around. Besides a couple homeless people sleeping out by the street, and about a thousand cars zooming by, she found no taxis.

Sutcliff wandered into the mini-mart and talked to the woman at the front register who seemed extremely put-out that someone would ask her a question.

"Do taxis ever wait here for bus passengers?" Sutcliff asked.

"I don't pay any attention to what the buses or the passengers do," said the forty-something woman in a gravelly voice. "Most just disappear after the bus dumps them here. And NO, you can't use the restroom."

Sutcliff felt like saying, "Hey, bitch. I didn't ask to use the restroom." But she decided not to waste her breath.

She looked around, saw a city bus go by and wondered if one of those would get her to where she needed to go. Instead, she turned on her phone again, found a number for a cab company, and called them. Sutcliff thought about ordering an Uber but didn't want to use her credit card because she thought the officials might be tracking it.

The cab showed up fifteen minutes later.

"Where to?" the driver asked. He was a good fifty pounds overweight.

"Department of Fish and Wildlife offices," Sutcliff said, then handed the man a slip with the address.

"Oh, yeah. I know where that is. Over by the airport. You applying for a job or something?"

"Or something," Sutcliff said.

"My sister-in-law worked for them for a couple of years. Good place to work. State job, so you have lots of benefits, and they take off every holiday and then some. Where you from?"

"Omaha," Sutcliff said, just pulling a town name out of the blue.

"Kansas, huh? Never been there."

Sutcliff almost asked, "Is everyone around here fat and stupid?" but decided it would do no good.

"Could you let me off about a block before we get to the office?" Sutcliff asked. "I have a few minutes to kill and don't want to be too early."

"Sure," the driver said. "I'll let you out at the cemetery."

"Perfect," Sutcliff said.

Chapter 37

McCain didn't plan on being at the office for too long, so he brought Jack with him. The yellow dog slept in the back seat of his truck, windows cracked to let a cool breeze blow through the cab. McCain, meanwhile, went in to handle a few items before heading back out into the field. Archery elk season was still open, and the fishing for fall Chinook salmon down on the Columbia River was heating up, so he needed to be out there checking on folks.

It was his first day back in the office after catching Carson Dobbs, so as soon as he walked in, several administrative staff members and biologists started asking him questions. He told the whole story, and they seemed genuinely amazed and concerned. Even Andrea Parker, a fish biologist who McCain had dated several years before, looked concerned when he told them how Dobbs was trying to kill him with the weird cougar-claw weapon.

"Jack saves the day again," Parker said at the end of the story.

One of the reasons McCain decided he and Parker weren't

compatible was because she didn't really like dogs. She, as McCain remembered, loved cats. That – and about seventeen other irritating little things she did – made it easy to tell her that he really wasn't interested in pursuing the relationship any further. She wasn't happy about his decision and for years gave him grief at work.

After the group was totally caught up on his exploits, he headed to his cubicle to take care of some reports, timecards, and emails that had piled up while he'd been searching for the tiger.

He saw the email from Sara with the photo of Cassidy Sutcliff but was so busy with the reports and answering emails, he hadn't taken two minutes to open it. McCain was just finishing up some timecards when the receptionist came down the hall and into the room where the enforcement officers had their cubicles. She found him at his desk and said, "Luke, you have a visitor."

"Any idea who it is?"

"Says she's a reporter for some wildlife magazine and hoped you might have a few minutes to chat."

"Aw, jeez. That's the last thing I want to do."

But McCain got up and followed the receptionist back to the lobby.

"Officer McCain," Cassidy Sutcliff said with an enchanting smile as McCain walked into the reception area. "I'm Janice Taylor, and I'm hoping to talk to you for a few minutes for a story I'm working on about the tiger that was set loose."

"Sure," McCain said. Talk about swimsuit models, he thought. This woman was stunning.

"Maybe we can step outside for a few minutes," Sutcliff said.

"What magazine did you say you are with?" McCain asked.

"Defenders of Wildlife," Sutcliff said. "We're a quarterly, working to stand up for wildlife species that have no say in their extinction or captivity."

"I left my phone on my desk," McCain said. "Let me go grab it and I'll be right with you."

He hustled back to his desk, jumped on his computer, and brought up the email he had received from Sinclair. He opened the attachment, and there in the driver's license photo was Janice Taylor, also known as Cassidy Sutcliff.

McCain quickly called Sara.

"Hey, what's up?" she asked as she answered her phone.

"You'll never guess who is standing in the parking lot of the Wildlife office."

"You know I hate when you ask that."

"Sorry. Here's a hint. *Sports Illustrated* swimsuit – "

"You're kidding? How'd she end up there? And what does she want?"

"No, I'm not kidding. And I have no idea. She gave me a false name and says she's a writer for some wildlife defender magazine."

"She's nuttier than a PayDay bar," Sinclair said. "You need to be extra careful with her. She probably saw you on TV and wants to make you pay."

"I thought about that. I'll keep an eye on her."

"Can't you go out there and arrest her?"

"I don't think so. I haven't seen anything that says they have a warrant out for her arrest."

"Hang tight, I'm on my way," Sinclair said.

"I think I can handle her," McCain said, but his wife was no longer on the line.

As McCain walked back out to the lobby, he slipped his Taser out of the holster on his belt and tucked it into the back of his pants so that it would be handy. He walked out the door and found Sutcliff standing on the other side of the parking lot under some trees.

"Can we talk over here?" she asked. "It's nice in the shade."

"You mind if I let my dog out?" McCain asked as he walked toward his truck. "He's been out here for a while."

"Oh, no, I love dogs," Sutcliff said as Jack hopped out of the back seat of the pickup. "He's beautiful. I understand he helped you find the tiger up there in the mountains."

"Well, the tiger kind of found us," McCain said. "But Jack did attack a guy who was trying to kill me, so I guess I'll keep feeding him for a while."

Sutcliff gave McCain the cutest little laugh, along with a very fetching smile. She walked over to him and got very close. Uncomfortably close, as far as McCain was concerned.

She reached out and grabbed his right bicep and said, "You're a well-built man, Officer McCain."

McCain took a step back. She took a step forward.

"Listen, Miss Sutcliff. I know who you are."

In a millisecond, McCain saw the look on Sutcliff's face go from sweet and kind to pure evil.

"I know you and your boyfriend were the ones who stole the cat-show trailer and released the tiger into the National Forest," he continued. "And I know you were the person who released the cats at the fair in Puyallup and almost got that security guard killed."

Sutcliff looked at him and then she put her face in her hands and started to sob. She slowly melted to the ground until she was sitting on the curb. McCain's first inclination was to comfort her, but something told him to resist the urge and stay alert.

As she sobbed, head down on her knees, Sutcliff slipped her right hand into her boot and grabbed her knife. She wailed a bit louder, hoping the officer would come closer to put an arm around her shoulder.

Jack had been off sniffing the line of trees, and now he came running over. McCain put his hand out, signaling the dog to stop and stay. Then he reached back and grabbed the Taser.

"You can pull that hog sticker if you'd like," he said. "But all it will get you is fifty thousand volts of electricity. You'll go limp and, more than likely, piss your pants."

As he was talking, Sutcliff magically stopped crying and lifted her head to look at him. He again saw that evil look spread across her face.

"Now, throw the knife over there," McCain said, pointing to the parking lot. "And roll over on your stomach, hands behind your back."

Sutcliff studied him, trying to figure out what her next step might be. Then she gave him the smile that had won over a hundred men, like a magical potion that would allow her to get them to do whatever she wanted.

"That's not going to work on me," McCain said. "Now, you can try to attack me, which will get you at least a good dog bite, and maybe an incredible shock. Or you can run, and although I might miss with this Taser, Jack will catch you, no problem. Or you can do as I say and roll over with your hands behind your back."

The smile left Sutcliff's face. McCain could see her thinking. Finally, she threw the knife onto the pavement and rolled over on her stomach.

McCain was just starting to walk over to the now-prone woman when a big, black Chrysler sedan rolled into the parking lot and stopped abruptly. Sinclair quickly climbed out of the car, her pistol in one hand.

"Just in time, Agent Sinclair," McCain said. "I believe we have our cat burglar. Miss Sutcliff, I believe you know FBI Agent Sinclair. She's the one who tracked you to the restaurant in Seattle."

Sutcliff didn't move.

"I was about to cuff her. Keep her covered."

McCain walked over, knelt, and placed the handcuffs on Sutcliff. As he was helping her to her feet, she leaned in and whispered a few words into his ear. It made him blush.

McCain put her in the back of Sinclair's sedan.

"Can you take her down to the sheriff's office?" McCain asked Sinclair. "One of the YSO deputies can run her to Kittitas County. I'm sure the sheriff there will happily figure out the charges to file on Miss Sutcliff for the theft of the truck and trailer, among other things."

"I'd be glad to," Sinclair said. "Then Ronald McDonald can go on TV one more time and tell the world they caught the mastermind of the exotic cat heist."

Sinclair climbed into the driver's seat, fired up the Chrysler, rolled down the window, and said goodbye to Jack. Then she turned to McCain and said, "Will you be home for dinner, honey?"

"Sure will," McCain said as he leaned in and gave Sinclair a kiss. As he was backing away, he glanced at Sutcliff. For the third time in about ten minutes, he witnessed the evilest look he had ever seen.

Chapter 38

"I'm sure glad you sent me the photo of Cassidy Sutcliff," McCain said as they worked on getting dinner ready that evening. McCain was grilling some halibut. "The second I saw her standing in the office reception area, I had an inkling it was her. But I couldn't figure out how she had found me or what she wanted with me."

"I think I know what she wanted with you," Sinclair said. "I swear, if she'd made even the slightest move, I was going to shoot her."

McCain laughed. "I don't think you would have done that."

"Oh, you don't, huh? I saw her whisper something in your ear. I'm guessing she wasn't thanking you for taking her into custody."

McCain didn't say anything.

"Come on, what did she say?"

"I didn't really catch it," McCain mumbled.

"Oh, baloney! You were blushing!"

"No, really!" McCain said, trying not to laugh. "She whispered into my bad ear, so it was all garbled."

"You don't have a bad ear."

"What's that?" McCain said, with a goofy look on his face, pointing to his right ear.

"That's not the ear she whispered into."

"Crap," McCain said. "I should never argue with an attorney-turned-FBI-agent. Hey, what did you find out about SO-AM Tradex?"

"I found out some very interesting information. We need to keep an eye on that Charlie guy. So, what did that woman whisper to you?"

"She said she really liked Jack."

"Oh, for crying out loud," Sinclair said. "That woman came from wherever the hell she was, and she was looking to hook up with you."

"That's very flattering," McCain said. "Isn't it great that your husband attracted such a mentally stable person?"

"You gotta admit, she was very attractive."

"Not in the least," McCain said. He wasn't falling into that trap.

"Oh, come on!" Sinclair said. "She is beautiful. Stunning, I would say."

"Beauty is only skin deep. I try not to judge a woman by her looks."

Then McCain started laughing. And he laughed even harder when he looked over and saw Sara with the bread carving knife in her hand, pointing it at him.

"What did she say?" she asked in a demanding voice.

McCain was laughing so hard he couldn't talk.

"You're right about one thing," Sinclair said. "If she wanted a goofball like you, she must be mentally unstable."

And then they both laughed until tears were streaming down their cheeks. Jack, hearing all the commotion, came in to see what was going on. That made them laugh even harder.

Finally, as they caught their breath and wiped the tears away, it got very quiet.

"Now, what did she say?" Sinclair asked.
And they started laughing all over again.

CPSIA information can be obtained
at www.ICGtesting.com
Printed in the USA
FSHW010947200721
83251FS